L. C. ple

║█║█║█║█║█║█║█║█║█║█║█║█║█║█║█║
◁ **W9-ASQ-852**

SAVED
FROM TRAGEDY

Hatless, her hair blowing in the wind, Mary bent over the neck of her runaway horse. Frantically she tried to regain control, to turn the horse back onto the trail. For unless she did, she would be plunged over the rim of the Mesa to a horrible death on the rocks below.

Suddenly another horse and rider appeared out of nowhere, racing toward Mary as the jagged edge loomed nearer and nearer. Leaping to the ground, the stranger grabbed for the runaway's head in a desperate attempt to avert the tragedy.

Books by Zane Grey

Arizona Ames	The Mysterious Rider
The Arizona Clan	Raiders of Spanish Peaks
Black Mesa	The Rainbow Trail
The Border Legion	Rawhide Justice
Boulder Dam	The Reward
The Call of the Canyon	Robbers' Roost
Captives of the Desert	Rogue River Feud
Code of the West	Shadow on the Trail
The Deer Stalker	Stranger from the Tonto
Desert Gold	Sunset Pass
Drift Fence	Thunder Mountain
Forlorn River	To the Last Man
The Fugitive Trail	The Trail Driver
The Hash Knife Outfit	Twin Sombreros
The Heritage of the Desert	Under the Tonto Rim
Horse Heaven Hill	The U.P. Trail
Knights of the Range	Valley of Wild Horses
The Light of the Western Stars	Wanderer of the Wasteland
Lone Star Ranger	Western Union
Last Pueblo	Wilderness Trek
The Lost Wagon Train	Wyoming
The Man of the Forest	

Published by POCKET BOOKS

 Are there paperbound books you want but cannot find in your retail stores?

You can get any title in print in **POCKET BOOK** editions. Simply send retail price, local sales tax, if any, plus 35¢ per book to cover mailing and handling costs, to:

MAIL SERVICE DEPARTMENT
POCKET BOOKS • A Division of Simon & Schuster, Inc.
1230 Avenue of the Americas • New York, New York 10020.

Please send check or money order. We cannot be responsible for cash. *Catalogue sent free on request.*

Titles in this series are also available at discounts in quantity lots for industrial or sales-promotional use. For details write our Special Products Department: Department AR, POCKET BOOKS, 1230 Avenue of the Americas, New York, New York 10020.

ZANE GREY

Captives

of the

Desert

A KANGAROO BOOK
PUBLISHED BY POCKET BOOKS NEW YORK

CAPTIVES OF THE DESERT

POCKET BOOK edition published December, 1977

This story was published serially under
the title *Desert Bound.*

This POCKET BOOK edition includes every word contained in
the original, higher-priced edition. It is printed from brand-
new plates made from completely reset, clear, easy-to-read type.
POCKET BOOK editions are published by
POCKET BOOKS,
a Simon & Schuster Division of
GULF & WESTERN CORPORATION
1230 Avenue of the Americas,
New York, N.Y. 10020.
Trademarks registered in the United States
and other countries.

ISBN: 0-671-81829-5.
Library of Congress Catalog Card Number: 52-5441.
This POCKET BOOK edition is published by arrangement
with Harper & Row, Publishers, Inc. Copyright, 1925, 1926,
by McCall Company. Copyright renewed, 1953, 1954, by
Lina Elise Grey. All rights reserved. This book, or portions
thereof, may not be reproduced by any means without permission of the publisher: Harper & Row, Publishers, Inc.,
10 East 53rd Street, New York, N.Y. 10022.

Printed in the U.S.A.

Captives
of the
Desert

1

KATHARINE resented further disruption of her enjoyment of the color and beauty and loneliness of the Arizona desert. But again she was dragged back to reality by the irritating presence of her friend's husband.

Wilbur Newton kicked a swirl of sand toward the offending automobile and glowered from the disconsolate driver to the ladies in the party: "That carburetor again! . . . Now we'll miss the Snake Dance. Exactly what I expected, though."

Obviously it was unspeakable inpudence for anyone or anything to interrupt the even tenor of Wilbur's lordly life. His face, his tone, his strutting gait, now all revealed his pettish anger as he swung away from the unpleasant scene and the car that had betrayed him.

Mary Newton sighed audibly.

Sighs could not always be stifled, thought Katharine, pressing her friend's hand. "Personally," she said aloud, "I think it's a lark to break down on the desert. It's the unexpected that's fun. Surely other motorists will make the Snake Dance by this trail. They'll help us."

There was no response from Mary. Katharine's gaze followed hers to the boulder some two hundred feet away, where the object of the sigh had halted. The balancing rock against which he stood shaded the tall, lean figure, but the sun, splitting its rays over and under the rock, threw pools of light on his sombrero and spurs, making them exceptionally evident.

"A big hat and a pair of spurs," murmured Katharine with startling audacity.

"Yes, a big hat and a pair of spurs—and nothing be-

7

tween. That's what I married," Mary replied. Her voice was as light and dry as the desert breeze.

"It ain't so bad, Miss," the driver explained. "But it's expert help I need. Now if we could make thet Indian school at Leupp. Still and all, it's fifteen miles off."

"Is it likely that a car will pass this way before night-fall?" Katharine asked.

"Might be days before a car'd come by this spot."

The man's reply stirred Katharine strangely. She wanted to learn more.

"Then we might be left here to starve or die of thirst?" she asked excitedly. "And our bones to be bleached by the desert sun?"

"No, Marm. Leupp's too near. Walkin's good at night if it comes to thet."

But the driver's reassurance could not destroy the romance of their situation for the Eastern girl. "Why, we'd enjoy being marooned," laughed Katharine. "Mrs. Newton and I will be just as dramatic as we please. We'll find some high place on these boulders where we can watch and pray for help. See, Mary, won't that make a jolly lookout?"

Mary entered into the spirit of Katharine's play, and raced with her toward the slope she had indicated.

"Now—what—did—we want to do that for?" panted Mary as they reached their objective. "Running in this sun—when we have a climb—ahead."

"To put distance between the world and us," Katharine replied, with a sidelong glance toward Wilbur's remote figure. How still the man stood, like a painted thing! Was he thinking? If so, what was he thinking about? No, he could not be thinking, for all his usual profound appearance. Mary was right. There was nothing between his hat and his spurs.

The girls climbed the trailless slope, zigzagging between boulders toward the red-rimmed rock of the domineering mound that rose above them. The higher they climbed, the more difficult became their breathing, and they were forced to pause sooner than they had anticipated.

Katharine dropped to a seat on a flat rock. "I'm actually —puffing!" she said.

Then, lost in a transport of joy, she caught her breath. The desert drew and held her eye—leagues and leagues of sand, pink-toned, shimmering, like an opal ocean in dead calm, the dim distant purple cloud banks resting on the rim of the horizon. It seemed that any moment they might lift and disappear.

"Oh, Mary, you were such a dear to include me in this trip!" Katharine declared ecstatically.

"I hope we can inspire you with a love for Arizona, dear. It may happen that you will have to live here always—for Alice's sake."

Katharine had never pretended that it was anything but terrifying for her to face the decision to accompany her frail sister to live in Arizona. When the family doctor had declared that Alice might be able to combat the dread tubercular malady which had followed her siege of pneumonia out here, she was sure that she would never have capitulated if Mary's letters had not been so full of optimism and her own example of courage so radiant. Katharine looked with admiration at the straight, slim figure by her side. There was something of Spartan strength in Mary's fine features, in her gallant carriage, in the simple, severe way she wore her hair. And five years of a new life had developed Spartan qualities of soul as well. Neither disappointment nor defeat would ever make this brave woman bitter!

"Wilbur isn't so sociable that he really wanted our company," said Mary, breaking the silence. "The trip materialized only because Hanley wanted Wilbur to meet him there. Hanley pulls a string and Wilbur dances. What this dance is I don't know. I reminded Wilbur that four years ago he promised we would make this trip, and therefore he should take me. You were dragged in by the heels."

"Well, at least I'm being dragged willingly," said Katharine.

"Oh, I wanted you, dear. But I had to scheme. It would be so nice for me to have company when he conferred with Hanley. You know—that sort of thing. All the while I wanted you just for your precious self, even more than I wanted the trip."

"For what you could give my 'precious self,' " Katharine corrected her.

Mary turned away with a lithe stride. "Come on, we've dawdled long enough. The higher we get, the more beautiful the prospect."

Katharine labored bravely upward, half-envious of Mary's ease in action. Manifestly her friend was desert-tried. As she climbed, her excited oh's and ah's were punctuated by little puffs of breath.

"Take it easy. You're not used to it. Don't mind me," Mary called over her shoulder.

It was fully twenty minutes before the girls met on the summit of the red-rimmed rock. It had developed greater proportions as they climbed, as had the desert increased in its staggering magnitude. Now the world was a huge irregular bowl, sand-lined and of translucent pink, an uneven purple fresco painted on its broken rim.

"How gorgeous!" Katharine exclaimed, breathing hard.

"To me it is peace—infinite peace," murmured Mary. She smiled dreamily. "Somehow having you here reminds me of when we were youngsters. Remember our secret places? Remember Desert Island—a huge rock in a meadow of daisies? It was there we confided all our secrets to each other."

"And how vast that daisy field seemed. How tremendous our island rock!" replied Katharine.

"Our childish troubles, so insurmountable before we reached the rock, vanished like magic once we made it. That's what happens when I climb a high place on the desert. Desert magic, I call it. And it is one of the things that hold me."

During the three weeks in which the girls had renewed their friendship, a time when most girls would have enjoyed the delightful intimacy of talking about themselves, Mary conscientiously had avoided personal references. It was of other people she spoke, with an all-consuming interest in detail. It might have been that she was aware that the life she was living spoke for itself. Today was the first time—and for an instant only—that she had opened the door of her heart and let Katharine look in.

When a half-score of years ago Mary left New York to live with relatives in the South because her father feared conflict between his eighteen-year-old daughter and her temperamental stepmother, a girl scarcely five years his daughter's senior, Katharine had felt that nothing good would come from so cruel a situation. The thought of proud, aloof Mary being thrust upon relatives whom she hardly knew because there was no place for her in her father's home had seemed impossible to her. Had Mary been trained to economic independence there would have been a chance of escape. But, no, true to a life-long habit of selfishness, her father had chained her to him to satisfy his creature comforts when her mother's usefulness had ended in death. Small wonder that Mary had met romance too quickly—that she became Mrs. Wilbur Newton before a year had passed. "I'm marrying a Texan," she had written, "of a branch of one of the oldest Southern families, a man of sterling qualities, not above becoming a rancher to help retrieve the family fortune. It will be such a wonderful opportunity for service, to help him in the upward climb. I'm so wonderfully in love. I'll never forget how thrilled I was when I met him for the first time. I heard a clink of spurs, and then I turned and a great big sombrero caught my eye, and underneath a face—really, I haven't the power to describe him—such kindliness, such reserve, you know, the kind of reserve that suggests silent power. Not dashing, but infinitely daring!"

Six months later there came word that Mr. Wilbur Newton had failed in the ranch enterprise, though Mary had struggled to keep up her end. Of course, so proud a man as he had to flee from his disgrace, so they migrated to southern Arizona. Two years later his farming project in some remote Arizona valley was abandoned—for what reason Katharine never knew—and they transferred their meager possessions to Taho, on the Navaho Indian Reservation, where the man of infinite daring prospered on a salary as assistant to a trader. He was the kind of person who would prosper under any condition, where his wife could scrape and sweat. Katharine had seen. Indignation burned within her. Once Katharine had written from the East, admonishing Mary not to wait too long with news of a little Wilbur Junior. Such news never came, nor any comment on Katharine's suggestion. The time had come when Katharine was profoundly grateful: neither dogs nor children liked Wilbur.

"The desert is thought-provoking, isn't it?" Mary's even words broke through her stormy meditation.

Katharine flushed and hastily replied that it was. But Mary's eyes, quick and roving, had left her.

"Look!" the older girl cried. "There's Leupp. See that windmill? See those specks? They're the government buildings."

"But that isn't fifteen miles away!" Katharine protested.

"Oh, yes, good long desert miles. Distances are deceiv-

ing, and so is the general topography of this country.
Notice that brownish line like a thread dropped carelessly—
about halfway between here and Leupp? That's Canyon
Diablo, a great deep canyon. We must cross it to make
Leupp."

"Canyon Diablo? Devil's Canyon, I presume. Oh, how
thrilling! Who'd ever guess this desert below us was anything but a perfectly level floor? . . . Now I know I'll be
broken-hearted if we aren't rescued soon!"

"It's a strange thing to consider," Mary explained, "that
Indians at Leupp doubtless know this very minute that a
party of four people, two men and two women, are stalled
on the desert near—well, whatever they call this particular
landmark. . . . More of what I call desert magic. I never yet
traveled anywhere on the desert that news of my coming
did not precede me."

"Oh, how spooky!" Katharine cried, thrilled to the mar-
row. "We are being watched, you mean. While we sit here
thinking we are the only souls for miles around, Indian eyes
are peering at us and riders are carrying word of our
coming."

Mary laughed, a low, pleasing musical laugh. "There's
not an Indian behind every greasewood bush and cactus
patch," she corrected. "But rest assured, the eyes of the
desert are on you."

"Would the Indians be likely to send back help from
Leupp?" queried Katharine.

"No, unless some white friend were expecting a party of
our description. That doesn't happen to be our luck."

"Anyway, it's a lark, whatever comes." Katharine's
words were profoundly sincere. She was seeing so much,
living so much, learning so much. "Tell me some more
about your fascinating Indians," she begged.

And as they sat there, looking out over the wasteland,
Mary related much that she had learned about the desert
dwellers, explaining graphically the dissimilar customs of
the gypsy-like, nomadic Navahos and the civic-spirited
Hopis who were planning for the solemn snake dance
rituals. As Katherine listened she watched the gray tide of
cloud shadow slowly advance before a lowering sun. Now
the desert appeared more defined through dissolving haze.
The distant irregular purple frieze grew bold in profile.
Shadow lay upon it like folds pressed in velvet.

"You have only to watch evening come to the desert to

understand what stirs these Indians to such religious fervor," concluded Mary.

"Can we stay here till the sun goes down?" Katherine asked.

"Heavens, no!" returned Mary, swinging to her feet with a start. "There are things to do."

"Things to do? Surely the only thing to do is wait, watch and enjoy."

"Yes. Campfire to make—supper to get. The driver will rustle some wood. I'll handle the rest."

"And Wilbur, poor dear, what will he do? . . . Ah, think, no doubt!" Katharine mimicked the slow, even drawl of the man she ridiculed, then added tartly, "Someday he'll die from what the observer might call overthoughtfulness, but at the post-mortem it will be discovered that his brains are only cotton wool!"

"Katharine!" begged Mary, with just the least sign of reproach in her searching gray eyes. "I'm sure Wilbur's a good camper when he's alone on the trail, or with men. But when I'm along . . ."

"Oh, yes, dear. I understand, and I'm sorry. But I feel like the bubble in that fairy story my mother used to tell us—the bubble who wanted to burst and couldn't. You remember: 'One day the poor bubble got giddy and gay.' Well, look out!"

"But the consequences were dire," remarked Mary thoughtfully. "The bubble found that things could never be the same again."

The full weight of the remark escaped Katharine. Far off in the direction from which they had ridden, she espied a slow-moving object. Could it be a car?

"Look!" she cried.

"That's a car," Mary declared. "It's moving faster than it appears to be. Still pretty far away; but I think it will get to us before dark. Come along now."

The descent was easy and swift, and they covered the ground between the slope and the stalled car with buoyant steps. The driver was asleep curled over his wheel. Wilbur was nowhere in sight.

"Fine!" thought Katharine. Aloud she said, "Don't wake the driver. I'll find wood. These clumps of dead greasewood will do, won't they?"

Katharine's fire was not much of a success at first, but was saved under Mary's instructions.

"Anyone as stubbornly persistent as you will learn," laughed Mary.

She had laid a small rug at a comfortable distance from the fire and spread camp tableware and a tempting picnic lunch. Katharine sauntered over, feeling very important now that her fire was burning.

"What's that black iron-pot affair?" she asked curiously.

"Dutch oven," Mary replied.

"Dutch oven?" Katharine echoed.

"The joy of a cowboy's existence," added Mary.

She was busy with flour and water and baking powder, and Katharine watched her quick fingers prepare a biscuit dough.

"One uses different proportions of ingredients in this altitude," Mary explained. "I could have bombarded a town with the first biscuits I made here by the rule I used back East. . . . Now you can help by poking out some hot cinders from the bed of your fire. Make a nice little nest of them alongside. That's for the Dutch oven."

Katharine applied herself thoughtfully to the task. Poking hot coals from a fire was terrifying. The burning wood above had a way of collapsing and sending out showers of sparks when part of its support was dug away. She was concentrating so intently that when a voice sounded at her elbow she gave a violent start.

"I ain't being much help to you." It was the driver, looking decidedly sheepish.

"Oh, I'm enjoying this!"

Her sally was cut with an exclamation of approval from Mary who was coming toward them, the oven swinging from one hand, its lid in the other.

"Splendid work. It isn't every cook who has an assistant like you. . . . Look here!"

She swung the oven toward Katharine. Neat little mounds of dough lay compact on the bottom of the pot. Mary set the pot on the bed of cinders, then, laying the lid on a stone conveniently near the fire, she raked out more coals and with a swiftness that excited Katharine's admiration transferred them to the iron lid. A protecting edge an inch high held the coals safe. Refusing the driver's protest to let him do that, she thrust a stout stick through the handle of the lid, and balancing it carefully, lifted and fastened it over the pot. Not a coal moved.

"That supplies heat from above!" declared Katharine, with as much pride as if she had invented the ingenious oven herself.

"When the biscuits are done, I'll put some bacon in," Mary returned. "It cooks in no time. I really prefer to sizzle mine on a stick. But Wilbur likes everything ready when he sits down."

The mention of Wilbur jarred on Katharine. She glanced about furtively, wondering what had become of the man. There he was, not far away, a blot against a patch of greasewood. He had a stick in his hand and was moving slowly toward the fire, jogging little jets of dust before him. Vivid light on the rock behind him made Katharine look toward the direction from which it came. The sun was setting between fleecy clouds low over the horizon, chiffon clouds of pink and gold; and the lonely desert was bathed in rosy light showered from purple mesa to purple mesa, through the silent legions of miles.

"And we were getting supper while all this was happening!" thought Katharine, flinging a resentful glance toward the man who walked with his eyes to the ground. She knew he would not speak unless he were addressed, so she called to him as gaily as she could, "Wilbur, isn't that sunset exquisite?"

He looked up slowly. Ah, that studied grandiose expression of dignity! She hated it. Did it never irritate Mary?

"Hadn't noticed. . . . Yeah, it's pretty fine, I guess. You'll get used to them," he drawled.

"Did you sight that car?" Mary greeted Wilbur with the quickness of speech she customarily used when addressing him, perhaps to lay subtle suggestion or to strike a balance, or—and this had not occurred to Katharine before— perhaps from sheer nervousness.

"Mmm. About twenty minutes ago."

The car was not in sight now. There was a perceptible rise in the desert floor approaching their location, though, as Katharine had noted from above, the whole valley appeared to be level.

"Better hustle through supper," suggested Wilbur languidly.

"I was trying to delay it until that car came," Mary explained. "It may carry some hungry people. I've made lots of biscuits and lots of coffee. We can be spare with the other things."

Wilbur's eyes narrowed and flashed steely blue. "We're not setting up a desert barbecue. There may be seven or eight people in thet car."

How evenly he talked! His irritation showed only in his eyes. Mary glanced apprehensively at the driver. Katharine, feeling her friend's discomfort, wanted to assure her that the stranger had missed Wilbur's words.

No sooner had they gathered round the campfire in response to Mary's call than the roar of a motor sounded.

"They've been steppin' on it, thet outfit, like they wanted to get somewhere," Wilbur commented. "I suppose they'll be a bunch of cranks who won't want to tow us. Anyway, they can get word to Leupp and send back a government truck. . . . Don't you mention supper, Mary. The quicker they get to Leupp, the quicker we'll get help."

The car was in sight now, approaching fast. Two points of light flashed across the sand. Another minute later, with a grind of brakes, it came to a stop along the trail.

"Halloo!" called a cheery voice. "That you, Newton? Trouble, eh? Heard you passed through Tolcheco this morning."

The people in the car were gray figures in the gray light. Katharine discerned three passengers in the back. The man who spoke rode alone in front. Taking a sudden leap, he cleared the door of the car without opening it and the violent movement sent him half running toward them. As he stepped into the circle of light Katharine experienced a pleasant thrill. She seemed to know this man, as one recognizes a composite of pleasing personalities. He was tall and broad-shouldered yet possessed an athletic slimness, and the fine swing of his gait was the mark of perfect control and muscular coordination. What rugged strength of features! He wore no hat. Katharine looked quickly from dark eyes under bushy brows to a stubborn crown of brown hair, then for a second time the flashing white smile and easy presence captivated her attention. Wilbur, addressing him as "Curry," explained that they had trouble with their carburetor and could not go on.

"Meet the ladies," Wilbur drawled. "My wife . . . oh, beg pardon, you know her, don't you? . . . This is Miss Winfield, Miss Katharine Winfield, from New York."

Katharine's fingers were paralyzed by the vicelike grip of Curry's hand.

"I'm right glad to meet you, Miss Winfield. You're a long way from home, but you're in good company."

Katharine glanced at Mary. Her face was flushed. Greeting people never seemed to excite her. Was she afraid of what her husband might say? That likely was the trouble.

"We do want to make the Snake Dance, if possible," Mary offered. "More for Miss Winfield's sake than our own."

"You're making it right now!" Curry declared. "I'll see you through. You bet! Wish I had my own car. I'd tow you. This car I'm driving is borrowed. The folks from the post have mine. I had to come around by way of Flaggerston and pick up my party there this morning—nice middle-aged people. Couldn't waste my seven-passenger on a party of three. Now I can't risk another fellow's car by towing your load." He ran his fingers through his hair with a jerking pull at the unruly locks, as if by so doing he could assemble ideas more quickly in his mind.

"Here's how! I'll take you ladies and send back a truck for the car and men. We're planning on a bed at Leupp for tonight. I can tinker with your car when it gets there. In the morning all hands will be ready to ford the Little Colorado. We'll make Oraibi early in the afternoon. Nice to have the Snake Dance at Oraibi for a change."

Wilbur cleared his throat. "Couldn't get me in somehow on this load?" A frown accompanied his question.

"Not very well. Running board packed with bedding, and valises stacked in back. We'll be riding three to the front seat as it is, and that narrow back seat is none too comfortable now. Got to consider my party some. They're paying for this. And crossing Canyon Diablo with an overloaded car is pretty bad business."

"You're shore to send someone back?" drawled Wilbur.

"Sure as a decent man's word," Curry retorted.

Katharine was aware that a man like Curry could not take Wilbur's insolence easily. Suddenly a daring idea stimulated her. "Oh, Mr. Curry," she said in her most affable manner. "Mr. Newton was suggesting before that we had plenty of supper for an additional *small* party. I'm sure you folks are hungry."

"Now, that's sure fine of you, Newton. Like to sit down with you, but my party's counting on a big layout at Leupp. They ate lunch late—not powerful hungry yet. You ladies go and get it. My engine needs a little cooling off. Meanwhile I'll look at that carburetor."

Wilbur was silent through the hurried meal. He had specific silences for specific occasions. This one bore like a heavy hand. Later, Wilbur's too emphatic words, supposed to be for Mary's ears alone, carried to Katharine where she stood brushing crumbs from her skirt.

"Mind me! You let Katharine sit next to thet man. I won't have you squeezin' close to him. Better leave the conversation to her, too. She's got enough tongue to do for two women."

2

THE people in Curry's party, a professor from the University of Chicago and his maiden sisters, made the girls welcome. They were glad to be of service. It all only went to show, they explained piecemeal between them, that nothing man could devise would ever conquer the desert. What good was a car? Had the girls been marooned in a more remote part of the desert, they might have starved to death!

Katharine wanted to tell them about desert magic, how the Indians who kept watch might be saviors under such a circumstance, but she always hated to repeat information just received. Unfortunately Mary seemed too preoccupied to enlighten them.

"A horse is the thing for this country," spoke up Curry. "When a fellow's car's broken down on the road and Indians ride up and look on from their saddles, you know sure as life they're figuring they have the best of the bargain. And they have. A horse can get where a car can't. Sure, he may break a leg when he's traveling, but if he's your own you'd just as soon starve to death right there anyway."

"You know how that hurts, don't you, Mr. Curry?" said Mary softly.

"You bet I do!"

For a moment Katharine was perplexed. There was a strange import in the look that flashed between her seatmates on their exchange of words, an incident that led her to believe they shared something more than a casual acquaintance—an experience, perhaps. Her conjecture seemed trivial, but she wanted to justify their amity. It came to Katharine then that the imperturbable Wilbur had been stirred to an unusual vehemence of speech when he mentioned Curry to his wife.

Katharine fell suddenly thoughtful. She stared out into the dusk. A mellow glow pervaded. There would be no severe blackness such as she had experienced early in her visit at Taho. The desert was a pale-tinted opal in moonlight, gently tenacious of the radiance of day. Everywhere shadows were fleeing before the goddess of the night. One lone star twinkled above the blue-black rim of the world. Katharine found herself listening to silence—an intense silence that seemed to muffle the sound of the car. Was it through such a silence as this that one could hear the voice of God? She thought of the prophets of old who went to the wilderness to commune with God. How terrifying to think of one small soul alone with the Creator—not alone as in prayer, but mute, voiceless, waiting for His word! Did anyone really ever seek such an experience? She, herself, would have fled from it. She was grateful not to be alone in this silence, so alone that there would be only God. . . . She stole furtive glances at her companions. Suppose they could read her thoughts! How puerile they would seem! . . . Nothing could change the silence—it hovered heavily over the desert night. Her companions, too, had become part of it.

Finally Curry spoke, breaking a long lull. "You'll be a little skeery crossing Canyon Diablo, Miss Winfield. We make automobiles do funny things in this country. We've got to."

"Scare me if you can!" said Katharine. "Bring on your old canyon!"

Curry laughed so heartily that one of the ladies burst out with a nervous "What was that?"

"We have a young lady along who's sure enthusiastic about that canyon I was hoping we'd make before sunset," explained Curry. "She's all primed for a fight."

"For a fright, you mean," retorted Katharine. "I don't feel as brave as I sound."

"Better grit your teeth then, she's a-comin'!"

"Where? I don't see anything."

"You will as soon as we cover this rise."

Katharine studied the trail. Could it be that close beyond the gentle rise of ground a canyon yawned? She leaned forward expectantly. They sped along through the silent, mysterious night—pale night, yellow night, ghostly night. Star-gleam ahead, and the canyon! They came upon it soon, a jagged black gulf, a pit of darkness over which they seemed to hang. Light caught slantwise from the moon penetrated part way down the opposite wall, and below was naked gloom. Devil's Canyon, indeed!

"We're going down into that—with this car!" exclaimed Katharine incredulously.

"We are, or we'll never make Leupp till bridge builders get out here!" replied Curry stoutly. "You'll get shaken up some."

Katharine braced her feet, a perilous performance in itself, with the emergency brake so close, and spread her arms behind Curry and Mary to get a strong hold from the rear. Mary sat in perfect relaxation. Canyons had no terrors for her.

Strong headlights made the tortuous trail visible over a short area, but below yawned the bottomless black pit. And black walls loomed suddenly before them. From these, they turned and rode on through their shadows, only to meet others, leaning, towering. The automobile pitched and swung and shook, and brakes groaned. Katharine felt as if she were falling, slipping down into the dark abyss. They rode at a perilous angle, fretting their way between rock and boulder in perilous descent. They were subjected to about fifteen minutes of this before the car swung around with a tremendous shake and slid out on a level place where Curry shut down hard on the brakes. A gasp of relief escaped Katharine.

"And now that we've come this far, what are we going to do?" she asked.

"Climb out, goose," returned Mary.

"You can get out of the car and stretch, if you like," Curry informed her. "I'm walking up a little way to look over a piece of that trail. Sometimes it's in a poor way. I might have to build it up some." With what equanimity this strong desert man talked of Herculean things! Katharine smiled on him in admiration.

"May Mrs. Newton and I come along?"

"Sure, anybody can come."

The ladies and gentleman from Chicago declined; they were still breathing hard from the already too adventuresome excursion. But Mary would miss no chance to explore. She and Katharine toiled up the trail together, following the gleam of Curry's flashlight. The sandy basin of the canyon was narrow and gorgelike and they came quickly to the precipitous trail up the far wall. Katharine looked up. Dim lavender light sifted down through the rent, and far beyond the jagged purple rim a long, narrow welt of sky gleamed like darkened steel. Yellow stars shone though the blue void, still and cold. The all-pervading silence was almost frightening.

"Isn't it too awesome for words!" Katharine managed to murmur to her companions. "As if we'd found the gateway to Dante's Inferno!"

"Night makes the setting more somber," said Mary. "Day is kinder and doesn't show the canyon in such a terrifying aspect. This is like being buried alive in a tomb."

The place Curry was examining was not more than two hundred feet up the trail; still they felt the strain of their climb over the rock-strewn slope. Katharine could see at once how narrow the roadway was at this point. A stout log and jammed rocks built up the edge wide enough to assure the passage of the car.

"We've got the world by the tail!" announced Curry. "Someone's put in a good job here. We can buck right over her!"

"I wonder how often this part of the trail has been rebuilt," said Katharine thoughtfully.

"As often as there comes a good rain," Curry replied.

The New York girl looked at him in amazement.

"Every break in that rim becomes a waterfall then," Mary explained, "and a torrent of water roars through the canyon. Look straight up to that break which looks like a cross-canyon. . . . Can't you imagine the water pouring over that ledge? All the dirt beneath that pile of rocks would be washed away, and it would be impossible to cross the trail here."

"Well, I should say so!" declared Katharine, while deploring in her mind such destruction by the elements of the fruits of men's labors. "The desert must be unconquerable. That might explain its charm."

"How do you like our canyon?" queried Curry.

"Yours and the devil's, you mean," said Katharine before she could curb her unruly tongue. "As people in Taho would say, 'I like it fine.' But heaven forbid that I ever have to cross it on a dark and stormy night! I want the moon."

"Next time you come through, I'll see you have a moon.
I'll fix it up with the government agent at Leupp. He's an
obliging cuss."

"You're both incorrigible!" Mary declared, laughing as
she spoke.

Immediately upon their return to the automobile, two
timorous passengers questioned them about the safety in
venturing farther over the terrible road.

Curry told them there would be no trouble. "We'll eat
it up. The place I was worrying about is in perfect condition."

Thus assured, the ladies lapsed into silence, and soon
the automobile was moving again, gasping and grinding
up the grade. Once when the motor went dead, Katharine's
heart stopped too. Only after Curry recovered control and
regained the few feet they had slid could she find breath or
voice.

At last they gained the canyon rim and the car
shot out upon the desert. Mary clapped her hands in
approval of Curry's masterly handling of the car. One of
the ladies quavered, "Well, I never!" a sentiment which
the Eastern girl heartily endorsed.

"I'll let the old nag cool off a bit and then I'll stick
my spurs in her and make her run," said Curry. "It's a
pretty even stretch now all the way to Leupp. We ought
to make it in a half-hour."

Katharine's impression of Leupp from a distance was
of a treeless community of toy buildings set haphazardly
on pale yellow cardboard. But the buildings, which surrounded a formal walk, took substantial proportions as
they approached. Several were dark, vacant structures.

"School buildings and dormitories," Curry informed
them, indicating the largest of the group. "No youngsters
here now. Vacation. Teachers gone too, I guess. Leupp's
sure a dead place in summer."

They drove by the buildings and on toward a square
brick house where a light shone. There they stopped.

"Hey!" yelled Curry. "Anybody home?"

"You betcher!" bellowed a voice from the doorway.
A man of giant stature strode out to greet them. He was
grizzled and desert-worn, and had a homely, good-natured
face.

"Howdy, everybody!" he said in thundering tones. "Want a lodging for the night?"

Mr. Curry introduced the man to his party. His name was Jenkins. He was the government agent at Leupp.

"Aw, shaw! And to think Mrs. Jenkins is in Taho when there's ladies to entertain!" His disappointment was so genuine that Katharine could not help sharing it.

"Miss Winfield and I are from Taho," spoke up Mary. "Sorry I haven't met Mrs. Jenkins there. Guess she's newly arrived."

"Yes, she shore is. But if you ain't away for long you'll have lots of time to be good to her. She's to spend a month there with the Burnhams. You know 'em, I guess. You can't live in Taho and not know everybody."

"Indeed I do know Mrs. Burnham. It's certain we'll meet your wife."

While the ladies accepted Jenkins' invitation to "step out and shake your skirts," Curry explained Wilbur Newton's plight.

"Shore. I'll pull him out," agreed Jenkins. "Likely he's diggin' a pair of spurs into a rock somewheres. Ain't he the dandy? Arizona couldn't support two of him."

Curry's effort to stop the man before he had his full say was futile. Half-whispered words passed between them; then Katharine caught, "Well I'll be damned! I didn't get it that she was the missus. Now, ain't some men lucky, and some women fools!"

Mary was serene through it all, as if she had not heard.

Their arrival had interrupted a card game in which sat a professor from Harvard University and two students, all of archeological bent. This information came unsolicited with the introductions. Jenkins was proud of his guests.

After professor had met professor, no one could separate them, and much to the consternation of the students it became their lot to decide who should accompany Jenkins on his relief expedition. It was obvious that they preferred the company of the ladies. Katharine did not wonder at it, marooned as they were in this remote place where they likely had not seen a girl for many weeks. Finally, in heroic brothers-in-arms fashion they agreed that they both would go.

Jenkins turned the house over to the ladies. They were to do with it what they pleased. There was a kitchen stocked with any amount of canned food. They could cook, play the victrola—at this the students exchanged despairing glances —look through his albums and guest book, or anything else that took their fancy. When it came to sleeping time they could send the men folks to the dormitories where they would find a dozen beds apiece. There were three bedrooms for which the ladies could draw. He wanted them to be sure to "make themselves to home."

Guided by their host's suggestion, Mary and Katharine explored the rooms as soon as he left. No small home could have been more complete than the Jenkins' desert place. And it was spotlessly neat. In the kitchen the girls found Curry, sleeves rolled above his elbow, laying out food supplies he had brought in from the car.

"You've had no supper," said Mary. "You and your party must be starved!"

"Just watch me rustle some grub!" Curry grinned happily.

"Let us do it!" Katharine begged.

"Not while I've got legs to stand on."

"Then let us help," chimed in Mary. "It will hurry things."

Curry swung one arm high in surrender. "That's putting it too straight for me. Dip in if you want to."

If it had been a competition, Katharine would have had difficulty in deciding whether Curry or Mary were the better cook. While she herself awkwardly carried out the tasks they directed her to do, Mary and Curry were talking as they worked and yet accomplished twice as much. Between the three the work was dispatched quickly.

Mary and Katharine waited table against the protest of the others. Attention of this kind, they declared, would spoil them forever.

Never had Katharine felt such joy in service; never had people seemed so necessary to each other, their interdependence been more clearly established, than here, far from the civilized world. The desert had a power over men, linking their destinies or pulling them far asunder. People met as friends or enemies. There was no intermediate bond.

After supper the maiden ladies retired to their room. They much preferred the room with a double bed to the separate rooms and single beds. The desert seemed to have made them conscious of their impotence, and they clung to each other for strength. Youth had greater vigor and less fear.

Katharine stepped out into the pale yellow night. The droning voices of the two professors came to her. She wanted to hear their interesting conversation on the subject of archeology. But even more than this she wanted the moonlight of the desert and its strange impelling silence; so she walked down the barren path that led to the trail.

This desert solitude was the storehouse of unlived years, the hush of the world at the hour of its creation. It was solemn, grand, incorruptible. It did something to one, something inexplicable; it drew one's narrow soul from out oneself, and poured in something big, so big it was almost too great to bear. It set one's heart beating faster. Tears came too, and a strange yearning. Was it the desire to be in tune with the Infinite? Was it self trying to meet God? Was it God trying to storm her soul? Had Mary surrendered to this force, this power, this unnamable magic, that she could find in the desert infinite peace? . . . "Come unto me all ye who are heavy-laden, and I will give you rest." . . . It must be that Mary meant that God had received her in the desert, that she too could find Him there. But Katharine was too unsure. This vast, solemn, ageless sepulcher was voiceless and fearsome, and too merciless in aspect. The stars looked down coldly, and the moon. The Eastern girl found companionship in her shadow; and watching it before her, she returned slowly to the house.

Curry and Mary were alone on the porch; he sat against a pillar; she, at the far end of the steps, seemingly unconscious of his presence, was wrapped in deep meditation. Neither was aware of Katharine's approach until her voice brought them to their feet.

"I didn't mean to run off. I simply couldn't resist it."

"The desert has a way of wooing all its own," said Mary. "However, I knew you weren't far."

"It's wonderful and so terrifying! Do you ever feel that way about it, Mr. Curry?" Katharine asked.

"I've lived on it for years, and I don't savvy it yet," Curry returned.

"Someday you will," put in Mary, turning to him.

"Do *you?* You sound like you meant that you do."

"I think so. And I want to continue to think so, because it means peace—it makes me brave enough to meet life.... It's something a person has to find out for himself."

Mary rose with a quick smile. "The moon is so lovely," she continued. "I'd like to stay with it forever, but I'd only fall asleep and miss it all. I'm not a desert owl like you, Katharine. I'm a very domestic bird, and go to my roost early. Will you say good night to Wilbur for me and explain that the men are to sleep in the dormitories?"

Katharine understood Mary's message. For her sake she stayed and talked with Curry until Wilbur had come, and she had told him, and he had seen.

The next morning Curry and Jenkins were moving about before the sun came up. Katharine, from her room in the rear, heard them enter the kitchen by the back way, and then whispers and the opening of cupboards and an occasional clatter followed by an exclamation of disgust. She identified the voices. The two were stealing a march— preparing breakfast while everyone else still slept. Katharine was amused and delighted at the idea of two men cooking breakfast for four capable women, and such truly masculine men, too! The whole social order seemed reversed. She rose hurriedly.

Mary appeared before Katharine was fully dressed. She was an early riser, accustomed daily to greet the sun. And presently Mr. Jenkins gave a tremendous bellow which ended in the summons, "Time to get up!"

The girls set the table, though Mr. Jenkins at first objected, claiming they had no right to have risen so soon and to spoil half his fun.

How different this man was from Wilbur, who came in when breakfast was half over, expressing mild surprise that he was the last to arrive. It pleased Katharine that the young students, not wholly without guile, had seated themselves one on each side of Mary. Katharine sat next, with Curry on her right. They were well barricaded. Wilbur, frowningly, took the vacant chair opposite.

The offending carburetor having been repaired by Curry the minute it was hauled to the shed at Leupp, everything was in readiness for both parties to move on. A silent rage evidently was burning within Wilbur that he must continue to accept Curry's favors. Katharine could tell by the two red spots that showed in his usually pale face. Curry offered to ride at the pace Wilbur set all the way to Oraibi, so he could be of assistance if necessary, and Wilbur received the courteous offer boorishly.

Mr. Jenkins, driving the government truck, went with them as far as the Little Colorado, whither at his request several Navaho Indians had come with a team and a high-bodied wagon. The wagon fascinated Katharine. It was a tremendous wooden box set on wheels and without protective covering.

Ford the Little Colorado! She was beginning to understand what such a thrilling experience would mean. Mary explained that although the river seemed wide it was low and shallow, a fact easily conceivable, after studying the topography of the land. For compared to the great, wide sandy wash through which it moved so sluggishly, the river had indeed but a narrow span, and the long slopes from the bank of the wash showed how far from its flood height the river had receded.

"It's the quicksand that's worrisome," said Mary. "These Navahos know the river well, but that doesn't eliminate the risk."

The Indians awaited orders with stolid indifference. They were exceptionally picturesque in their bright velvet tunics and the careless twist of gay bands that encircled their foreheads. One wore elaborate silver ornaments and another a string of turquoise. Prosperous Navahos these obviously were.

Jenkins told them to ride on across the wash to the place they had picked as a crossing while the cars followed. The horses and wagon traveled easily over the trail, but at times the wheels of the automobiles, buried deep in the sand, spun ineffectually. When at last the two cars reached the river their engines had to be cooled before attempting the ford.

"Now folks," dictated Jenkins, "the cars must be cleared of everything and everybody except the drivers. We'll get them over first, and then cart you and the baggage in the wagon. I reckon we'd better make two trips of that, too."

The New York girl understood the process as soon as she saw Jenkins and the Indians hitching the team to Curry's car. The automobiles could not make the crossing under their own power. They must be towed.

Viewed from the river bank, the country was barren. The only visible breaks in the monotonous stretch of terrain were a few clumps of greasewood on the rim of the wash which made lacy prints against the sky. Katharine thought of the majestic view she had had yesterday from the top of the red butte, that now they had left far behind them in the desert. How remote they were from civilization!

Curry and the professor unloaded the cars. Wilbur meanwhile kept busy giving unnecessary advice to Jenkins and the Indians. Katharine, with Mary and the older women, looked about for a shady secluded place, and finding none took refuge in the shadow of the wagon. From there they watched the activities of the men.

As soon as the horses were securely hitched, each was mounted by an Indian, and Curry took his place behind the wheel of the first car. With shouts and kicks the Indians got their horses started. The car progressed ever so slowly under its own power until the front wheels slid into the water; then Curry turned off the ignition. The rest was up to the horses. They strained and pulled and panted, and breasted the lazy current stoutly. The advance was scarcely perceptible; but slowly the water rose around the wheels of the machine, reached the hubs, and crept up to submerge the four wheels.

"Won't that water flood the body and engine and everything?" Katharine asked. She was really more worried about the Indians and Curry, but pretended that it was the car about which she was concerned.

"Indeed it will flood the body," returned Mary. "The cover Mr. Curry put over the hood and radiator will protect the engine some. He'll open everything up the minute he makes the other side. The sun will dry things in no time."

"Talked it all over with Curry, I suppose," drawled Wilbur. "Oh, he's shore smart, and he'd waste no time telling you about it."

Jenkins, who was standing near, wheeled quickly. "Look-a-here, Newton, what that hombre is talks so loud in all the fine things he does that he don't have to go round shootin' his mouth off about himself to folks."

One of the maiden ladies peered at them, and Katharine wished devoutly that she had not asked her stupid question.

"Look! They're stuck, aren't they?" Mary exclaimed.

Katharine followed Mary's intent gaze past Wilbur,

whose suddenly compressed lips and narrowed eyes expressed malevolent pleasure, out to the middle of the river where the horses tossed heads and strained without advancing. The car might have been a boat anchored in midstream. Only part of the body was visible. The Indians yelled and beat the horses frantically. Behind them Curry held fast to the wheel.

"Quicksand! I'll be blowed!" muttered Jenkins.

"Head 'em with the current, you fools!" he shouted. And when the Indians turned, he gesticulated wildly, pointing downstream.

There were more high staccato yells and frantic blows. The bewildered beasts staggered and swayed. Each time they jerked their heads forward they met the water. Curry was straining at the steering wheel to turn the front wheels of the car. His action seemed to frighten the horses, a lucky circumstance, because they pawed and reared so violently that the car moved with them and they were on their way again, making surer progress on to firmer bottom. A few rods, and the horses and the car began slowly to emerge from the muddied stream.

Katharine gasped her relief and turned to find a similar expression of relief registered in Mary's eyes. The professor and his sisters too were showing their concern.

"That's a terribly dangerous crossing, Mr. Jenkins," one of the women declared. "I'm not so sure that I want to try it."

"Don't you be worryin', Miss. It's them cars that play the devil. They're so heavy. You'll mostly float over in the wagon. . . . Funny for them Indians to make straight for that quicksand! Usual they test a place first, and pick out a landmark to put 'em right. You see that big clump of greasewood yonder? Likely they was workin' one or t'other side of that and got to operatin' on the wrong side. They won't be forgettin' next time."

"Well, I hope not," returned the woman severely.

Soon the automobile was safe on the dry sand of the wash. The Indians dismounted to help Curry take down the top and lay the engine open to the sun. Then they waded their horses across the river.

The second car was lighter, and under better piloting made the trip without difficulty.

By the time the Indians had returned, the professor's

sisters had recovered somewhat from their anxiety, but unblushingly requested that Mr. and Mrs. Newton and Katharine precede them across the river. The New York girl caught a twinkle in Mr. Jenkins' eye.

"Shore, you folks came a year too soon," he said dryly. "There's talk of a bridge going up here, mebbe next summer."

"This will be interesting to talk about afterward," returned the heretofore uncommunicative sister, "having to ford a river and do such terribly primitive things. But I don't know that an airplane wouldn't suit me any better."

Katharine bade good-by to Mr. Jenkins, and followed by Mary and Wilbur climbed into the high hearselike box of the wagon. The side boards were almost five feet high, and to these they had to cling. There were no seats provided. A narrow shelf across the back supported their baggage, but so insecurely that Wilbur had to stand against it to hold the things in place.

"You look exactly as if you were on the way to be hanged," came an unemotional comment from below. And Katharine laughed out loud.

This time the Indian riders rested, and one of their companions mounted the wagon, took the reins over the high board and gave a shrill cry to the horses. The wagon rolled easily on its way. The horses started to wade in the shallow water and the wheels of the wagon scattered spray. The farther they advanced, the higher the water rose and the more swiftly it swirled and eddied about them. The river was swifter than it had appeared from the bank. Suddenly the wagon pitched and everyone was jerked violently about. There was a sudden drop in midstream they had not figured on. The water rose above the level of the wagon bottom, and a little seeped in, wetting their shoes. Wilbur swore. Katharine, on the contrary, would have been pleased to find herself ankle deep in water. It was all so thrilling, yet she would have it even more so. She almost envied Curry his misadventure. The water continued to rise, but not for long. The horses were moving quickly in their eagerness to make the bank again, and the river fell away below them. In a short time they were straining and tugging the heavy vehicle up the last few yards to the place where the cars were standing. Curry was alongside the minute the panting horses came to a stop. He helped the girls to descend. Newton swore again, but this time it was just a breath between closed teeth.

As Curry had predicted, it was late afternoon when the cars reached the foot of Oraibi Mesa. For miles Katharine had seen the great promontory take form and color, growing higher, bolder, more sweeping in length, coming out of its lavender haze, warmly red and shimmering. A jagged cliff lifted itself high above the desert, and atop it, on a perch lofty as an eagle's, rose the red walls of the old Indian village of Oraibi.

While Wilbur dozed, Mary told Katharine the traditions of the place toward which they were climbing. In the ancient village, life was going on much as it had a hundred years ago; old Indians, and the young who adhered to the faith of their fathers, frowned upon the automobiles of the white man, on the encroachment of a modern civilization, hating the recently erected Hopi dwellings at the foot of their noble mesa. The Indians who lived in the despised places had a smattering of education and enough knowledge of the white man's trade and traffic to copy his commercialism. It was they who encouraged the white man to appear at the Snake Dance ceremonies, so they might rent their houses and horses and sell their handiwork.

The houses at the foot of the mesa were boxlike, one-story structures, some square, some rectangular, all built of adobe pink-red in color. The dwellings were few and widely scattered. Some of the surrounding terrain was under cultivation.

The driver, looking back to see that Curry was close behind, picked a house with a central location and stopped. Curry drew up alongside. Other cars were parked near by on the open desert. A dozen white people were in evidence. Several, not ten yards away, were bargaining with an Indian for a gay-looking basket. A party of six, gathered round a campfire preparing their evening meal, shouted a cheerful welcome to Curry.

"That's Mr. and Mrs. Weston and guests from the trading post at Black Mesa. Fine people, the Westons," said Mary.

"Mebbe it would be better to rustle right now, and take stock of folks later," Wilbur suggested.

Mary opened the car door for him, then she and Katharine stepped out.

Curry, busy with his own party, called over, "See you later, friends! Mosey over to the Westons' fire for a while this evening."

"Like hell we will," muttered Wilbur to himself.

Meanwhile two young women and a man appeared from the doorway of the adobe house. The girls were dressed in riding habits of the latest cut. Their faces beneath small tailored hats were comely. The man was brutish in build, tall, thick-bodied, shoulders heavy and broad, and his legs were bowed, a condition that intensified his likeness to a bulldog. Under a large sombrero which might have been twin to Wilbur's bulged a wide-jowled, square-cut face. The man was laughing at something one of the girls said, and Katharine beheld a perfect though unconscious imitation of a ventriloquist's yapping doll.

"There's Hanley now," said Wilbur. "Hello, pard," he called.

That name struck association in Katharine's mind— Hanley! The man Mary spoke of yesterday!

He looked up and saluted. "Be right over, Newton."

After a word to the girls he doffed his sombrero and came to join Wilbur. Katharine and Mary forthwith re-treated a few yards to where the baggage lay.

"There go two thoroughbred fillies!" Hanley greeted Wilbur, indicating the girls he had just left. His gaze swept down the trim figures of the women, audaciously, specula-tively.

Katharine shrank from the prospect of meeting this man, but it could not be avoided for at once Hanley abandoned Wilbur for them, and Mary was forced to perform the amenities.

"Folks come a long way to see them Indians cut up," he said. "An' it sure is interestin'. Never seen it before, either of you, I reckon."

Mary said they had not.

"Don't miss none of it," Hanley continued. "Make the old man take you up to the race tomorrow mornin'." He turned to Wilbur. "You're takin' 'em, ain't you?"

"Race? I haven't heard anything about a race."

"Sure! Most everybody goes. You got to get up about four-thirty to make it. It's on top of the mesa, at sunrise. The Indians will bring your horses in time if you tell 'em."

"That lets us out. We're not getting up at four-thirty to see a fool Indian race!" declared Wilbur.

As far as he was concerned, the matter was settled. Mary looked before her, not daring to express an opinion.

"You lazy son-of-a-gun," Hanley exclaimed, his small eyes snapping. "You might ask the ladies what they'd like to do."

Katharine felt indebted to him for his remark. She would have said as much to Wilbur, though not quite so forcibly. Hanley was not wholly abominable.

Wilbur scowled, but made no comment.

"I'll take the ladies, if they'd like to go," Hanley went on. "I'm goin' up with the Weston outfit, and likely some other folks'll join us."

"That's very kind of you," Katharine hurried to say. "I'd love to go, and I'm sure Mrs. Newton would too."

She had not the slightest desire to encourage companionship with Hanley. She knew what Wilbur's reaction would be, so she purposely compromised him, enjoying her duplicity.

"If Mrs. Newton goes, I go!" declared Wilbur, a thin cutting edge to his words.

Katharine smiled inwardly.

"Of course, we'll all go, and gladly," said Mary quietly. "I appreciate your suggestion, Mr. Hanley. Mr. Newton never did have much zest in anticipation, but he is always glad afterward that someone has dragged him into a thing."

Hanley declared he could arrange quarters for them easily. The girls he had just left—the Blakely girls, he called them—would share with Miss Winfield and Mrs. Newton the adobe house across the road which they had just bargained for. Wilbur could make camp with him, and the driver would shift for himself.

From Katharine's point of view, any place was perfect that gave Mary to her for a while without Wilbur's presence added.

"The Blakelys are kind of society," said Hanley. "Don't like campin' much an' don't want to be alone. I promised I'd look 'em up some nice companions."

Hanley transferred their baggage and bed-rolls at once. That done, he and Wilbur left the girls and went to search for some Indians from whom they could rent horses.

The adobe house was a barren place, just the four pink-red walls and roof, and a doorway with no door—not a stick of furniture, not a single decoration. Whoever lived there must have taken his few possessions with him before he vacated it. Hard clay hut, clean and cool, was the way Katharine described it to herself. It was at most a shelter, if shelter were necessary, though why, Katharine could not imagine, she herself preferring the stars.

"There's nothing to do here but sit on our bed-rolls and talk," said Mary. "Wilbur didn't specify whether we were to wait here or not. Let's go out to the car. He can't be provoked at that."

Once outside, they discovered a short, slight man in riding outfit foraging through their car, dipping into the pockets on the doors in a most dogged fashion and without stealth.

"What does he think he's doing?" exclaimed Mary, hurrying forward.

Katharine, too surprised to answer, quickened her steps to keep pace with Mary.

As they approached, the man straightened to meet them, jerking into position much like a soldier about to salute. He was very solemn and very important for a man of such a negative type, and appeared offended rather than the offender.

"So this is your car!" he said. "I was wondering. I was looking for liquor."

"Dreadfully sorry we can't accommodate you," said Mary with gentle irony.

The man's look of injury deepened. "You misunderstand me, Madam! I am the government agent. I am trying to locate liquor. Some has already been passed on to the Indians. Liquor on the reservation is absolutely against the law, and I'm out to make a few arrests."

Katharine, reflecting on the size of the only lawmen she knew—husky New York policemen—smiled.

"It's no smiling matter, Madam!" the government agent continued. "It's really very grave. You'll pardon me if I make absolutely sure there is nothing in this car?"

He investigated again as thoroughly as before, and came up red in the face.

"We wear no coats and have no hip pockets," said Katharine demurely.

But he ignored her with perfect dignity.

Then came a volley of questions: "Who drives this car? How many in the party? What are the names? Any hand baggage? How long do you intend to stay? Have you any cameras? If so you'll have to turn them over until tomorrow evening. No photographing allowed on Oraibi Mesa at the Snake Dance!"

From them he stalked impressively to Curry's car. The girls watched him, amused beyond words. How shocked the professor and the maiden ladies would have been to discover themselves looked upon as liquor suspects!

Katharine turned to see Wilbur and Hanley returning. Hanley was carrying a burlap from which protruded an ear of corn.

"Didn't happen to see the government agent around, did you?" asked Wilbur.

"Yes, very much in evidence," Mary returned. "He searched the car for liquor."

"Been by, has he? Went right on down the line, I suppose," supplemented Wilbur. "He's a sketch, isn't he?"

Hanley sidled over to Curry's car. "Guess he'll want some of this corn," he said, as if to himself, and hoisted the bag over onto the floor of the car.

A minute later, as if from nowhere, Curry himself strode up. He had eyes only for the car, and to Katharine they seemed ablaze. He flung open the door, dragged out the burlap bag, and stalked over to the men.

"Hanley! That's a skunk trick. I came 'round that adobe house in time to see you. You'll risk my reputation instead of yours, will you? Take your dirty liquor!"

"Liquor?—why—why, it's corn!" declared Mary, her eyes wide with astonishment.

"John *Barley* Corn, Mrs. Newton, the inseparable companion of Mr. Hanley and his friends."

"That's a lie! It's not liquor," stormed Hanley, reaching for the bag.

Curry drew it away. "No, not yet, Hanley. I'd better drop the bag and demonstrate to the ladies."

"For God's sake, don't!" Hanley muttered. "Think of what might happen. Think of it sensibly—the ladies and everythin'."

"You and Newton have given them a heap of consideration, haven't you?" retorted Curry. He thrust the bag toward the heavy-set man. "I'm sorry they are forced into such company."

With that he strode off.

Katharine glanced covertly at Mary. She sensed the

humiliation her friend was suffering, saw color rise and recede in her still face. Wilbur was white with the paleness of wrath. But Hanley seemed untouched, now that he possessed the bag.

"Can you imagine anyone messin' up such a row about another feller's private stock?" he asked. "Everybody knows he don't drink, and in an emergency he could have helped a feller out."

To a man of Hanley's intelligence quotient, that was all the defense his action required.

Mary, head high, walked past Hanley. "You better come with me, Katharine," she said.

Wilbur grasped Mary's wrist as she stepped past him. "Where are you going?"

"To the house," Mary replied quietly. "I've quite lost my appetite. I'll not eat anything this evening. Perhaps Katharine will join you. Call her when you're ready."

"But Mary, nothing's happened," protested Katharine. "Don't be so upset."

Mary sat on a bed-roll, her head tilted back against the wall, the lovely curve of her lips lost in a tight line.

"You've told me that Wilbur isn't a drinking man," said Katharine. "That's one of the good things about him. Mr. Curry apparently doesn't know Wilbur very well."

"It's the duplicity," moaned Mary. "It's Hanley—his influence. I'm afraid of it. Wilbur is selfish, egotistical, weak in many ways, but there used to be a sweetness, and at times even a bigness, in things sacred just to him and me. At least I *thought* so. But Hanley isn't good for him. Hanley has no real regard for women. It's superficial— play-acting. He's the kind who thinks all women fundamentally weak because he could brutally ruin a few. He's poisoned Wilbur's mind to such an extent that my husband distrusts me."

"Why does Wilbur hate Curry so?" Katharine asked bluntly. "He's the kind of man, it seems to me, that one would choose for a friend."

"Because of the way I first met Curry." Mary was lost in thought a minute, then she went on, "I went riding alone one day out to a place called Cliff Rocks. I had wanted to go for a year. I knew that I would never get there if I didn't try it alone. It was twelve miles, but I had a good horse. I wasn't afraid. The Indians, seen and unseen, are a protection to anyone among them. And Wilbur didn't care much that I went. . . . I made it beautifully. Then something drew me to ride farther, just a mile to investigate a curious boulder. I thought a deep wash lay beyond. As I came near the boulder, I thought I smelled blood. Suddenly my horse reared and snorted, and then, Katharine—oh, I'll never forget it—I saw a horse, recently shot, not fifty feet away down in the wash, and just beyond, a man, stretched full length, and face down in the sand. He was groaning. He hadn't heard me. I was petrified. I thought a thousand harrowing things. I think I cried out, 'Oh, what's the matter?' or something like that—some childish, thoughtless words. Anyway, the man looked up. He seemed dazed. I didn't know at first whether he saw me or not. It was Curry, though I didn't know him then. I had never seen him before. It seems he'd been on a mad race from Castle Mesa to get the doctor at Taho to save some poor Indian youngster's life. His horse tried to clear the wash and missed, and broke two legs in the fall, and pitched Curry against the rocks. Curry was bruised and cut, and his ankle was sprained. He had to shoot his horse and that broke his heart. He had ridden him for years.

"There we were, two people alone on the desert, with one horse. He wouldn't take my horse and let me walk, and he couldn't walk, I knew, though he pretended he could. I mounted and told him I was going for help. I'd seen a hogan about a mile from the trail four miles back, and I figured the Navahos would have horses. I met them, a young boy and an older man, mounted and about to leave the place. I had an awful time making them understand that I wanted only one to go along with me, but that I needed an extra horse. The boy luckily understood a little English. He explained and the older man agreed he should go. I told the boy about the sick youngster at Castle Mesa, and when we had reached the trail I managed to coax him to give the extra horse to me, and go on alone, riding fast to Taho to get the doctor. I was so excited that I never thought about sending a message back to Wilbur."

Mary paused. Her eyes were soft, dark and eloquent. Her mouth had lost its hard set look. Never had Katharine seen her look so beautiful.

"I rode back to Curry," she continued presently, "and he managed to mount somehow, and we rode to Taho together. Katharine, that night the sun set perfectly. I will never forget the desert as it looked to me then. And poor Curry, after he explained who he was, that he was a guide and packer for Mr. Weston and lived at Black Mesa half of the year, was silent all the rest of the way. I knew he was in pain. I don't mean pain from his injuries—the pain of bereavement. It was dark when we got in. Wilbur, lantern in hand, watched us ride up to the post. He was in an ugly mood—wretchedly ugly—but Curry didn't know because men who had collected to search for me, surrounded him and rode him off to the government hospital. Two weeks later Curry called, and Wilbur deliberately walked out the back way when he saw him come in. Curry brought his bridle to present to me. He said he could never use it on another horse—wanted me to have it as a token of appreciation for what I had done. Later Wilbur hacked it to pieces with a knife. That is all there was to it."

"That is all!" Long after Mary's recital, Katharine repeated these words to the night. Mary had retired, and the Eastern girl was alone in her restlessness. The Blakely girls had not come in yet. They were still at the remote red dot of fire that marked the Westons' camp. Gay voices carried through the night from the spot. Mary should have been there with them, happy and giving happiness. Curry, perhaps, would be there, too. Mary and Curry! Why couldn't it have been such a man as he that Mary had loved and married? How ghastly to have to live one's life out with a man like Wilbur, and how difficult to keep one's soul from dry rot under such a bondage!

3

It was only at intervals that Katharine slept. She heard the Blakely girls come in about an hour after she had taken to her sleeping bag, and this and successive events interrupted her repose. Once she awoke with a start, cold perspiration breaking out over her at the clammy wet touch of something moving against her hand. It was only a stray dog, inquisitive about her presence and which seemed ashamed that he had wakened her. She had scarcely recovered from her fright when a step outside pulled her back from the fringe of sleep, and she started violently at sight of the somber figure of an Indian peering in through the open doorway. Would he dare to come in, or was he, from some sense of guardianship, making sure that all was well? He could not know that she was observing him; she was in the dark, he in the moonglow of the doorway. After a while he left as quietly as he had come. The illuminated dial of her watch read two-fifteen. Sleep continued to evade her. She reached out for comforting contact with Mary, which action, reassuring in its effect, drew Katharine slowly from consciousness to rest. Later a sudden grasp on her arm threw her once more into a spasm of fear until she discovered that it was Mary, pulling herself out of the horror of a dream. That was too much. Sleep no longer was possible, and Mary, now wide-eyed too, was satisfied to hear Katharine's whispered account of the night. At a little past four they dressed, donning riding clothes, each taking turns standing guard at the door.

While Katharine kept post she observed a woman dressed in khaki advancing through the dusk of early dawn from the direction of the camping grounds, where several fires still blazed brightly. Katharine imagined, watching her, that she had come to wake the Blakely girls, and such was the case. The woman was Mrs. Weston. She was a rather short, stout person with a round face, peach-pink, and a brisk bright smile that came freely. She accepted Katharine as she must have accepted everyone, like a mother suddenly recognizing a strayed member of her brood.

"You must visit me at Black Mesa!" she said with a degree of accusation in her voice which made Katharine feel remiss for not having journeyed to Black Mesa earlier. Mary, who was included in the invitation, assured Mrs. Weston that her several attempts to get there always had been thwarted.

For the Blakely girls, who had slept in almost full attire, dressing was a simple matter—a comb run through bobbed hair, and boots pulled on over rumpled riding-breeches—and they left with Mrs. Weston before Hanley and Wilbur appeared.

Stars were paling and the moon was low, and a sweet dry smell, carried on a light breeze, filled the early morning air. More fires were blazing on the campground. Mounted Indians moved like shadows down the road, leading strings of horses. Here and there some on foot slipped in and out of doorways and corrals, behind automobiles and wagons, quiet, purposeful, fleet in action. To observe the scene was more like dreaming the experience than living it. Hanley and Wilbur breaking into the picture made it all too real. Hanley came only part way, then struck off toward the Westons' camp.

Whether it was merely because Wilbur had slept well that there was in his manner an unusually gentle deference to Mary, or because, capable of shame, he wished to re-establish himself in a more kindly light in his wife's regard, Katharine could not decide. But he was proving a most attentive spouse. A campfire and breakfast awaited the girls; and while they partook of the meal, an Indian rode up with their horses. Two of them, like most Indian horses, were small pintos, but the third was a rangy bay.

"Him bad devil, sometime good," said the Indian of the sturdier of the two pintos, and with a wave of his hand seemed to relegate that particular mount to Wilbur.

However, it was Mary, at Wilbur's suggestion, who rode the "bad devil." Wilbur expressed preference for the bay, and after adjusting the stirrups of the other pinto for Katharine, Wilbur mounted his own horse.

One day at Taho Wilbur had expressed great disdain for "the rats of Indian horses that make a man-size hombre look like a fool." It was evident that under no exigency would he risk such an appearance; rather he would prefer to risk his wife's safety. There was no doubt the bay became him, added to his pompousness quite as much as he could have desired, and brought out to full advantage his equestrian skill.

When they set out on the long winding trail up Oraibi Mesa the stars were fast disappearing; the daylight was spreading over the farthermost reaches of the desert. Small parties were assembling from everywhere, both Indians and whites, and riding in slow procession along the trail like silent shadows in a silent world. Below them on the plains, white twisted wraiths of smoke blew from dying fires.

The air was cool, clean, sweet. Katharine turned her cheek to catch the caress of the breeze, and breathed deeply. Her entire body warmed with the glow of mounting excitement. What had she ever experienced that gave her such complete delight? She thought of New York, of the hustling, jostling crowds, the hurry-hurry-hurry that beat itself into one's pulse, the terrible never-ending strife into which the individual plunged and was lost; then she summoned visions of green fields, glades, laughing brooks and mountains, only to let them pass too. The desert was incomparable, its solitude more intimate than that of cities, woods and hills.

The horses needed no guiding. They climbed at a leisurely pace. Tails flicked and heads bobbed as they swung along the steep trail. They came to a fork in the trail, where, for no particular reason, in view of the fact that both branches led to the village, Wilbur took the steepest, roughest way, along a rocky ledge of the mesa. Back from the mesa rim rose the severe outline of the village of Oraibi. A village hewn from one great mound of rock, it seemed, its walls long since blasted by invaders. But what appeared to be breaks were places where the continuous walls were terraced, some of the long low houses rising a story higher than the rest, and no roof being level with another. The tops of crude ladders showed over the highest roofs. Though Oraibi loomed grim and dark against the steely sky like a towering fortress, it in truth housed a peaceful people, home-loving and deeply religious. They were assembled now along the rim of rock, men and women, youths and maidens, and small children too solemn for their years.

The men's attire varied from ordinary overalls, also plain white cotton shirts hanging over woolen trousers, to khaki and denim trousers slit up the side, all worn with velvet tunics of the type common to the Navahos. The women and girls were arrayed in gay calico dresses, with high necks, long sleeves, and full skirts; or in a strikingly simple native garment of a dark blue hand-woven material, obviously made in one piece with a single opening through which the head slipped, allowing the folds partly to cover the arms and to fall below the knees where a touch of color showed in a line of red. This motif at the hem was repeated in the woven girdle which bound the garment loosely at the waist.

Some of the women were barefooted, others wore moccasins, while those in native dress—and they were in majority among the younger girls—wore loosely bound strips of buckskin from ankle to knee, giving their legs a stiff and shapeless look. The older women parted their hair in the center and bound it, with threads of red wool interwoven, in two long forward-hanging braids. The girls either braided their black locks the simplest way, or had them dressed in large shining whorls that covered their ears, and stuck out picturesquely. Contrasted with the variety of dress worn by their elders was the complete nakedness of most of the children, even eight- and ten-year-olds.

Sex segregation seemed a studied practice. Boys and girls were not mingling, though some stood in respectful groups apart from their elders. Others were under the quiet chaperonage of their parents. Holiday spirit was in the air, but no great manifestation of delight. In the light of the hubbub created by the white people, the conduct of the Indians themselves seemed almost subdued.

Katharine and Mary dismounted, and Wilbur led their horses off, then presently returned to direct the girls to a spot safely remote from the places where other white visitors were gathering. Hanley saluted them from afar. Curry, hovering near the Weston outfit, was occupied with the horses for a time, but later joined a man who Katharine decided must be Mr. Weston.

Mary was bubbling with anticipation of the event. The

starting point of the race was on the valley floor below, and
the entire ground to be traversed was two miles, ending at
the rock rim of the mesa. The first sign of the sun above
the horizon was the signal for the start. About every
quarter of a mile along the staked ground Indian maidens
stood with huge cornstalks to stroke the passing contestants
and urge them on their way. One could see the girls plainly
through the fast-coming brightness of the morning, and
beyond, small creatures in the distance, were gathered the
fleet-footed men of the tribe, awaiting the starting signal.
There would be perhaps a dozen competing. Not far from
the starting point stood a priest, ready with a small sack of
corn to be snatched by whoever had the lead, and carried
on by him until a fleeter runner seized it in passing. The
winner of the race, so current legend had it, could choose
for a bride whatever girl of the tribe he desired.

A hush pervaded the mesa. Everyone awaited the signal
from the sun. It came with startling suddenness. At the
edge of the saffron-spread eastern horizon appeared a thin
line of red-gold that curved into a bow and continued to
curve until by sudden magic it changed into an inverted
golden bowl. Then a shout rang out, followed by a chorus
of shrill staccato cries. They were off! The race had begun!
Small objects moved in close formation on the desert
below. One runner valiantly kept the lead for a long time,
but at last someone passed him with upflung arm. A third
crept up, gained on the new leader and swept by him. The
girls with the cornstalks formed a rear guard, falling in
behind the runners, only slowly to drop back. Now the lead
was indisputable, and judging from the nature of the exclamations of the crowd a favorite among them was on his
way to victory. The most difficult part of the event was still
before the contestants, a racing climb to the top of the
mesa up a tortuous footpath, far more arduous than the
trail.

When the runners rounded the foot of the cliff they were
lost from sight. The crowd moved in a body toward the
goal to get a better view. Suddenly over the rim the
onlookers could see an Indian bearing the bag of meal. He
was naked save for a breechclout and moccasins, and his
bronze body shone wet with sweat. His face was masklike,
nostrils distended, eyes wide and staring, lips curled back,
frozen in a smile half agony, half triumph. Again a shout
rose from the crowd. Other naked forms now appeared,

struggling, panting, but they could not overtake their leader. His sure feet carried him over the jagged rocks, between cactus spines, around brush and greasewood, on and up unflaggingly. Cries of encouragement showered on him from above. Girls reached out in their excitement as if to drag him up. He leaped a rock. Small stones sped away from under him. At last he cleared some brush, miraculously escaping a fall, and came out on a stretch of trail clear of obstacles all the way to the rim. A hundred yards, and he covered the distance to a gate of maidens holding waving cornstalks, and dashed through it to victory! Pandemonium broke loose, and alas for the segregation of the sexes! Indian girls swarmed from everywhere to attack the winner and snatch the precious bag from him. Holding the prize high, he fought them back with only his right arm for defense, until one slim creature pushing her way through made her presence known to him with a glad cry, and the bag of meal dropped into her uplifted hands. The victor had made his choice, and the chosen one had anticipated him.

As soon as the other runners reached the mesa top, they rushed upon the scene waving cornstalks high in the air, inviting tussles with the girls such as the winner had experienced; and they fought desperately against the violence of the homely, less graceful maidens, as if indeed surrender might mean the jeopardizing of their future, and contrariwise yielded all too easily when the objects of their desire appeared before them. Romance, it was quite evident, was not prohibited at Oraibi.

Not all the girls of the village joined in the scramble. Apparently the younger maidens were excluded. It seemed to Katharine that all the girls who encircled the men wore their hair in whorls. She asked Mary if that headdress had any particular significance, and Mary replied that the whorl was a symbol of the squash blossom in bloom, and a manifestation that the girls were of age to be courted. Whereas the long braids represented the fruit of the squash and revealed their wearers as the wives of the tribe.

Good will prevailed. Defeat was received as happily as success, as the screams of laughter betokened. Slowly the commotion subsided. The crowds of Indians dispersed, disappeared quietly, as if serious anticipation of the religious ceremony of the afternoon was now in order. A few inquisitive Navahos remained to mingle with the whites.

Because he was surrounded by acquaintances, Wilbur was forced to be agreeable, to meet the Blakely girls and talk to the professor and his sisters and to Mrs. Weston, who brought her husband and guests to be introduced to the others.

Mr. Weston delighted the New York girl. He was what she had always imagined a desert scout might be like. A man of medium build, thickset yet lithe, with a face made intense by dark eyes under shaggy brows and scar lines of suffering and toil, and in appearance somewhat untidy, he was gruff yet kindly in manner. The guests were an artist, Miss Miller by name, a cartoonist and his wife, and the cartoonist's young brother, a long-legged lad of perhaps eighteen years.

Katharine missed Curry and Hanley, and unable to explain their absence, was inclined to hope that they might be locking fists somewhere, Hanley, of course, getting the worst of it. She blamed Hanley for the new complexities which burdened Mary, for the pressure of anxiety that Mary was struggling to disguise under false gaiety. Wilbur, she felt, was not so much to blame. He was negative, a weak instrument for Hanley, and therefore pitiable. She did not want to abandon her faith in his one outstanding virtue, his complete abstinence from all kinds of liquor. She had established her faith on Mary's own declaration of this fact. Now she was beginning to have misgivings. Did not Mary herself doubt him after last night's episode?

At the moment attention was focused on Miss Miller who, Mrs. Weston declared, was to start a painting of Oraibi Mesa shortly, and had to find the best perspective, but was afraid to scout around alone. Mrs. Weston was ready to accompany her if she could find some other recruits. Wilbur, to Katharine's amazement, suggested that she and Mary go along. And when Mary agreed, Mrs. Weston was delighted.

So it happened that an hour later their little party of four set out on horseback, prepared for a lengthy excursion by a picnic lunch, and promising that they would return in plenty of time for the dance. Wilbur was left to his own resources—and Hanley's.

When Katharine and Mary rode up Oraibi Mesa the second time, Wilbur did not accompany them. He failed to appear when and where he had stipulated, and after giving him a half-hour's grace, Mary accepted Mrs. Weston's invitation to join her party. Under the circumstances meeting Curry was inevitable. He was again the ingratiating person of Katharine's first acquaintance. The altercation of last night might never have happened. Manifestly it was forgotten.

"I'd been thinking that Miss Winfield might want a rattlesnake to take home for a pet," he said when, as he rode along with the girls for a brief time, Katharine had confessed to him her utter horror of snakes. "They're really good-natured snakes. I like them. They're square. Always give a fellow a chance to get out of the way, rattle their tails like they were tootin' horns. These Hopis love them—worship them. You'd never catch them killing a rattler."

"How ever do they catch them for the dance?" Katharine asked.

"Just like an eagle swooping down. They sneak up on them and nab them just behind the head and press so hard that the snake can't twist around to strike. You'll see them at the dance, dropping the snakes and catching them again."

The Eastern girl considered Curry's words thoughtfully. "And the snakes are not doped for the dance nor their fangs removed nor anything?"

Curry received the question with a smile. "No Hopi would ever molest a rattlesnake or dope him either. The dancers take precaution by fasting and drinking something they prepare from desert plants, but even that doesn't make them immune from the effects of a bite. It slows up the working of the poison, and after the dance is over they take one of their strange antidotes. In fact, they all take it whether they need it or not."

"It's all so solemn and sacred to them," murmured Mary. "It's an appeal to the snake god, who, in their belief, controls the rains. Drought is their one great fear."

"Then how terrible it would be for them, believing this, if the dance were prohibited. There's all sorts of legislation on foot about it now," Katharine demurred. "Why can't we keep our noses out of other people's business, particularly when they are not citizens and live only by sufferance?"

"Because since the beginning of time man has wanted to take the mote out of his neighbor's eye before he casts the beam out of his own," replied Mary. "Perhaps on an average of once in ten years an Indian might die from a rattlesnake bite received at a snake dance, but any white man's town, east or west, the size of Oraibi, has two or three fatalities a year because the enforcement of traffic laws is so lax or because no laws exist. We are very, very inconsistent mortals."

Curry enjoyed Mary's tirade immensely. "And all this time I've been thinking you were a reformer." The twinkle in his eye belied his words.

"I try to see things whole," was Mary's reply.

The dance was to be held in a large square court hemmed in partly by the walls of the pueblo where the Indians were already gathered. Katharine was impressed with the solemnity of the occasion. She felt that she was treading on holy ground amid reverent, worshipful souls. She could not pretend to understand the childish manifestations of the Hopis' belief, but their apparent faith was nonetheless beautiful, and commanded her respect. She had come to join them in their church. They sat crowded along the roofs, some high, some low, waiting in silence. A few black cotton umbrellas, glaringly incongruous, spread blotches of shade here and there. Surely they were not necessary to a people who loved the sun; rather they were enviable possessions proudly flaunted on special occasions. Even the Indians wore their all to church.

Separation of members of the Weston party could not be avoided because the few available points of vantage were scattered. For Mary and Katharine, Curry chose a low roof, partly shaded by an adjacent wall. The spot was secure, comfortable, and with an unobstructed view. He left them to return to the professor and his sisters. "Now let Wilbur show up if he must," thought Katharine grimly.

Mary seemed to divine what passed through Katharine's mind. "I wonder what is keeping Wilbur?" she whispered.

"Hanley, likely," returned her friend. "Haven't you missed him and——" She bit her tongue in irritation over her vast stupidity.

"The Blakely girls?" supplemented Mary. "Yes. But that's not particularly significant. They've witnessed the Snake Dance several times, you know. Wilbur has never seen it."

The New York girl meditated on the situation. The

cartoonist spoke of the Blakely girls as a pretty fast pair from Phoenix, the Phoenix summer variety he said, whatever that might mean. Well, she'd bite her tongue out before she would tell that to Mary!

She felt herself staring steadily at a hut not large enough for a person to enter standing, which stood in the center of the court; she wondered about its use. Something like heavy burlap hung over the place designed for an entrance. Somehow she did not want to question Mary about it. Mary might not know. If, as she suspected, an Indian would suddenly pop out his head, Katharine would have been delighted. However, no such thing happened, and presently a nudge from Mary drew her attention to a corner of the court where a strangely costumed group of Indians came pouring through a doorway in single file.

"These must be the men of the antelope order," Mary whispered low. "They dance first, I believe."

They were certainly most extraordinary-looking. An odd block design of black and white paint, applied thickly to their faces, made their heads seem broader than they were long. One noticed at once that they were naked to the waist because their bodies had been treated with an intensely red stain. They wore knee-length dance skirts, and dangling from the waist, tail-fashion, long beautiful foxskins. Their feet were encased in tight-fitting moccasins, and bird feathers were caught in their long black hair. In their hands they carried gourds that rattled with each step. Keeping place as they had emerged, the antelope men marched around the court several times, then drew up in double file, forming a path to the opening of the hut. There they swung from one foot to the other with a quick tapping step, shaking the gourds, and defining each movement with a decided toss of the head. This monotonous performance continued for almost ten minutes, after which time the antelope men dispersed to clear the court for a new procession of dancers, who Katharine surmised must be the snake priests. Their costumes were similar to those of the antelope men. She was too fascinated to try to note any minor dissimilarity, and very concerned about the absence of snakes. The last four to appear were boys not over twelve years of age.

These dancers, too, paraded the court, perhaps half a dozen times, but with speedier movement. They appeared a trifle more impressive than their predecessors. Every time they passed the hut—the *kisi*, Mary called it—the dancers stamped hard with the right foot on a plank that lay before it. This surely was some special invocation to the gods. Soon they gathered at the entrance to the *kisi*, in no particular formation, but dancing the tapping step of the antelope men. One among them stood before the *kisi*, and at once Katharine realized that the great moment had come. Now the purpose of the *kisi* was revealed. It housed the snakes, and the priest who stood there was to dole them out. He was welcome to his office, Katharine thought. She did not envy him. He lifted the curtain part way and thrust in his arm. Never could he know how prayerfully a certain young lady regarded his movements. In another moment he withdrew his arm, and there, suspended from the firm grip of his fingers in the paralyzing hold of which Curry had spoken, was a rattlesnake fully five feet long, which, quick as a flash, he passed along to the nearest dancer. Skillfully the dancer grasped the snake without giving him an instant's freedom. What followed filled Katharine with such intense horror that at first she could not believe her own eyes. The man newly possessed of the snake lifted it to his mouth, snapped his lips hard over the place where he had taken the finger hold, and slipping his hand down over the full length of the writhing reptile, looped it up free of the ground. In this manner he held it, tight fast in mouth and hands, the head a few inches from his cheek, but powerless to turn and use its fangs.

Meanwhile the man at the *kisi* had doled out another snake, and a second dancer seized it in his mouth; and the performance was repeated again and again until each dancer had a snake, even the small boys, who were given the shortest ones.

Now the place swarmed with antelope dancers again, they too participating in this most formal procedure of all. Each snake dancer had an antelope man as a sort of custodian partner who took his place behind him, one hand resting lightly on his shoulder, the other gently stroking him with the feather-tipped rod he held in his hand. Advancing in a circuitous route, they danced a hopping step, four beats on the ball of one foot, the last being accentuated, then four on the ball of the other with a strange swaying motion accompanying the change. As they swayed the snakes swayed, and on and on and on. There was no drum, no music, just the beat of feet. Occasionally a dancer liberated a snake, why Katharine could not tell, and the first time it happened it appeared an accident. But quickly she saw that the extra antelope men on the outskirts of the court were there on guard to catch the liberated snake, pouncing on them much like a cat on a mouse and even more sure of their strike. The snake dancer, unmindful of the snake he had freed, would go directly to the *kisi* for a fresh one.

The four boys were brave and apparently tireless. They clung fiercely to their snakes and their small feet beat hard upon the ground. Katharine, following the leader with her eyes, saw two forms slip quickly before him and leap to a place on the walls—the Blakely girls, making their belated appearance.

The dance went on—the beat of feet continued. It grew monotonous. The Eastern girl felt that fatigue must surely be creeping over the dancers. Yet she had been so interested that she had not noticed the sun dropping low, withdrawing its heat and flinging shadows across the court.

"This performance will end with the sunset," said Mary, which made Katharine aware that day was drawing to a close.

She pitied the little boys. "Are they watching the sun?" she wondered. And in the next moment she rejoiced that they were still dancing safely. No dancer had been struck. Was it because they had believed they would not be? Was it more desert faith? More desert magic?

Presently the dancers hesitated, the sound of feet lost momentum just as the tick of a huge clock that is suddenly stopped; then came a stir of action and high cries, and every snake man, raising his snake aloft, fled from the court and out beyond the village upon the open spaces of the mesa. The long-awaited ceremonial dance was ended.

Everyone seemed eager to rise, to exercise cramped limbs. Katharine and Mary slipped easily to the ground. Mrs. Weston, who was perched up on a high wall, signaled Curry for assistance.

"I see the Blakely girls arrived," said Mary.

That they had was unmistakable. They were scrambling over roofs in high glee, attracting solemn stares from the Indians.

Katharine recognized the trend of Mary's thoughts. "But Wilbur has not come yet." Then she added hastily, "Yes, they've been here quite a while."

This brought a strange, quizzical smile to Mary's eyes. "Katharine, you're a dear," was all she said.

Mrs. Weston descended upon them suddenly. "Whatever happened to Mr. Newton?" she asked. "He sure wanted to see the Snake Dance bad enough. I'll kidnap the two of you if he doesn't show up soon."

"Do please kidnap us temporarily," suggested Mary. "I think we have been passed on to you, anyway."

With a word and a nod here and there, Mrs. Weston gathered together her friends and the professor and his sisters, and led them on a tour of the village, while Curry and Mr. Weston went off to bring up the horses. To study the village was to understand how primitively the desert-bound Hopis lived, yet Katharine was half-ashamed to poke around, uninvited, in their homes. It seemed audacious to her. Because they were white, they assumed the privilege was theirs, but that in nowise made it right.

On the outskirts of the pueblo Curry met them with the horses. By the time he came over to the girls, he found Mary already mounted. A frown puckered his forehead.

"Mrs. Newton, I don't like the way that horse of yours lays his ears back and shows his teeth," he said. "I'm afraid he's a mean cuss. Perhaps you better ride him around a little before we try the trail."

"Make her be careful," he said aside to Katharine as he helped her to mount. "See she walks that horse."

The horse did not want to be walked, but Mary, who had always been perfect in command on a horse, held him in. They rode out slowly beyond the village, single file, Mary in the lead, along a footpath worn deep by generations of Indians. It was the trail the snake men had followed. They saw the Indians far ahead assembled on the plain.

"We had better not get too far away from the others," Katharine suggested.

Mary turned in her saddle. "I am trying to get away from Wilbur," she said in a low tone which only Katharine could hear. "He was coming up over that rocky trail with Hanley when we left. I don't believe he saw us, and I want to avoid any insulting remarks to me and possibly to Mr. Curry. When Mrs. Weston sees Wilbur, she won't expect us. People are not stupid. No one here, except Hanley, really desires Wilbur's company."

Mary was right, so all Katharine added was, "He'll see us now. Let him follow. He'll hardly drag Hanley along."

In their direction came an Indian rider who had detached himself from the group of snake men. As he approached the girls, he checked his horse and turned him sidewise to block the trail. He gesticulated and uttered strange words, and then at the very moment when it dawned on Katharine that he was trying to tell them that they must go no farther, he swung from his saddle, grasped Mary's bridle and with a sharp lash from his quirt turned her horse and sent him through the brush and cactus, racing madly back toward the village.

Immediately Katharine wheeled her horse. Memory of Curry's warning made her fearful of the sight of Mary clinging to the infuriated horse. She tried to keep pace. Her own horse, spurred on by a desire to race, sped swiftly in pursuit; but Mary's horse plainly was running away. He tore cross-country, heedless of the cruel growths that snatched at him. He was making straight for the rim trail. Or was it for the rim itself? Katharine's blood froze. The distance widened between them. She urged her horse to greater speed, beat at him frantically with her quirt. Out of the tail of her eye she saw the pueblo village approaching nearer. But all of her attention was on Mary, hatless now, and bent low over the neck of her runaway horse. Soon he would strike the trail. Would he turn? The alternative was too horrible to consider. . . . But what was that ahead? Katharine felt her eyes straining wide in their sockets. A rider, racing from Mary's left to head her off at the rim! Now they were almost at the mesa rim! Katharine fought to hold back a shriek of terror. She could not tell which of the racing horses was gaining. Already the rim with its jagged edge seemed only a few steps from either rider.

Then something happened, too quickly for Katharine to see in detail. She only knew that the horses had met at the rim, that the stranger had leaped from his mount and was on foot dragging hard at the runaway's head. Curry, it was, and when she recognized him she went limp with relief. Curry would save her. Everything would be all right now. In another second he was striding from the rim with Mary in his arms. When he sat her down gently on her feet, she collapsed against him. Katharine rode up, her eyes smarting with tears.

"My God, that was close," Curry cried hoarsely to the girl, but he was looking at Mary's pale face resting against his shoulder. There was something more than tenderness in his eyes, something that bordered on despair. "I thought there'd be two of you to handle. Didn't savvy you had control".

"An Indian turned us back down there and lashed Mrs. Newton's horse. I don't know what I was going to do. I was following, trying my best to overtake her," murmured Katharine, fighting back the tears.

"It's my fault," Curry declared. "I should have told you not to go so far in that direction. That's the cleaning field. Sacred ceremonies going on down there, and they won't stand to have any of us butting in."

Would he never look away from Mary? People were approaching mounted and on foot, and Wilbur was riding in the lead. Distracted, Katharine was about to tell him they were not alone. But Mary stirred, opened her eyes and swayed from him.

"Why did you do it?" she asked dazedly. "Why did you risk your life for me?"

Curry met her question serenely. "I'd have done as much for Miss Winfield, or any other woman, I reckon. Only with you it was different. I was sure I'd save you. I had to. I was plain selfish about it. You've done a lot for me. I've got to keep on knowing that you're on this same desert with me even if it happened that I never saw you again."

"I—I—" Mary's attempt to reply failed. Then Wilbur came striding toward her.

"Can't you be left alone for a few hours without trying to make a fool of yourself and me?" he demanded.

"Newton, don't you know horses well enough to prevent your wife from riding an animal like that?" interrupted Curry. "Blame yourself instead of blaming her."

"No one's asking any advice from you, Curry," Wilbur replied coldly. "Seems to me that you and my wife are staging quite a few of these horseback affairs. How about it?"

Curry would have struck Wilbur if Mary had not quickly stepped between the two angry men. It was Curry she faced, and to him she said, "Won't you please escort me down from the mesa, Mr. Curry. I'll ride your horse if

you don't mind. Mr. Newton will escort Miss Winfield."
Then she walked away, and Curry followed her.

When the others came up, Katharine was talking animatedly about the Snake Dance, plainly aware that the absent-minded, disconcerted man to whom she spoke did not hear a word.

4

WHENEVER Mary displeased Wilbur there always followed days of contemptuous silence, during which, to emphasize his displeasure, Wilbur made himself as much as possible her companion. Always during such periods Mary waited on her husband hand and foot. All the little attentions that she had given Wilbur freely in their early days of love, but which had long since lost their flavor because of his greedy and thankless acceptance of them, she continued to give mechanically, because she felt it her duty to satisfy his surly demands. But Wilbur's contemptuous silences made these duties almost unbearable. Pleasing her husband became a hateful task.

It was noon of the seventh day after their return from the Snake Dance that Wilbur found his tongue again. Mary had brought his cigarettes to the table and started to clear away the lunch dishes when suddenly he spoke.

"Lenora is coming to Taho today on the mail stage," he said.

"Lenora? Your sister?" Mary asked, more startled by his announcement than by the fact that he had chosen to break his silence.

"Yes. I'm going to be away in the Black Mesa country for a couple of weeks buying up silver for MacDonald. Tourists going through have cleaned us out at the post."

"You didn't have to send for Lenora—all the way from Texas. I've been alone before. Katharine and Alice could have stayed with me," Mary protested.

"You'd rather have them, I reckon, than a lady from the South who happens to be my sister."

"But I hardly know Lenora."

"Well, I'm giving you a chance to get to know her."

What little Mary had seen of Lenora was not enough to endear her to her sister-in-law.

"Why, Wilbur! You sent Lenora the fare to make the trip." Mary's words came as quickly and accusingly as the thought. "Your people can't afford to send her! And here I've scrimped and saved and kept poultry to sell and slaved in a garden—just for that—for your sister's pleasure."

"It's kind of early to say how much pleasure she'll get out of staying here with you. I'm aboot convinced it won't be much, seeing how glad you are to have her. I want you to understand that she's coming as a very special favor to me."

Mary had nothing more to say, but her hands shook as she carried away the dishes. Two weeks when she might have lived blissfully without Wilbur! Two weeks when she might have had Katharine with her, or spent most of the days on the desert! How could he send for Lenora without consulting her? And the money! Where would the winter coat come from which she needed so badly? Her poultry savings would go for the running expenses of the house. Wilbur would demand it, and if she refused would run up some never-to-be-paid bills. The ghost of debt visited them in continual duns from southern Arizona. Mary had been meeting these bit by bit out of her poultry money. They were beneath Wilbur's consideration, of course. According to his point of view, his creditors deserved to be hung for annoying him.

Mary plunged her hands into the steaming dishwater. She did not mind the burn. Physical things were inconsequential. . . . In a few hours Lenora would arrive. Would Wilbur want to give up the bedroom to her at once? He might. He was very considerate in his relations with his own family. She had better proceed on that assumption and change the linen, and make up the living room cot for herself and Wilbur. And she'd have to rush through with the cleaning, and polish the lamp chimneys and the few pieces of silver, and wash out the napkins they had used for breakfast. The pillow cases, too! She was short on pillow cases. Katharine was off on a picnic so she could not borrow from her.

Wilbur walked past Mary and slammed the kitchen screen door behind him. Such was the nature of his goodby. An unpleasant odor wafted in. That chicken house!

Wilbur had promised to clean it before they went to Oraibi. After continued failures to keep such promises it had resolved itself into Mary's job, a job she detested, and this time she had let it go in the hope that he would be forced by the unpleasantness of the condition to attend to it. No chance for him to do it that afternoon. He had to return to the trading post and be on hand to meet Lenora. Lenora, a lady from the South, as Wilbur called her, would have scorned to consider the chicken house a woman's job. Just the same, Mary would have taken care of it if Wilbur had only warned her of his sister's arrival.

By two o'clock Mary's sense of shame for Wilbur got the best of her, and having completed most of her other tasks by dint of driving herself until exhausted, she descended on the chicken house with scraper, scrubbing brush and deodorant powder. . . . Sometimes the stage was late.

Shortly after four Mary dragged her weary body into the living room and sank into Wilbur's armchair. She had worked so fast and so hard that her clothes were soaked with perspiration. It was terribly hot in the low, frame chicken house outside. All her energy had been sapped. She felt that she could not even raise her arms to arrange her hair.

She heard steps on the porch and smiled grimly. What luck to have Lenora come now! She was facing the door, could make out the girl's form and Wilbur through the close mesh of the screen. Immediately she rose to meet them. Seldom had Wilbur seen her appear so untidy. His look of annoyance testified to that. Lenora stared at her sister-in-law from the perfect defense of her china-doll daintiness, her big blue eyes looking more stupidly surprised than usual.

"Hel-lo, Mary," she said with such a startling pause between "hel" and "lo" that the tired Mary wanted to laugh and weep at the same time. "Did I come before you were expecting me?"

"No, not at all. I just worked too late," returned Mary, recovering her poise.

Lenora fluttered around her like a bird around a part-rotten cherry which it could not quite make up its mind to peck.

"No, no! Don't kiss me," said Mary. "I'm much too awfully dirty."

"You shore look as if you were going into the pig business," snapped Wilbur.

"You mean the chicken business, don't you, dear?" she replied.

Lenora's presence had a strange effect upon Mary. She had two people to defend herself from now. "It's the most delicious fun to get really dirty once in a while, Wilbur. You ought to try it." Mary felt at the moment as if Katharine's pert nature had taken complete possession of her. "Did you ever?" she added to Lenora, in a disarmingly sincere way.

"No, I never did," replied Lenora somewhat sourly. "Mother says that even when I was little I never would play in the dirt."

"The mark of true aristocracy, I suppose." Katharine was speaking through Mary again. "You know, because I love earthy things I've always had a haunting suspicion that I come from a long line of grave-diggers."

Mary was directing the way to the bedroom as she talked. "I think you'll be comfortable here," she said, pausing at the door to step aside so Lenora could enter. Wilbur entered too, just over the sill, to pass judgment on the condition of the room, and after a tender word to Lenora about seeing her at dinner brushed past Mary and disappeared.

"We have no modern conveniences," Mary explained from the doorway. "You'll find water in the pitcher and I'll bring some hot in a few minutes from the kitchen. Then if you'll excuse me I'll freshen up and dress."

"Now, don't you let me be any trouble," lisped Lenora with a sugar-sweet drawl.

"No trouble," said Mary, trying to feel as kind as she sounded. "I've been heating some for myself and there's enough for us both."

No matter how fatigued she felt, a good wash and a vigorous brushing of her hair always gave new life to Mary. The touch of a cool, clean lawn dress was likewise refreshing; and later, casting a last glance in her mirror, she was satisfied that the meditative image reflected there was neat and comely.

She encountered Lenora in the living room, curled up like a kitten in Wilbur's chair.

"What tons and tons of hair you have!" Lenora commented half-enviously. "And it has that wonderful least little bit of a wave in it. Why don't you wear it bobbed? They say it's the thing in warm weather. It's awfully French, you know."

"Yes, only I'm not so sure the French ladies wear it that way." Mary was trying to decide what was wrong with Lenora's hair.

To Mary's surprise Lenora burst out unexpectedly, "How do you like it?"

"What?"

"My hair. It's bobbed. Don't you think it's adorable? A little thin, but I think bobbing it will thicken it."

"Oh, yes, undoubtedly it will!" said Mary, absently.

"Now don't let me interfere in any way," Lenora begged sweetly. "I've brought several books to read. You don't have to entertain me. Run along and do what you have to do. And don't go to too much trouble for dinner tonight. I'm just one of the family, you know."

Mary set the table, ironed napkins, prepared vegetables and cooked while the third member of the family buried herself in a book, one with a glaring jacket on which a strangely doomed young couple of rather odd physical proportions seemed engaged in an eternal kiss.

Wilbur joined them at dinner, very properly groomed and wearing a brand-new tie.

Mary might not have noticed the tie, engrossed as she was in her duties as wife and hostess, if it had not been for Lenora.

"What a heavenly blue, Wilbur! Just like your eyes! Wasn't he smart to get a tie to match his eyes, Mary?" she effused. "And did you ever see more beautiful eyes than his?"

At one time Mary had thought them attractive too. Too often, however, since then she had seen them glint with the blue of cold steel, had watched them grow cold and lifeless as soiled snow.

"How am I ever going to marry if I can't find a man with eyes like Wilbur's?" Lenora babbled on. "Mother says when he was a baby everyone used to stop his nurse in the street to look at his eyes."

Wilbur, to Mary's surprise, seemed to be enjoying Lenora's childish prattle.

All dinner conversation was created by Lenora, who clung tenderly to the topic of Wilbur, starting from baby-hood and reaching—some little time after dessert had been served—that terrible day when Mary took him away from them. Never in all the world or in all time could there have been two men like Wilbur, judging from what Lenora had to say.

"Does she really believe it?" Mary wondered. She looked back from the kitchen after carrying away the dessert plates and saw brother and sister close together, he chucking her under the chin, lifting her little face close under his lowered head. They might have been sweethearts. Presently they walked arm and arm out to the porch. Mary proceeded to wash the dishes, happy to be alone.

She took it for granted that they wanted her to join them later; therefore, as soon as her work was finished, she went outdoors. They were not on the porch, so she walked around to the rear of the house. Maybe Wilbur was showing Lenora the garden. But they were not in the garden either, and Mary, baffled by their complete disregard of her, was about to return to the house when voices floated up to her from under the cottonwood beyond the wire fence. She paused irresolutely. The dead hush of young evening had touched the desert. Clearly through the warm air came the sound of voices—whispers overloud.

First Lenora: "Well, I'll bet she's got money and she's holding out on you. A tricky Northerner, that's what she is."

Then Wilbur: "No, Norry, you've got that wrong. I thought so once. There's where I got fooled."

Tricky Northerner! Tricky Northerner holding out on Wilbur! They meant her! Of course they meant her! Oh, no, it was too sordid, too sordid and too cruel. She could not have heard aright. Mary did not enjoy her role of eavesdropper. She walked noisily along the wire fence. The voices lowered on her approach.

She knew that she was flushed and breathing hard when she approached them, and that her "So there you are!" did not sound as casual as she planned it. It did not astonish her that she had surprised them.

"I came out here to have a little talk with Lenora," said Wilbur.

"Just Lenora?" asked Mary with a catch in her voice.

"Yes, just Lenora. I'm going away tomorrow and there are things we want to talk about that won't be of interest to you."

"You don't mind, dear, do you?" Lenora's sweetness was exasperating.

"Oh, please don't consider my feelings in the matter," returned Mary with a laugh that was not at all gay. "I am used to being put in my place. I wish you both a pleasant evening."

She left before they could hear the sob that rose to her lips. "I'm tired—too tired," Mary said to herself, outrunning threatening tears on the way to the porch. There they fell in a quick rush. It made her unhappy to be tired and lonely. The burden of it weighed upon her. But Mary was not given to tears for long. Tears meant surrender, and to surrender was to be weak.

She walked out to the broad avenue, the one and only thoroughfare of Taho, and along it to the desert in which it ended. Theirs was the last house on the avenue, a circumstance that afforded Mary pleasure in her times of stress—the desert close and intimate, and people all behind her, lost in their own petty interests and unconcerned with hers. The desert was like a father, profound in unspoken consolation, in the understanding of the loneliness of one's soul, wise with the wisdom of years, sad with the sorrow of age.

Mary's eyes grew accustomed to the darkness which had fallen with the suddenness of the desert. She felt the great loneliness about her, she heard the whispered rustle of a breeze in the brush and the chirp of a cricket, melancholy, sad. She came across a discarded government wagon which would soon go under the ax, and she climbed to the high seat, from which she could look down and through the solemn glory that she loved.

Out there was Castle Mesa and fifty miles beyond Black Mesa, and Curry was there—Curry, the only person who had ever expressed a feeling for her that sprang from the needs of the soul.

The next day Wilbur left. Lenora shed a few tears and promised she would take care of her sister-in-law. "He's asked me to," she confided to Mary.

Mary felt that Wilbur's admonition was pretense and wished with all her hungry heart that it could have sprung from tender solicitude. As she went about her work with the energy of a healthy, vigorous woman, she was aware of Lenora's scrutiny from time to time.

"You ought to live in Texas where you can get help cheap," Lenora suggested over the top of her book from the depths of Wilbur's chair. "We couldn't exist if we had to do our own housework."

Mary smiled at this remark from the Texas lady. Lenora had no idea that her own grandmother had referred to the junior Newtons as a lazy shiftless lot, the frayed-out stock of a broken-down aristocracy, and had explained that their continual indebtedness came from such unnecessary luxuries as a general-work girl, or a procession of them who came and left, left usually with a threat to sue for their back wages. How that proud impoverished old lady deplored her son's deterioration and the hopeless wasters his shiftless wife had brought into the world! Yet her complaints had come over soft, fluffy dresses with which her rheumatic fingers struggled and which her conscience excused with the saying that the girls couldn't go naked. How Mary had pitied the generous old soul!

Day after day, Lenora, when not reading, lounged under the cottonwood tree that spread its shade into Mary's front yard from the edge of the broad avenue. Her gay-colored dresses were signals of her presence there. They drew attention from Taho's citizens and the few strangers who passed through. Following her appearance, several people called on Mary, people not usually given to social intercourse. It developed that Lenora had spoken to them and pressed them to come to the house for tea. She took it upon herself to go to the post and purchase some fancy crackers which she charged to Wilbur.

Soon Mary noticed that several cowboys, engaged in building a government barn across the road, spent the fag-end of their lunch hours along the roadside under the shade of the cottonwood, not far from Lenora's customary place to which she retreated the minute lunch was over. Presently Lenora announced there was going to be a dance at the government mess and she guessed she would go, though Mary could not, Wilbur being away.

It was a fine-looking half-breed Indian, an educated young man in government employ, who brought Lenora home from the dance. He talked so audibly during scattered moments of the hour that he lingered with Lenora on the porch, that Mary, in the room beyond, recognized his voice and could not sleep.

"Nice set of young folks for such a small place," Lenora

commented the next morning. "But I haven't seen a man yet who could give me a thrill. There must be some nice ones around somewhere."

Mary gave Lenora a look that was too honest for the Texas girl to take.

"Oh, I don't mean that I could marry and live out here," she hurried to say. "That would be all right if I were a native, to settle in a place like this, but with family, I've got to marry family, and someone with money too."

The remark savored of something that had passed between her and Wilbur that night before he had left, and Mary suffered a strange sinking sensation for a moment.

"Wouldn't you like to ride some day?" Mary asked by way of changing the conversation. "I can borrow some horses."

"I've got such delicate skin and I'd ruin it out in the sun. Now, if we could ride along in the shade . . ." Lenora left her conclusions for her sister-in-law to surmise.

Mary made no comment. Lenora, giggling foolishly, started on another tack.

"There's one condition under which I would go in a minute."

"What's that?" Mary asked with no great show of interest.

"If a certain cowboy asked me."

The remark failed to arouse any curiosity in Mary.

"Does he come this way often?" Lenora purred.

Mary recalled the three cowboys who were now on such easy speaking terms with Lenora. "Which one?" she asked.

"Curry—Mr. John Curry!"

Mary was staggered. She felt the blood mount to her face.

"Now, what are you blushing about?" Lenora taunted. "You—a married woman! That's why I want to meet him. He must be a wonder. You're usually so straight-laced, Mary, and if you've gone and fallen for him . . ."

As the girl went on with her merciless harangue, thoughts, strange and terrible, flashed through Mary's mind.

"You—have—met Mr. Curry?" Mary faltered.

"No, but I'm dying to. . . . Wilbur told me how completely he had turned your head, and he wants me here to keep him off."

"Oh-h-h!" Mary's exclamation was almost a wail. "And you believe your brother's slanderous, jealous talk! You dare to intimate that I—that I—would ... You are here to watch, to spy, to take care of me—you poor, silly little fool! Why I despise you, I pity you!"

Mary slammed the screen door and hurried out beyond the garden, down along the irrigation ditch toward the little house where Katharine lived. Brush caught at her skirt and tore her stockings. She tore it free and ran. A neighbor called a greeting to her and she shouted a response, but her feet carried her on faster and faster. Katharine at last! She stumbled over the low step and flung herself against the door. It gave way. Katharine, standing at the stove, a spoon in one hand suspended over a pot, was staring at her in amazement.

"Mary, dear, what's wrong!"

The spoon fell with a clatter. Mary, safe in Katharine's arms, sobbed out, "Oh, Katharine, it's too much for me! I tell you, it's just too much."

5

JOHN CURRY maintained his popularity among the cowboys at the Black Mesa trading post by demonstrating his need of their counsel. He was their leader by virtue of his power to control and because of his position of trust with Mr. Weston as chief of the outfit. Though he never pressed his authority, he exercised it wisely. Among the boys he was "good old John," the buddy of every fellow on the place. An unconscious recognition of John Curry's leadership was expressed in the epithet "old," for John, who had just reached twenty-eight, was younger than four or five of his own men.

That the leader of the outfit looked upon High-Lo as his own special charge endeared him even more to the rough, desert-bred men. High-Lo had become completely disassociated from his Christian name by his preference for the nickname John had given him. When addressed as Alex Hardy, he seldom responded. Readdressed as High-Lo, his characteristic grin immediately appeared. Alex Hardy lost his identity one day when Hicks, a cross-eyed, red-haired cowboy, came to John protesting, "I've looked for that dumb fool Alex high an' low an' I can't find him anywheres." Such was the usual state of affairs. Whenever Alex was especially needed, everyone had to join in a search for him, and as Hicks expressed it, "look high and low." The truant was often found far from camp, high in spirits because he had been up to some deviltry, or low in the torture of self-abnegation, stricken with a sense of his own uselessness. High-Lo, John had decided, was a good name for Alex.

66

High-Lo was a handsome young fellow short of twenty, with a tremendous store of energy which, in his early youth, had been misdirected. When he was a lad of seven or eight his father had introduced him to the delights of a whisky flash and had nourished in him the false notion that the true measure of a man was his ability to drink heavily without losing his sensibilities. High-Lo had tried his best to measure up to this standard, but seldom succeeded in meeting the required restriction. Consequently he was outlawed before he was eighteen by the man who had ruined him and the community in which he lived. He had faced the county judge once too often. Before High-Lo left the family homestead in Colorado, he rustled three of the county judge's own maverick calves, marked them with his father's brand, and personally presented them to the judge as a gift from a father who wished to show his appreciation for the judge's leniency toward his wayward boy.

It was on High-Lo's momentous exodus from his home state to nowhere, at which time he was intoxicatedly careless about whether he happened to be riding into Utah or Arizona, that he encountered John Curry journeying to Black Mesa from his brother's ranch in Colorado. The incident of their meeting opened a new chapter in the boy's life. High-Lo made the aimlessness of his ride known, and later sobbed out his troubles over a campfire. John adopted the boy at once, nursed him through his drunken sickness, then when he found him drinking again, after making an impressive ceremony of destroying High-Lo's stock, thrashed him soundly. At the close of a ten-day journey he brought in a thoroughly steadied new hand for Mr. Weston's outfit. The new hand developed into a much-loved nuisance, at once the best and the worst cowboy Black Mesa trading post had ever acquired.

At the Black Mesa post, contact with tourists made the cowboys fastidious about their attire, but High-Lo was not affected in like manner. He was individual enough not to care that his hair stuck through a hole in his sombrero, that his boots were seldom blacked and were run down at the heels. However, when John returned from Oraibi, High-Lo met him resplendent in new boots and sombrero and a painfully starched white cotton shirt, and with the confession that he had "fallen for the society stuff." John was not impressed. The source of High-Lo's inspiration was too obviously the Blakely girls. They had turned more than one cowboy's head, and each victim had complained to John of the folly of two nice pretty girls wasting their time on Hank Hanley. Hank Hanley's kind of girl was no kind for High-Lo. John worried for a week. At last he resolved to protest.

He looked for High-Lo in the store, the kitchen, the laundry, the toolshed, among the men and Indians who were idling before the door of the trading post, and finally, at Hicks's suggestion, sought him at the corral where he was headed when last seen.

The corral could not be seen from the trading post. The store and the cluster of buildings about it were arranged snugly against the slope of a great curving hill that swung down from the floor of the main valley. The corral was above on the high level, where an enchanting sweep of country never failed to delight John's love of scenic grandeur. Great hummocky mountains of red rock lifted above the ridges that confined the snug v-shaped lowland and hid the post, and bound the larger valley on the east. Four or five miles westward Black Mesa, dark with its growth of cedar, loomed majestically, presenting its impregnable corrugated front as far as the eye could see; and from the intercepting mesas of the north, the tremendous length of the valley broadened to a vast and limitless plain above which towered two great monuments of rock, one red, one black and gray. Greasewood, green from a good season of rain, carpeted the country with color. The air had been sweetened by a shower that had come in the night, and it carried the delicate fragrance of desert flowers.

High-Lo, intent on shoeing a horse, did not see John approach.

"So that's how you're putting in your time, cowboy!" John called to him.

High-Lo grinned. "Shore! I ain't wastin' none of my time when the boss is around. You want these fellers shoed, don't you?"

"Yes, the new tourists will be hitting the trail day after tomorrow."

"I'll show the outfit I can shoe a horse prettier'n the rest. Them lazy cusses was puttin' it off fer tomorrer."

High-Lo slipped some nails between his teeth and continued busily with his task.

"Think I'll send you out on the trail this time," John began.

The nails were blown wide, and High-Lo almost gave up his hold on the hoof between his legs. "What? Me? Again?" he expostulated. "It ain't my turn! What's the row? You goin'?"

"No, I'm not going."

"If that's the goods I'm not worryin' none about me goin'."

"I'm dead serious. I ought to keep Stuffy home, and you'll have to go in his place," John protested.

"There's nothin' wrong with Stuffy 'cept he's been eatin' too much. It'll be good for him to go out. He'll have to go easy on grub then." High-Lo was hammering hard again.

"That's all right, High-Lo. I'm entitled to an opinion once in a while," returned John.

High-Lo contemplated his boss a minute. "Say, ain't you hidin' suthin' under your saddle blanket?" he blurted out at last.

John did not meet the question directly. "I'm trying to hide a feeling that you're about ready to bust loose again."

"Lordy, cowboy, you hit it!" cried High-Lo. "That's what I am. An' I'll be even worse on the trail. You better keep me close to home. I hate to tell you, John, but I've took to liquor again."

John laughed out loud. "Anyone as smart as you deserves to be let out. Taken to liquor! This place is bone dry. A fellow could safely assure booze fighters that a vacation out here would cure them. You're not in Colorado. You're on an Indian Reservation in Arizona. I'd hate to be riding steady since you took your last drop."

"Then you're gettin' tender. I took my last drop yestiddy."

When High-Lo spoke the truth, he never failed to convince.

"Hey, cowboy, can't you tell me you're lying?" asked John uneasily.

High-Lo let go the horse's leg, led him into the corral and then swung to a seat on the timbers. "Not this time, John," he announced from his high place. "But don't get riled. I'll tell you about it. Honest, it's sort of funny."

John was not prepared to see it that way, but he listened.

"Yestiddy there wasn't no one to take the Blakely girls ridin', so I ups and offers my services."

"That's another thing," interrupted John, "Stub should have taken them."

"Stub couldn't. Someone shaved his hair off, an' he's hidin' like a settin' hen. Natural-like, with so many of the boys out, I had to take his place."

Inasmuch as High-Lo sounded so like injured innocence, John could not refrain from saying accusingly, "You're the hombre who tied Stub and shaved his head, you son-of-a-gun, because he was too popular with the Blakely sisters."

"Say!" burst out High-Lo, "I thought I was tellin' you suthin'! You're gettin' me off my trail."

"Beg your pardon," said John, aware that he himself was being sidetracked now.

"At the last minute one of the girls ups and guesses she won't go, and leaves me with the other, the youngest and prettiest one," continued High-Lo. "So me and my sweetie goes ridin' alone. When we get down in the Red Canyon Wash, she guesses she'll have a drink, and me not havin' a canteen thinks she's plumb crazy and has in mind that muddy water. But, John, she had a little canteen under her slicker no bigger'n a pint. She offers it to me and I thanks her and says no. Then she comes back that she won't take none unless I do and paralyzes me with a stare from them big calf eyes of her'n. So I hauled off for a swaller, and, by golly, John, I like to died. I spit all over the place. It wasn't water she handed me, it was good old Scotch. I was sick at the thought of wastin' it."

John swore mildly. High-Lo, ignoring him, went on. "She says, 'What did you think it was? Milk? I'm past my teethin' days and I only use water to wash in.' Honest, that girl that I thought must sure be awful nice said that to me. It was the first time I ever had anyone I thought was a lady offerin' me a snifter. I told her to help herself, an' then after I'd take another nip, an' I did."

"High-Lo, you were a skunk, to do that!" John shouted. "You missed a chance to let her know that all cowboys are not like Hanley. You should have told her what you just said to me—that it was the first time you ever had anyone you considered a lady offer you a drink of liquor. What's more, you broke your promise to me."

High-Lo leaped to the ground. "Don't be so damn quick to call me a skunk and to say I'm breakin' promises. I had a reason for wantin' to seem sociable. I would of told you, but I sure ain't goin' to now!"

"Suppose I suspect your reason," returned John. "Suppose that's the real reason why I'm sending you out on Wednesday."

"And suppose I won't go," muttered High-Lo.

"I'd have to fire you," retorted John, feeling despite his words an overwhelming affection for the boy.

"Would you?"

"Yes," replied John.

"Well, if you would, then you can!" At that High-Lo strode off. He ignored John's shouted order to come back.

Dozens of times in the past High-Lo had threatened to quit. Each time he had succeeded in rousing in John the fear that he might carry out his threat. Usually High-Lo's outbursts were followed by a two or three days' disappearance, then a return to his job with no reference to his absence, and a zeal for work never equaled by any other man at Black Mesa.

Today's bluster seemed less serious, though High-Lo did little save lounge around the post and avoid John every time he came into view. When he appeared for his meal at noon, he took Stuffy's vacant place instead of his own opposite Curry. Nevertheless John felt relieved.

All went well until late in the afternoon when John saw High-Lo riding out again with the younger Blakely girl. That was a significant climax to High-Lo's new mode of conduct. High-Lo knew he did not have to accompany Miss Blakely. There were half a dozen boys around who would have traded their horses to go in his place. It might be the girl or it might be the liquor, and one was as objectionable as the other from Curry's point of view. If it was High-Lo's way of punishing John, by giving him some anxious hours, he was certainly succeeding.

High-Lo was gone until sunset. John had ridden up to the ridge several times, unnecessarily, to scan the open country. His last trip had satisfied him that High-Lo would be in soon. When Curry caught sight of the pair loping their horses down the ridge, he loitered behind the saddle shed to watch High-Lo unobserved. The boy appeared soon, a saddle on each arm and singing lustily:

The old sow woke up in the morning,
And one of her pigs was dead.

His knowledge of the doggerel was limited to the two lines which he repeated over and over again. They, with the accompanying melody, were infallible signs of High-Lo's happiest moods, and these moods generally followed upon or led to mischief. His present levity, however, might have had its origin in Miss Blakely's canteen. John walked away. He did not want to encounter High-Lo right now.

In the hogan at the back of the post, a place used by John and several of the cowboys as a general dressing room, word was astir that an Indian had seen Hanley, who had left a few days before professedly on his way to Flaggerston, making camp twelve miles from Black Mesa in Cedar Pass. Hanley had lived a capricious existence ever since he had grown prosperous enough to hire someone to look after his sheep business; therefore a sudden change in his itinerary meant nothing. But the boys were wont to discuss Hanley on any provocation because they disliked him. John placed no credence in the suggestion that Hanley was laying for the couple of mules that had strayed from Mr. Weston's last camp in the pass.

The boys were loud in their deprecation of Topsy, one of the missing mules that nobody wanted to see again, when High-Lo arrived, looming tall in the doorway. His body seemed bronzed to the color of his curly hair. His eyes, blue and fiery, showed a dangerous twinkle. He looked about the hogan with grand contempt.

"How are yo'-all this evenin'?" he drawled. "I've been asked to announce as how Mr. Wilbur Newton has come to favor us at table, and tonight borrow some of our beddin' and our desert. I shore think yo'-all ought to be honored."

A born imitator, he cleverly caricatured Newton's voice and actions as he strode majestically into the hogan and seated himself, after haughty consideration, on a duffle bag that someone had flung in the center of the room.

"Now, yo'-all have been razzin' me aboot my new boots and hat, and someone was intimatin' around that they had a new pair of spurs for me. The time is come when I need them spurs, so take 'em right off, Beany, or I'll lay you low. I'm competin' for first prize as Arizona's dandy, and I've been stockin' up agin the day. Reckon I'm about to meet my sole competitor, and I've sure got to outshine him like the sun outshines the moon."

High-Lo turned to tow-headed Stub, whose short body was doubled up in laughter. "Here, yo', Stub! Black my boots." Then he turned to long, slim Waffles of the pock-marked face. "Here yo', Waffles! Brush my hat." He flung these articles of apparel airward.

Beany had paid no attention to the command issued to him, so High-Lo proceeded to fulfill his threat, and there would have been an even match in strength and brawn if John had not intercepted the onslaught, whereupon High-Lo drew himself up full height and said, "Reckon we've met before, stranger, so yo' bettah pack yore gun."

The boys howled.

"Quit your nonsense!" commanded John of High-Lo. "Has Newton really come?"

"Shore has. An' in full fancy regalie. He's buyin' up stuff from the Indians for the Taho post, but Pop Weston treats him like he's the best friend he ever had."

"You needn't worry that the Indians will sell their best things to Newton," spoke up Stub. "Pop Weston ain't worryin' none either."

At dinner High-Lo resumed his place opposite John, and Newton fell heir to Stuffy's vacancy. Guests, host and hostess, and the cowboys, thirty-two people in all, ate at one long table, so it was simple for Mrs. Weston to separate Newton far from the boys, and thus maintain peace.

John gave himself over to speculation during the meal. He did not like it that Hanley was camped at the pass when Newton arrived at Black Mesa. If Newton came through this afternoon he could not have missed Hanley. Somehow it looked prearranged. Hanley purposely had left Black Mesa before Newton arrived. He met him at the pass where no one but a chance Indian might see them. And Hanley would linger there until his friend's return. John felt sure of these conjectures. There was a reason why, at present, these men did not want to be seen in each other's company. Hanley had more important interests in mind than rustling a couple of outlaw mules. He found it less dangerous and more honest to cheat Indians in buying and selling sheep. His crooked deals with Hopis in the Taho country were well known. Newton, to all appearances a friend to the Indians, could win for Hanley the Navahos' confidence, and prepare the way for him to operate in new territory. That this was their game it was easy to believe. Let one Navaho complain of being cheated, then see what would happen to Hanley! The boys at Black Mesa loved the Navahos and meant to protect them.

Under John's distaste for Newton in his relations to men, boiled the resentment he bore him for his unworthiness of Mary. John had come to think of Newton's wife as Mary. That was his mother's name. He associated the mutual goodness of the two women with the simplicity and beauty and holiness of the name. He figured to himself how Newton would react were he aware of this, and pitied the man because he was incompetent to grasp the purity of such a regard. For Newton to force Mary to associate with a man like Hanley was a sacrilege; for him to become involved with the man in any deal that might illegitimately repair his fortunes was the rankest infidelity.

After dinner John took care to avoid Newton. He knew that Mr. Weston would not stand for any violence at the trading post, and that the only way to insure peace was to disappear. He went at once to the hogan in the hope that High-Lo might be there. But High-Lo was nowhere around. Nor had he shown up when John's watch registered ten o'clock. All the boys were hogan-shy tonight.

Long after ten Beany came in. "Oh, Lordy! You missed it!" he said. "That kid of yours is runnin' wild out there. He insulted Newton to his face and I was scared to death there would be nothin' short of gunplay, but that Texan's hide is so thick it didn't penetrate."

"What happened?" John's voice betrayed anxiety.

"We were all hanging around outside the post swappin' yarns, the Blakely girls and Mrs. Weston listenin' in, when High Lo, casual-like, says, 'By the way, Newton, I got a story you'll appreciate. It's about a feller who was tryin' for the governorship of one of the Western states. He come by train to a town where he expected to tell the folks how good an' grand he was, an' he got a jar when he found there wasn't no delegation there to meet him. He went paradin' up an' down the platform, his cutaway coattails swingin' madlike and his stovepipe hat jest set up straight like his hair was standin' up straight under it, when along comes a cowboy who'd been drinkin' more'n his ma said he could. He got kind of taken with the feller who was measurin' the platform and starts follerin' him up an' down, and sayin', "It's a lie! It's a lie!" He kept sayin' it so much that he got on the nerves of the high-an'-mighty can'idate, an' he swings around an' says, "What's a lie?" The cowboy hiccups a minute an' then says, "Mister, it's a lie! There ain't no one on God's earth as important as you look!" ' Would you believe it, Newton laughs first, everybody else holdin' back, and then lettin' loose like mad when they see it didn't hit him the way High-Lo intended!"

"High-Lo shouldn't have done that. He deserves a call!" It was not sympathy for Newton that brought the angry words from John. He was thinking of Mary, of how crushed she would be to know that everyone at Black Mesa was ready to ridicule the man she once loved enough to marry. He wanted to protect her from the people out there who had laughed. There was no question of the justice of their ridicule, it was a matter of injustice to her. He was furious with High-Lo.

"Hold on now, John, you know it was comin' to Newton," Beany expostulated. "Maybe he's jest slow to ketch on. Maybe he'll wake up to what High-Lo meant when he gets out on the trail, and take to shootin' rabbits for spite."

"Where's High-Lo now?" asked John.

"Sparkin' maybe."

"Sparkin'!" exclaimed John, falling into the vernacular.

"With that youngest Blakely girl he's so sweet on. She fell for his baby-blue eyes. I never had any real chance, but even if I did I'm sure a gone goose now." Beany sounded disconsolate. His round shoulders stooped beneath the burden of his despair and he bowed his black head in his hands.

John swore.

"You, too, heh?" commiserated the first sufferer. "No one would of thought it. You ain't much on the women. Still I was figurin' on what she'd do to you on that Snake Dance trip."

Beany's commiseration was too much for John. He went outdoors to walk and think; and he climbed the hill away from the corral. The night was dark. Few stars shone in the remote dome of the heavens. Clouds, blacker than the night, were massing over Black Mesa. A storm had slipped by them. A silence, cool and heavy like that of a sepulcher, hung over the valley. John was conscious of a deep pity working in his heart for boys like High-Lo and Beany whose values were so warped because of lack of education and experience. They could not recognize subtlety, they could not discriminate readily between girls like the Blakelys and a girl like Mary. They could classify the Blakely sisters with Mary because beauty of clothes and a polish greater than they knew baffled them. An experience like High-Lo's should serve as an awakening. High-Lo admitted that it did, but among desert men women were not so plentiful that their actions were judged too critically. These boys were bound by their simplicity and the ways of the desert.

The next day John's concern about High-Lo became a thing of the past. Before breakfast the boy begged a conference with his boss and apologized for yerterday's outbreak.

"I'll take Stuffy's place on the trail," he agreed. "I ain't got the right to tell you I won't. And you needn't to worry about the Blakely girls. They're drivin' their car to Taho today, an' Mrs. Weston says they're leavin' the reservation for good. And I'm shootin' straight, John, when I tell you that if they'd stayed a year, I'd never be seen with them again."

John felt a rush of pride in his cowboy. "Well, I'm glad to hear that, son," he said. "You won't have to take Stuffy's place. He's able to go himself. He's putting through a little bluff right now. If I got you to take his place, by Thursday Stuffy would be as lively as a frisky mule."

"But you're wrong," protested High-Lo. "Stuffy's awful sick. He had to take his bed inside last night. Said he had the chills. You better send me. Go ask Mrs. Weston, if you think I'm kiddin'!"

John smiled. "Mrs. Weston is overindulgent about you fellows. The fact is I know Stuffy. Stub found a plate in his tent last night from which a hearty meal had been polished—and he's supposed to be giving his stomach a rest! He hasn't a tenth of a degree of temperature. His chills come from the prospect of work. I ordered him up this morning."

"Send me out with him," ventured High-Lo. "He'd be no good if he took sick again. The boys would be short of help and things would move slow and this new party strikes me like a bunch of cranks."

"No need of that," John returned emphatically.

"Well, all I know is that you better think it over about sendin' me out," High-Lo persisted. "Let me know later."

For a moment John had misgivings about High-Lo. The boy's intimation of yesterday that he was supplied with liquor which he could consume on the trail flashed to mind. But the idea passed in John's shame for his doubting the young cowboy. High-Lo was just overzealous in his desire to make amends, an impulse that was typical of him.

Newton made ready to leave the post immediately after breakfast. High-Lo, observing his preparations from the toolshed, vouchsafed to John that Newton's departure would be good riddance. "Magdaline will be lonesome now," said the cowboy with a wink.

"Magdaline!" repeated John above the clink of the horseshoes he was tossing from a box.

"Yep, our little Indian friend, Magdaline, the pepper pot of the Navaho Reservation. Newton was walkin' an' talkin' with her last night. Can't testify to nothin' else."

John accepted High-Lo's news angrily. "I thought Magdaline was visiting her relatives at Sage Brush Springs."

"She was, but she come in last night. Where were you that you didn't see her?"

"How could Newton have ever met her?" asked John, ignoring High-Lo's question. "She was at school in California for three years, and she's only been home since June, and it was Mrs. Weston who brought her. This is Newton's first appearance at Black Mesa this summer."

"Newton didn't get quite that confidential with me," High-Lo replied sarcastically. "But I've got a hunch he ain't never seen her before. The oldest Blakely girl gave him the go-by for Beany, and he took what was left. Guess Magdaline was pretty willin'. An' you know, John, she does kind of get a feller somehow—for an Indian."

John was thoughtful for a moment before he spoke. "I'm afraid for her. She's too pretty for an Indian and too well versed in the ways of a white girl, and to add to the pathos of her situation, she has a mighty keen intellect. Her education is bound to make her suffer."

"What you're sayin' don't mean much to me," concluded High-Lo, obviously perplexed. "An Indian's an Indian. They're square shooters, an' I like 'em."

Boss and cowboy repaired to the corral, collecting other hands on the way to join them. There was always much to do on the eve of a party's leave-taking. John's attention was divided all through the day. He lost track of High-Lo. Indeed, he was grateful for his absence when it came time for the Blakely sisters to leave. They dallied at departure till John feared at the last moment that they might decide to stay. But at about three o'clock, much too late for them to make the rough road through to Taho by night, they called their good-bys and drove off.

"I'm not worried about them," said Mrs. Weston. "Let them camp alone if they must. I'm sure the devil takes care of his own."

John laughed to hear prudent Mrs. Weston talk that way.

High-Lo was not on time for supper, a fact John accounted for as the boy's wish to make amends through work. "Still," he argued to himself, as the meal progressed, "High-Lo owes it to Mrs. Weston to appear on time."

"Anybody here seen High-Lo?" he asked of no one in particular.

Stub spoke up at once. "Last I saw of him was about mid-afternoon when he jumped the corral fence and went racin' down the hill yellin' that damn song about the sow whose pig was dead." A red flush covered Stub's face and mounted to the crown of his shaven head. "Excuse me," he added, glancing furtively at the nearest guests, "I mean darn song."

"He must be cleaning up," said John. "Run up to the hogan, Stub, and tell him to shake a leg."

Stub was quick to comply and reappeared shortly. "He ain't there," he announced.

John tried to hide his annoyance. "Beany, you're through with your dessert," he said to the lanky youth next to him. "See if High-Lo is up at the corral."

To John's consternation, Beany's mission was as unfruitful as Stub's. He tried to assure himself that everything was well, but he had an uncomfortable feeling of alarm. He instituted a search for High-Lo in which the boys resentfully joined. Hicks, the oldest and most reliable cowboy, ended the quest in short order by offering certain deductions he had made.

"High-Lo's horse is missin'," he reported to John, "an' his saddle is nowhere around. Guess he's rarin' off somewheres."

"Thank you, Hicks," said John.

He strode off, prey to conflicting sensations. There was deviltry astir. High-Lo had left. What bothered him most was that the young cowboy had bluffed him to cover his intentions.

6

NEXT morning the cowboys rose early to round up the horses and mules that were going on the trail. No one mentioned High-Lo, at least not to John nor in his hearing; whereas John, with High-Lo filling his thoughts, was conscious of everyone's consideration.

As soon as the stock was brought down from the ridge, John assigned the boys tasks according to their efficiency. Unfortunately the best packer had left. Striving to forget this, John threw himself heartily into the work on hand.

Presently the foreground of the post became a place of color and action. Groups of horses and mules, neighing and hee-hawing, manifesting their rebellious spirits. The cowboys moved among them shouting, "Yo! . . . Hold 'em, cowboy! . . . Blast that lop-eared mule!" These and like exclamations came to John above the stamp of hoofs and the clink of spurs. Everywhere flashed the colorful designs of saddle blankets. On the edge of the scene Navahos in gay-colored tunics lolled about indolently.

John directed disposal of the piles of goods stacked outside the store—rolls of bedding, duffle bags, food supplies, Dutch ovens, pots and pans. Suddenly he became conscious of watchful eyes. He looked up to see Magdaline standing near and caught her warm glance and the gleam of her perfect white teeth. Her bronze face, unlike so many of her kin, was delicately molded.

"You, John Curry! You hide from me!"

John caught the coquetry in her lowered lashes. The whole charm of her was evident in that look, and in the fashionable cut of her cheap gingham dress.

"I've been busy," returned John in a matter-of-fact manner. "How are you, Magdaline?"

"Lonesome to see my friends," Magdaline replied, striving to woo his attention.

John met her words with silence.

"My friend High-Lo, no sooner I see him than he goes away," she persisted. "Why did he ride so fast?"

Her question startled John into immediate attention. "You saw him leave?"

"Yes. But he didn't see me. He went so like a thief that first I thought he was stealing a horse."

"What time did he go?"

"Four o'clock maybe. I was up on the ridge sitting by a mound waiting to jump out on you should you come that way. Then, too far away to speak, I saw High-Lo leading a horse. He stopped where a saddle was cached, saddled the horse, and rode away so quick the dust covered him."

"Which way?" queried John above her last words.

"Toward Four Mile Wash and maybe to the pass."

"Maybe to the pass," John repeated aloud. "Thank you, Magdaline."

"Then you didn't know at the time that he went. You didn't know why or where," Magdaline remarked thoughtfully.

John reflected that Magdaline's wits needed no sharpening. "Don't bother me just now," he returned. "I'll talk to you later."

"I wish you liked me as much as you like High-Lo," the girl went on stubbornly.

John, busy with new thoughts, was irritated by her perseverance. "Please run along, Magdaline," he said.

As she walked away, John heard one of the boys call her name. A merry response followed immediately. Tom, Dick, Harry—all were alike to her!

Magdaline's insinuation that High-Lo's goal was the pass provoked a surmise in John's mind which involved Hanley. He could conceive a desire on High-Lo's part to frustrate Hanley's plans, whatever they might be, by forcing his company on him; and he knew High-Lo would attempt such folly without thought of consequences. For this theory John disregarded his earlier ones wherein the Blakely girls had figured, but he failed to convince himself that he did so more from reasoning than from wishful thinking. His meditations led to a decision to follow High-Lo. Should his latest conjecture be wrong, a good half-day's ride lay between them, and High-Lo's destination and purpose would remain as uncertain as before. Someone had to cache grain in Noname Valley, miles beyond the pass. John decided that there was no reason why he could not undertake the mission himself. He would make no pretense about it. He would explain the twofold purpose of his journey to Mr. Weston. And if Mr. Weston protested, he would have to leave the man's employ. High-Lo's safety was worth that much to him.

He propounded the issue as soon as the outfit had departed and received prompt permission from his employer. Mr. Weston, too, demonstrated a steadfast affection for the troublesome but likeable High-Lo.

"Give yourself time. Hunt up the young scamp if you can," Mr. Weston said. "Don't worry about the post. Hicks will take care of things while you're away."

John moved with alacrity as he prepared his pack and loaded the string of pack mules with grain. The mules had to be driven and they would retard his progress; but better that his journey seem business-like to whomever he might meet on the way.

Less than an hour after the others had left, John was driving the mules over the ridge. Then he turned his back upon the tracks the others had made, and followed the trail to Four Mile Wash. The spirited animal in the lead set a brisk trot for the others to follow, which John encouraged with an occasional shout. They moved through the wide sweep of valley, along the interminable wall of Black Mesa on the left, hummocky red mountains and great jagged red peaks on the right, along a trail that cut through greasewood, green near by, gray-green in the distance toward the cedared flank of the mesa.

It was good to be alone. The beat of hoofs was music to John's ears. His nostrils welcomed the warm, fragrant breeze and his eyes watched its course through the brush. He looked up toward the mountains, thrilled by their majestic height. A pile of Navaho prayer rocks rose like a spiral of red flame on a distant promontory. John imagined a Navaho there looking down in peace over the land he loved, whispering the benediction his prayer bestowed:

Now all is well,
Now all is well.

But behind his meditations stirred uneasy thoughts of High-Lo, Hanley, the Blakely girls, and Newton, who, like disembodied spirits, remained in his consciousness. Then, the others fading before her, Mary Newton came to him, flooding his senses with her beauty and serenity. What comfort would come to him if he could only speak to her now, tell her about High-Lo, attempt to explain his devotion to the irresponsible but lovable boy! He could see the deepening serious look she would wear, hear her voice soften with sympathy and understanding. What a mother she would make for a boy like High-Lo! He could see Mary's black head bent over a fair one, reasoning patiently with such defiance as High-Lo must have shown when young. He could see her looking up from the child with a gentle confidence in her power, and a smile for him. Intimate, personal became Curry's thought, and a tender yearning possessed him. Unconsciously all the dreams of his youth were revived, and into them Mary had slipped, as the mother of his son, as his wife, into a place heretofore possessed only by an elusive, changing form and face. John felt hot blood mount upward through his throat.

"I'm loco," he muttered to his horse. "She's married. She belongs to another man. I swear to God I don't covet her. But I can't help seeing what she is. I can't help what my heart . . . And I can't let High-Lo go. I've got to have someone to take care of."

The leader of the mules, taking advantage of John's silence, had slowed down, but a single shout set him to trotting again and his lazy fellows mechanically fell into step.

John tried to evade the issue into which his thoughts had just betrayed him, but the dream persisted. There was no cause for shame. He loved where love was most needed. What had happened to High-Lo in his starved childhood was happening to Mary in young womanhood. Both had ill return for what they so freely gave. That, no doubt, was the thing that drew him to them most. Yet no word of Mary's had betrayed to him the things he knew. Newton's actions spoke for themselves. That day at the Snake Dance when for a moment he held her in his arms should have been a revelation to him. Why had it taken more than a week for him to recall the supreme joy of a moment now gone forever? Had the knowledge of her unattainableness come between him and the rapture of that moment? He owed thanks to the Almighty that it had. For John Curry, though he acknowledged his love of Mary Newton, in no way would stop to betray another man.

"Make every experience in your life count for good," his mother had said to him when as a boy a terrible disappointment had threatened his peace; and he had tried ever since to inculcate in his will the spirit of her words. He would make his love for Mary Newton count in that way. He would be a better man for having known her.

"Make me worthy to love her," he whispered, his eyes on the pile of prayer rocks. And forthwith to his heart came the knowledge that already the leaven of love was working for his good.

John came upon Four Mile Wash suddenly, so engrossed was he with his thoughts. The storm that had by-passed Black Mesa had made a turgid stream where normally only a dry bed showed. The mules declared their disapproval of the unexpected crossing by halting at the top of the steep declivity which led down into the wash, and refusing stubbornly to budge from their stand. John coaxed, urged, and at last resorted to his quirt. Failing in his efforts, he gathered some sharp stones and drove the animals forward with stinging blows. The wash was so familiar to him that a glance was enough to assure him that no more than three feet of water were passing through. He knew the mules could make it easily.

The Blakely girls' car had dug deep ruts where they had driven their way out of the wash the day before. And some half-baked horseshoe prints present there had probably been made by High-Lo's horse a little later in the day. These signs assured Curry that he was on the right trail, even though Hi-Lo's and the Blakely girls' trails seemed to be identical.

The mules' hoofs scattered dust over their wet thighs in their prodigious labor to gain the sunlight again. Gaining the top of the grade at last, they came to a panting stop. John favored their mood with a few minutes of rest, then sent them forward with a shout.

For a few miles the trail continued as level as a table top, and then began to climb. The rise was so imperceptible that only the distant acclivity could testify to the change. John always anticipated the change in altitude by watching for scrubby cedars and taller greasewood bushes. It was five miles to the pass from the place where the cedars first showed! New uplands bisected Black Mesa and the country of rolling rocks, and these uplands met far ahead where they formed the defile through which John must pass to reach Noname Valley. The trail led slightly to the left for a couple of miles, and Black Mesa seemed more remote the closer the intercepting highlands came. What seemed a mere angular junction viewed from the ridge above Black Mesa trading post became a huge arena encircled by massive walls of terraced red rock on which dwarf cedars grew.

Soon the leader mule was plodding up the steep part of the trail which wound around and over hillocks on its toilsome way up the mountain. From the higher level, where John again halted the pack animals for a rest, the country took on a new aspect. Black Mesa, for a while lost to view, now appeared again, grander, more indomitable than ever. The mountains of red rock were crowned with massive bald hummocks, and they turned aside to form the mouth of Noname Valley, across which cut a wonderful canyon, red-throated and marked with the green of cedar and greasewood. John continued the climb. The trail widened. Above the receding mountains of rock he saw golden spires, new red walls and startling eminences. Presently he was descending to a parklike opening bound on one side by the canyon, on the other by slopes of piñon and cedar. He had reached the camp site of Cedar Pass. Not for a moment did John entertain the thought that Hanley had camped in the open, or that he would be there now. Therefore he dismounted to reconnoiter.

He followed the hoofprints of a shod horse to a nestlike site hidden from the trail by a cluster of cedars and high brush. This place bore convincing evidence of a recent camp. Freshly opened cans, with fragments of their contents still moist, and the charred coals of a recent fire were conclusive proofs. Hoofprints of unshod horses showed on the rise above the camp, likely made by the Indians who had reported Hanley's presence in the pass. John made a careful survey of the immediate ground. Other and larger tracks showing from another direction proved that a second shod horse had ridden that way. The first tracks mingled with these others and led away in the direction from which the second horse had come. All these tracks had been made since the last rain. High-Lo, an unbidden guest at that camp, had ridden away with his host.

Straightway John went down the hillside, following the progress of the two riders. They had crossed to the sloping wall of the canyon and passed down the canyon trail. Either they were headed somewhere along the canyon or they had crossed over the valley. Curry sat motionless for several long moments, trying to determine which route the two riders had taken and why they had taken it together.

In short order he was on the move again. A broad sheet of water collected from the storms of the week had saturated the floor of the canyon, and made tracking through the adobe mud an easy thing. A bright stream wound its noisy way down the canyon. John watered his animals there. Forward across the canyon led the tracks of the two horsemen Curry was following. What a happy coincidence that they were heading for the valley! His plan of procedure was simple enough now. It was only six miles to the cave in which he intended to cache the grain. Once relieved of his load he could hobble the mules and turn them loose, and be free to go his own way.

With the canyon behind him, John followed the familiar trail between a deep wash and the more remote hummocky hills at the foot of the billowing swells of red rock. Cedar and piñon were plentiful, and high up on the slopes were stubby pines. Noname Valley actually was a succession of valleys, wide in sweep and colorful, opening one upon another at the very places where they seemed shut off by the abutments of the red mountains that encircled them. The trail soon led away from the wash toward the foothills and the nearest defile. Midway into the foothills was the cave John sought, and his practiced eye, keen though it was, often searched and researched the slopes before he could locate the cleverly concealed hiding place. There was no trail. The way led over bare rocks. A clump of trees marked the place where his detour began.

Arriving there, John dismounted for a careful study of the tracks he was about to leave. To his surprise he found prints of the shod hoofs of a third horse. At times they came between the other prints, at times they completely blotted them out. The third rider was not an Indian—that was certain. Could he be following the other two? Then it might not have been High-Lo who had joined Hanley at his camp! If not, who had? And where did this third party, if it *was* High-Lo, cut in? John upbraided himself for being so sure of the second rider's identity in the first instance. A

little doubt would have made him observe the trail more
closely.

Caching the grain was a task quickly dispatched, and
John did not linger to brood over his mistake or to analyze
the new complication. He mounted his horse and drove the
reluctant mules over the bald surfaces of the low foothills.
There was no sign of life about. The breeze had died out
completely. A vast silence was suspended from the blue
arch of the sky to the motionless physical features about
him. Nothing moved. Only the click of his horse's hoofs
against the rock broke the deep silence. Yet John's ear was
inclined for other sounds, a trained ear waiting to receive.
He had a strange apprehension that he was not as completely alone as appearances indicated. Suddenly a sharp
crack sounded. Something struck a rock behind the ridge he
was mounting. Crack, crack, crack, came the sound again.
John, intent on the direction from which the sound had
come, leaned forward in his saddle. The mules halted and
John rode ahead to the top of the ridge. Then he relaxed
with a laugh. On the other side of the ridge was the outlaw
mule, Topsy, standing with stupidly inquisitive eyes, one ear
erect, one flopping down, nonchalantly rapping her tail
against the brush. Topsy was trying to find the oft-trodden
way to the cave. She fell into line with a meekness that
would have made the boys at the post stare open-mouthed.
Her truancy had ended.

John had to rest the mules several times before he
reached the cave. But once he arrived, every motion he
made counted to bridge time between him and High-Lo.
Cedars protected the mouth of the cave and darkened its
interior. It was short of five feet in height, but extended
back for quite a distance, and it kept the grain secure from
any kind of exposure. John had to bend low to enter. The
cave was supposed to be cleared of grain, but he could see
in the semidarkness that something was stacked against the
wall. Immediately unburdening himself of the pack he
carried, he crawled back to investigate. He reached out
against the bulk before him and withdrew with a shudder of
revulsion. He had touched the form of a man that was
huddled like a sack against the wall. The thought of an
Indian sleeping there came as soon as the momentary
horror was dispelled; but he realized at once that this was
no Indian. Could it be—John's breath was held suspended
by the terrible thought. Quickly and none too gently he

reached for the man and dragged him to the light. Then a terrible helplessness took possession of him.

"My God! It *is* High-Lo!" he muttered.

There was blood on John's hand where he supported the boy's head.

"Foul play!" he said aloud. "Damn them, they'll pay for this!"

He backed out of the cave, drawing High-Lo with him. High-Lo, it soon was revealed, was not dead; his heart beat a low irregular rhythm and his pulse fluttered weakly. John was conscious of a strange rush of joy electrifying his shaken body. He could see that the blood which matted High-Lo's curly hair came from a wound near the crown of his head. It was not a bullet wound. He had been struck with something sharp, perhaps from behind. Curry could see that even in his unconsciousness the boy's lips were drawn tight in pain. No amount of cold water applications to his face and forehead served to revive him, so John set about cleaning the wound and binding it with strips from his cotton undershirt. Then he hobbled the mules, stacked the balance of the grain in the cave, slung High-Lo over his shoulder, and leading his horse by the reins walked with them down the slick mounds of rock to the clump of cedars that marked the trail. Eighteen miles to the post, and High-Lo unconscious—how long unconscious, only God knew! And he might never come out of it! That thought alone was staggering to John.

At the cedars he forced High-Lo into the saddle and mounted behind where he could brace the sagging form with his arms and body. Nugget was a good horse with a good trot, and John loved him more for the service he was about to render. But to trot even with the very best of horses was dangerous to anyone in High-Lo's condition. John saw at once that High-Lo's body, limp as a rag, registered each motion like a shock and realized that the banging contact of the boy's head and his shoulder must be avoided. Therefore he slowed Nugget to a walk. He estimated that it was close to three o'clock when they got started, and trusted that they would make the post before nine.

There were times when John feared that High-Lo had stopped breathing altogether, and there were anxious moments when his own breath came hard. He knew he could not stand to have High-Lo go. He found himself measuring

the boy's worth against many more fortunate men he had
known. All High-Lo's failings passed away before the vision
of the struggle the boy had made to abandon his old way of
life for things clean and wholesome. If the young cowboy
had been born into happier circumstances, with possibilities
of education and the right discipline for his willfulness, he
would have made a leader of men. At Black Mesa he
became the favorite of family and guests alike by reason of
his lovableness and happy nature.

In time John became aware that Topsy was mincing
along behind, which made him reflect that High-Lo was the
only cowboy who had ever been able to elicit any service
from the stubborn mule. Did she in her dumb-brute way
surrender because she was somehow aware of her master's
presence, or did she follow because she sensed that High-
Lo, the once mighty, was now in trouble? Mules were
strange beasts, stupid judging from appearance and conduct
common to them, yet capable on occasion of demonstrating
shrewd intelligence. Right then and there John formed a
lasting attachment for Topsy.

Never had the ride from the cave to the pass seemed so
interminable; the six miles between, to be sure, were generous cowboy miles. The valley was cool with the shadows of
late afternoon before the rim of the canyon showed. The
arm that held High-Lo in the saddle was numb, and riding
the trail that wound in and out of the canyon was a difficult
thing under the circumstances. It took all of Curry's power
of strength and will to keep High-Lo from shifting in the
saddle. Topsy still followed along.

While riding through the cedars of the pass John's attention was arrested by the beat of hoofs, and watching
intently in the direction from which the sound came, he
descried the shadowy forms of a horse and rider approaching. In another moment he identified the rider as a
woman. There was something so familiar about her and her
mount that he sensed immediately that the rider was Magdaline. Yet hours earlier he had left Magdaline with the
Westons at Black Mesa trading post. An unjustified irritation arose in John.

Though the girl was aware of his approach she gave no
sign of greeting until she dismounted several yards away
and came to him on foot, running. John checked his horse
and swayed uncomfortably in the saddle. Topsy at once
trotted off to a shady place under the cedars.

"What's—the matter—with High-Lo?" Magdaline panted, her eyes wide with fear.

"He's been hurt. Badly, I'm afraid. Maybe you can help."

"How far have you come?"

"Six miles down the valley."

"I see. I wondered why you were so long. Better let him down a while. I can ride like the wind to the post and send back a car. Are you not glad I came to meet you, John Curry?"

"I'm glad you happened to be here," John returned gruffly.

"Get down while I hold him," the girl commanded.

John dismounted heavily. A minute later he had High-Lo in his arms and was staggering to a place under a tree which Magdaline indicated.

"How long has he been unconscious?" she asked. Her manner was different now. She was impersonal and aloof.

"About two hours or more that I know of. He was unconscious when I found him."

"You go back to the canyon and get some cold fresh water," Magdaline ordered. "You need the exercise. I will work over High-Lo for a while. As soon as you come back I will ride to the post. I think you ought to wait here. I would not move High-Lo now. You may be making him worse."

She might have been an Indian princess from the manner in which she assumed command. Her dark eyes flashed proudly and her hand moved imperatively with that no-loss-of-motion grace peculiar to the Navahos. And she wasted no more time in foolish questioning; her desire to help was stronger than her curiosity. John warmed toward her, and acted on the advice she gave. He left them together, High-Lo's head resting on her thigh.

Quickly John dispatched his errand, and the weariness left him as Magdaline had said it would. When he came riding through the cedars again, he saw at once that High-Lo's position had changed, his face was turned away and an arm was flung over his head.

An assuring smile from Magdaline gladdened his return. "He moved and he spoke," she said. "But he has not his senses yet. He acts like a tired little boy."

There was something ineffably sweet about the Indian

girl at that moment. She was a mother with a child, a Mary of another race, moved by instincts common to all woman-kind. She had opeened High-Lo's blouse and exposed his breast, and now her hand moved slowly up and down along his side.

"I'm afraid he is hurt here worse than his head," she said. "Here is where his hand went to when he groaned."

John stooped over High-Lo and forced the canteen against his lips. Magdaline, to assist, tilted High-Lo's chin, and her action more than the water, which largely spat-tered down his cheek and breast, brought a sign of life from the boy. He writhed and his face screwed up in pain as simultaneously his arm came down in weak protest against her hand. Then he sank back with a groan and his eyelids fluttered in successive attempts to lift. Finally they held in a wide stare.

"Where am I?" High-Lo's question was accompanied by a sigh. He breathed in irregular jerks and each breath seemed to bring pain. "Where are those dirty sons-of-guns? . . . Quit pressin' my side, you idiot!" Not once while he spoke did his eyes leave John's face, but there was no recognition in the stony stare.

"Don't you know me, High-Lo?" John asked. "It's John."

High-Lo did not answer. His eyes followed Magdaline's arm and on up to her face, then returned to John. His brows knit in a perplexed frown. "Why is *she* here if you're John?"

"Come on, buddy," said John gently. "Try to think! This is your pal, John Curry. You ran away yesterday. I trailed you. I found you in a cave."

Just then Topsy brayed vociferously. Suddenly the first gleam of intelligence showed in High-Lo's eyes.

"Oh, shore, the cave!" he managed to articulate. "And that damn mule brayin' all the time. . . . Oh, my God, my side!" His hand went quickly to his side, the train of his thought broken. "John . . . John might come," he muttered after a while. His eyes traveled aimlessly until they met John's again. "You say John did come? Oh, yes, so you did."

Magdaline was a silent, pitying witness, but now she spoke. "He's coming out of it. Make him drink."

"Take a swallow, son," urged John, offering the can-teen.

High-Lo gave a wry smile. "Don't mind if I do."

He wanted the water, but it seemed to hurt him to swallow, and after a few gulps he pushed it away.

"Someone said something about the cave," he pursued, as if revived by the little water he had taken, and plainly endeavoring to collect his wits. "Shore, I was in the cave. How did I get here?"

"I brought you," said John. "But don't try to think about it now. Magdaline's going to the post for a car. We'll get you home as fast as we can."

"Magdaline ... home," repeated High-Lo. "Yes, and make it quick, cowboy. I think some of my ribs are broke."

"I was thinking that," said Magdaline. "You come here and take my place and get his shirt off."

"We've got to bind him with something," John insisted.

"Yes, I know," Magdaline returned. "You do what I say."

She left them and disappeared for a few minutes. When she came back she waved a white petticoat.

"This will make good bandage," she called.

In no time she prepared strips and presented them to John.

"Not too tight. . . . There! I'm going now. I'll send Hicks back too. Mrs. Weston says he can set broken bones."

She walked to her horse, mounted and rode away. One minute John saw a flash of a gingham dress, the next minute it was gone. Magdaline, true to her word, would race like the wind to the post.

John turned to High-Lo again and found the boy studying him intently.

"Good old John, so it *is* you," High-Lo said in glad recognition. "Things are comin' back to me now. I'll be able to tell you all about it soon."

"Let me finish this job first," John suggested. "And be sure you're up to it. It can wait, you know."

John had to knot the strips of cloth together to make his bandage effective, and he took infinite care that the knots came where they were least annoying.

"They're broke all right," winced High-Lo. "Careful of—that left side."

Next John unsaddled his horse to use the saddle and blanket as a prop for High-Lo's head.

"Wonder where my horse is," High-Lo said.

It was a question that had baffled John too, but he had long ago committed it to his ignorance of events.

"We won't worry about your horse," John returned. "He'll find his way home unless someone rustles him."

He settled down beside High-Lo and lit a cigarette.

"Cricket may be a mighty pore horse when he does get home," High-Lo reflected. "Let me tell you about it now."

John hesitated to encourage High-Lo, but the boy's impatience was proof of his normal activity of mind, so he capitulated with a warning to him against overexertion.

"Might as well begin from the beginnin', buddy," High-Lo declared. "It goes back a few days. Remember, we had words about that Blakely girl an' me drinkin'? That starts it. I did like her honest and fine for a bit till I got wonderin' how she could stand Hanley and how it come she knew him before she come to the reservation. I had a hunch about Hanley that I wasn't tellin' to no one. I'm naturally trustin' and when that fails me I'm always sure there's sumthin' wrong. Well, the mornin' of the first day I went ridin' with Miss Blakely I comes sudden on to her an' Hanley, and before they see me I hear Hanley say, 'You needn't be worryin' none. Newton's got a good excuse for comin' on the reservation. You an' your sister skip. The rest's easy.'

"That sounded to me like business and the kind of business I've been suspectin'. I didn't let on I seen them until after I heard. I let 'em think they saw me first. Right then I got awful anxious to go ridin' with that girl, an' I got what I wanted, an' I had to shave Stub's head to do it.

"I told you what happened—about her offerin' me a drink. I didn't get that far in my calcerlations, I didn't think she had any use for booze herself. I honest was staggered. An' I took the drink 'cause I wanted her ter think I was as cheap as herself—that I'd think her pert an' smart an' considerin' of me. I was aimin' for her to get confidential. It got as far as this—that she could get me some of the stuff awful easy an' she could get it to me soon. I took her up quick like I wanted it. But she didn't know the hombre she was buckin'. The next day, after you an' me locked horns, I took her ridin' again. I was after more information, but all I got was booze an' a glad eye. But I was layin' for Newton to come pretty soon, an' he did. I had an idea of follerin' up what was goin' on, an' you had to bust it by comin' along that mornin' sayin' I had to go along on the trail. That's where the row come in. I was goin' to tell you everythin', but you made me bullheaded.

"Well, after Newton come—the girls keepin' away from him like they didn't want to know him better—I knew I had to trail him an' Hanley, an' where I'd find the one bad egg the other'd be in the same nest. It come to me it was just as well I didn't tell you things. You'd been afraid to let me go, an' you'd gone yourself, so I tried the goin' in Stuffy's place idea just to get away from the post alone. I'd of gone a piece with them an' then quit the outfit flat, an' you wouldn't of known or been worryin'. I was desperate to make a killin' all by myself. You see, John, I've never done nothing worth while in my life before.

"I knew shore as mules kickin' when Newton headed out for Sage Brush Springs he'd no intention of goin' there. I could see him trailin' back around that other mesa an' goin' round about to Cedar Pass. I lay to make a getaway early, but them fool Blakely girls put off goin' until late an' I couldn't risk them passin' me on the trail. It just come dark when I got to the pass. I tied Cricket this side of where we camp, an' was goin' ahead on foot when I heard a horse neighin' down toward the canyon. I'd of killed Cricket if he answered. Guess he was too busy nippin' brush. Anyway he didn't answer an' I almost bust my eardrums listenin'. There were two horses makin' that canyon trail. I could hear their hoofs against the stones. I let 'em have the canyon to themselves, but I brought my horse over near to the rim. When them fellers got down into the canyon I could make out the sound of 'em clear as a bell. I give 'em lots of rope. I took my time startin' after, an' when I did I made my own trail way down the near side of the pass. When I come out the other side of the canyon I saw a fire about three miles down. An' it wasn't no squaw fire. Lucky, I knew every rock of the country clear to our cave. I picked my own trail way over toward the hills. Then I tied Cricket in a gully about a mile from that campfire an' I put out on foot.

"I didn't have to get too near the place. Hanley and Newton must've had a few drinks in them an' were talkin' loud. I heard all I needed in a short time. An' boilin' it down, it's this. They're in a liquor-runnin' deal with that Mormon horse wrangler, Tim Wake, over to Gallup, to sell booze to the Indians. An' they was on their way to meet

Wake at Canyon Bonito. Seems they was early an' had to waste time, Newton havin' to come when his boss sent him. Ain't he the skunk, stealin' time from MacDonald? An' say—the way I heard 'em talkin' about the Blakely girls who are mixed up in the buyin' end of the rot-gut booze an' of other women in general made me mad enough to shoot 'em down right there. John, I've heard men talk plenty dirty about women, but never nothing like that. An', believe it or not, John, they tell me that feller Newton has a mighty sweet wife, pretty as a picture and as good as she's pretty!"

A pang tore through Curry's breast. "Yes, I know. I've met her. . . . Go on with your story, High-Lo, and make it short. You're tiring yourself."

"Shore that they were stayin' the night," High-Lo continued, "I made camp a mile back where I'd left Cricket. I ate a bar of stale chocolate an' some crackers. It was the only grub I'd brought with me. Next mornin' I was up 'fore it was really light an' sittin' in a cedar I watched fer smoke from Hanley's camp. It come, but late. They was takin' their time. After a while they went on. I had to keep to the hills because they'd see me in that open country. I kept a good mile an' a half between us, an' that made me just about below the cave when they reached that narrer pass into the next valley. They was lopin' their horses then, an' I figured to do the same an' make even better time for fear they'd cut over the rocks an' disappear. I took straight down to the trail an' set Cricket scootin'.

"Then pretty soon I got mine. It was in that very narrer place where you pass between two cedars. Just as I made it Cricket done the funniest flop I ever seen, an' throwed me like a bullet so that I was wedged in a place between two rocks. I sort of remember Cricket comin' to her feet an' tearin' away like she was loco. Then I must of passed clean out. I come to pretty dizzy an' with an awful pain in my head an' side. I whistled for Cricket, but Lord knows where he went to. Then I walked over to the cedars, an' I'm tellin' you, I cussed! Hanley an' Newton had fouled me. They must of got wind that someone was follerin', an' hurryin' to the pass they stretched a len'th of bobwire across the trail from tree to tree about three feet from the ground. It was so cussed gray there in the shade that it didn't show. By Judas, when I think of what that damn bobwire must of done to Cricket's legs! An' it like to killed me besides. Now just

suppose I'd been an innocent son-of-a-gun Indian? I
thought of that when I took the blame wire down. I cached
it near the tree. Maybe I'll find use for it some day.

"I knew'd I was pretty bad hurt an' sick to my stomach,
an' in a devil of a hole at that. It come to me that someone
would be cachin' grain today, an' then, too, I got a crazy
notion you might be comin' with it a-purpose, so I dragged
myself to that cave. I must of been out of my head 'fore I
got there. I remember singin' goin' over them rocks. 'The
old sow,' I guess I was singin', an' a mule hee-hawed back
at me an' kept keepin' on. I figure I must of fainted in the
cave with that infernal hee-hawin' buzzin' in my ears."

As High-Lo talked, John had been connecting the liquor
episode at Oraibi with Hanley's and Newton's present
activities.

"So that's their game," he muttered. "And they might
have killed you and the next fellow who came that way
with their barbwire trap. Someday we'll tie those fellows up
with their own wire and turn them over to the sheriff in
Flaggerston. I never dreamed that fool Newton would have
the guts to stage such an outrage, but I guess he's pretty
much of a slave to Hanley's whims."

Curry noticed then that High-Lo's head had slipped from
the saddle. The boy seemed too tired and weak to care,
now that his story had ended.

"Let me make you a little more comfortable, son. You've
exhausted yourself talking," John said, as he lifted High-
Lo's head to the rolled-up blanket. "It will be getting cool
with that sun going down so I'd better rustle some
wood."

High-Lo winced when John moved him, but declared
with a grin that he was lucky to be alive. "It'll take
consid'able killin' to finish me," he said between clenched
teeth.

Red and gold streaked the sky, and through the cedars
remote spires and peaks gleamed above vermilion mountains. A breeze sprang up and sighed through cedars and
brush. Soon the sun sank, the afterglow faded, and Curry's
fire split the gloom of twilight. High-Lo had fallen into a
heavy, troubled sleep. Occasionally John caught the sound
of Topsy and Nugget grazing nearby, the rattle of a stone,
the scraping of hoof against a rock. But aside from these
peaceful sounds and the increasing moan of the desert wind
there was silence.

John rehearsed the things High-Lo had related. As the dirty schemes of the two men began to register more clearly in his consciousness, he felt an overwhelming desire someday to catch Hanley and Newton red-handed so he and High-Lo would have the satisfaction of turning them over to the authorities. But he had not thought of Mary then. Suddenly what it would mean to her crowded everything else from his mind. He owed her his protection. Yet how best to protect her was a problem. After all, a man like Newton had to be brought to justice—both he and Hanley—for the harm they could do among the Indians was incalculable. But in that event Mary would be the crushed and broken wife of a man publicly dishonored. Could he have a hand in her disgrace?

Accompanying his thoughts came the mournful sound of the night wind crying its travail through the trees. Hours passed during which John watched, waited, and replenished the fire. After a long time there came the distant sound of a complaining motor climbing a steep grade. John rose, stretched his stiff limbs and walked down to the trail to meet the car.

7

By tacit agreement, though no compact existed between them, neither John nor High-Lo explained the misadventure in Noname Valley beyond the brief statements that High-Lo had been thrown from his horse and his horse had taken to the hills. If Magdaline had been impressed by the things High-Lo uttered in his delirium, she certainly kept rigid silence. The affair blew over quickly, as had many of High-Lo's escapades in the past, the boy's rapid recovery being the sole reminder of his latest adventure. The doctor from Taho had pronounced the extent of the injuries to be a slight concussion and several broken ribs, and rest was prescribed for the cure.

High-Lo, who was deft at hand work, occupied part of his enforced leisure by weaving a quirt for Magdaline out of leather strips. It was his way of expressing his gratitude to the Indian girl. However, when the quirt was completed, he inflicted upon John the duty of its presentation.

"Give it to her with my compliments," said High-Lo, "an' tell her it's the first quirt I ever made for any girl."

John could not find Magdaline at once, so the quirt was cached in the store. Later, down by the windmill, he came upon her watering her horse. The girl's dark face did not wear the usual smile. A questioning glance constituted her only greeting.

"I've been looking for you," John called.

She waited for him to draw near. "For me? I thought you had forgotten me. Your time is so busy. You seldom have a word for Magdaline like the other boys."

With her large, luminous eyes upon him and her pretty

olive face in sad repose, it was difficult for John to imagine anyone neglecting Magdaline.

"Oh, come now!" he teased. "Don't I always say good morning?"

"Yes, I almost forgot that," she replied with a touch of irony in her low voice. "But I have not forgotten how kind High-Lo is. How is he?"

"Much better, thank God!"

"Why thank God?" Magdaline inquired half-angrily. "Why not thank yourself, and me, and the doctor?"

John was amused by the remark until he was struck by Magdaline's gravity.

"I do not think there is a God, John Curry, and if there is, what can He have to do with our little lives?" she pursued. "I have been thinking of that all morning. Why, if there is a God, did He make races, one to conquer the other, one to be superior to the other, one to break the hearts of the other?"

"Good heavens, girl! What has set you thinking this way?" John exclaimed.

"Well, is it not so? Did not the white man conquer my people? Are they not trying to force their superiority upon us? Look at me! Would I not be happier just an Indian in the hogan of my father with a name that belongs to my people? Who am I? Magdaline! Why Magdaline? Because somebody at the white man's school cannot say my Indian name, finds it too long and hard to write. So I am Magdaline, a stranger to myself after they make the change. I am taken away from my people, like a dog made to change his master and name. I am put with many other Indian children who are given names that mean nothing to them. For years I go to the white man's school, first to Taho, then far away to Riverside where for years I do not see my people. And you give me knowledge, you wake something that has been asleep in the breast of my race. You make me desire to learn more and more. But all the things I learn, one on the other, I build up between my people and me like a mountain that has no trails. And when my mountain is high against the sky, you send me back. You say, 'Now climb this terrible mountain. Your people are on the other side. They will meet you there.' But you are wrong. I can never meet my people ever again."

John realized the poignant truth of this tragic-eyed girl's accusations. Months of brooding were behind the passion of her words and once the long-inhibited ideas were released, she had no will to check them.

"When I came home from Riverside to my people I shook like a cottonwood leaf in a storm I was so glad. 'Home!' I thought. 'Home!' I sang the word over and over. I was not then aware of the mountain. I forgot I had not been living close to the earth as my people do. I forgot the hogan, ill-smelling to those who were no longer used to it. I forgot the customs of my people—the sheep killed before the hogan and immediately served half-cooked. I forgot that they slept on the ground with sometimes no blanket beneath them. I forgot that living close to animals breeds lice and pests for the body. I had been eating the white man's food. I had been sleeping in the white man's bed. I had been living in the white man's way. I had been thinking much as he thinks even to his God, who was forced upon me and whom I do not understand."

There were tears of grief and anger in the girl's eyes as she continued: "And when I came because of these things, I did not know my people—that is, I could not reach them with my love, and they surely did not know me. They did not want to hear the things I had to tell. How ever could they have understood them? I could not get over the mountain to my people, and they could not get over to me. I stood it only for a night and a day. Then I came to Mrs. Weston who is very good. She seemed to understand and said, 'Go back and help them, little by little. Teach them the things you know.' When she spoke I remembered the electric washing machine with which we were taught to wash. And at the same time I remembered my father's hogan. And my knowledge was like that washing machine. There was no place for it in my father's hogan. There was no usefulness for one there or ever would be. A washing machine would need electricity, like my knowledge for operation needed desire from my parents. They have no such desire. They are satisfied as they are. And they are strangers to me. They watch me with half-distrust as they would an unknown white woman. My education has made me an outcast. My people have no place for me; and what place has the white man? I can go to his towns and cities and be a servant in the homes, paid much less than a white servant. That I learned at Riverside. I do not want to be an underpaid servant to white people. I do not want to be a servant in that sense. For Mrs. Weston I would work just

for love, but she does not need help always—only through
the spring and summer months. In the winter I must go
back to the hogan—sealed up in a hogan I must be with my
family who do not understand me, with my family whose
customs are so strange to me now. . . . And winter is
coming soon."

A stick he had whittled to the thinness of a wafer fell
from John's fingers. He deliberated a moment over his
knife as he struggled for words that might console the
unhappy girl beside him.

"You won't always live in the hogan of your father,
Magdaline. Some day one of the schoolboys will come
home and see what a beautiful girl his old playmate has
become and he will fall in love with you and ask you to
become his wife."

She laughed a thin, unnatural laugh. "And because he
loves me, I will be supposed to love him and go to his
hogan and kill sheep to half-cook for him. Where are your
eyes not to see that education makes no difference to the
men of my race? They go back quickly to old customs. But
I am a girl—a woman. I am altogether different. I could go
back, yes, like a slave. But what would it do for me? Some
of the girls go back and seem happy. Yes, they are happy in
losing one leg to have the other. Some people are that
way."

"But would you trade your desert for the white man's
cities?" John asked.

"No. But I am really unfit for both now. By birth and
tradition I am part of the desert. Perhaps that is why you
send us back to the desert when you are through changing
us. Yet there is such a terrible loneliness in the desert when
you are different from your people and like nobody else!
Sometimes I am afraid, I am so lonely. I feel a great burst
of pain in my heart. I feel as if the great walls of rock
under which my people love to ride would fall and crush
me if I went close."

"Poor Magdaline!" John said, his voice very low and
very tender. "How you must hate us for all our mistakes!
Try to believe that it is only our blindness—that we mean
well. You call us a superior race. Intellectually, yes! But
morally and spiritually, no! And while we try to develop
your intellect we give you an insight to our moral and
spiritual weaknesses, and you see the terrible futility of so
much that we live and do. We do not, alas, live the lives we

profess in our religion. And you wonder because your own
people fit their lives to their own faith instead of ours. You
are justly contemptuous. . . . But, Magdaline, it is not our
God you do not understand. It is our lives you do not
understand—our failure to conform to our professed
teachings. I know we preach to you to convert your people
from their own beliefs, and that's a great mistake. Suppose
you tried. You wouldn't convert them, you would only
confound them. Even the children we take into the schools
become confounded. We say you must believe, and try to
tell you that your fathers are damned because they think
differently. We are terribly, terribly wrong in this. . . . But
the white people are coming more and more into your
lives, into your desert. Change in your people is inevitable,
just as inevitable as the progress of what we like to call
civilization. Your change will be a part of that progress. Of
late years we have been forcing radical changes in your
lives, and you, Magdaline, belong to the generation upon
whom the change is going to be inflicted. You will suffer
most. You are young and your feelings are unbridled. Your
parents are suffering, too, Magdaline, but they have a
resignation that comes with age. They know they must die
soon and that with them must go many of the traditions of
their race. To them death will be an escape. On the other
hand, your children and the children of your sister now at
school in Taho will never know how you and she have
suffered. You will make circumstances easier for them."

"Then I do not matter? I am only a sacrifice!" retorted
Magdaline bitterly. "How I feel is nothing."

"How you feel is very important, indeed, to consider,"
John parried. "Just by watching you I understood. I have
been sorry and helpless. I would do everything for you, and
I can do nothing."

From fiery wells of reproach Magdaline's eyes cooled to
gentle gratitude.

"You have been watching me," she said unsteadily. "You
have been sorry for me. . . . I did not know that."

Curry looked away to the familiar red slopes. Waves of
heat rose from the glaring surfaces. They were almost like
a visible expression of Magdaline's trembling voice. Her
words themselves were lost to John. Suddenly he felt her
hand on his in silent appeal to give back his arrested
attention. As soon as she had brought his eyes to hers again,

she spoke. Her voice was very low. Her dark eyes never left his.

"There is something you can do for me, John. Marry me. Do so because I love you, because you understand and are sorry and care. Do not make me go to a hogan—or to worse things—to those fears I cannot explain even to myself."

Her very directness rendered Curry unprepared to meet the startling and moving proposal she had made to him. Nothing could have been further from his thoughts than the solution she was offering with such simplicity and appealing directness that a mist came suddenly to his eyes.

"Magdaline, I can't marry you," he said unhappily, taking her hand in his.

The girl turned her eyes away from him, and fixed them as if in careful scrutiny upon a far golden spire.

"Because I am Indian and you are white?"

"Because I don't love you," John answered simply.

"That should be enough," Magdaline said, her eyes still intent on the distant spire. "But maybe I could make you love me."

"No, Magdaline. You couldn't do that. And I say that with all finality," John replied helplessly. "But believe me, I am very very sorry for your unhappiness and for any part of it for which I am responsible."

Magdaline drew back and swept John with a long and troubled gaze.

"You love someone else," she said finally. "I thought your heart was empty and hungry like mine. . . . No, I do not want what you cannot give me."

She shrugged her shoulders, as if with that gesture she completely abandoned hope. Her eyes went back to stead-fast contemplation of the peak.

"There is no girl here whom you love. I would have known," she went on. "Whoever she is, she does not love you or you would be where she is. Or if she cared, or knew how you care, she would come to you, because she could not stay away. No one who loves you could stay away."

"I haven't said I love anyone else," John declared in an effort to defend himself against her intuition.

"Your sorriness for me tells me that you do. There is pain in your feeling for me because you too have suffered. Perhaps it is better to be sorry for me than for yourself."

Magdaline's voice trembled again. "Maybe I will try to be sorry for you, now."

"Count on me as a friend any time and any place," said John, nonetheless sincerely for his desire to change the direction of Magdaline's thoughts.

She looked about her quickly, seemingly in a desire to run from herself had the open barrenness of the desert not defied her.

"It is not that I am Indian that makes you hold back your love?" she pleaded once more.

"No!" John's reply was immediate. "That would make no difference if I cared."

"There are white men who marry Indian girls!" she insisted, fighting her last doubt. "But you are different from those white men, John, and it is the difference that I love."

Before John was aware of her intention she had grasped his hand and kissed it. Then she backed away toward her horse with a choking half-laugh, half-cry.

"Good-by, my friend," she called. "I am going to ride under the great wall that my people love. But if I knew where she lived I would go there first and kill her for not loving you."

Nimbly she mounted and whirled her horse in the direction of the golden spire. John watched her disappear smaller and smaller into the distance.

Everything he had known or thought concerning Magdaline rushed to him for approval or correction. Mrs. Weston had declared her exceptionally bright and well-read, and deplored that more complete educational advantages were not given to prepare such girls as she for social service work on the reservation, that her inadequate knowledge had not prepared her for such service, but had only rendered her helpless and miserable. And in this he had agreed. And watching Magdaline squander her smiles on any and every man who met her glance, he had feared to think what would become of her. He was convinced that she was a coquette, and fickle in fancy, and he knew too well the ways of men. Now Magdaline had startled him with her earnest protestations of love, and bared to him the strife and struggle in her soul. What would become of her, she whom life among her own filled with repulsion? He could not follow her and bring her back. She would misunderstand such a gesture. Perhaps ancestral pride would stir her blood, and dignity and stoicism help her over her present dark hour. Perhaps she fled to the mountains to summon courage to meet life. John prayed that she might find it.

He rounded up the horses he had brought down to water and drove them to the corral. Then reminded of the hour by the lunch gong, he went to the hogan to clean up. High-Lo hailed him jocularly.

"Did you see my sweetie?"

John was nonplused for a second. "Your sweetie?"

"Magdaline."

"Yes, I saw her. Why?"

"Well, didn't she act pleased when you gave her the quirt?"

The quirt! John rebuked himself for forgetting all about his mission for High-Lo. His expression must have betrayed him for High-Lo said at once, "You're a fine hombre. You forgot. What did you do with it?"

"Left it in the store."

"Be doin' Magdaline a lot of good there."

John felt High-Lo scrutinizing him closely.

"You seldom forget things," High-Lo continued. "It's only when you're worried that you do. I'm all right now, honest I am. I'll be around in another week lookin' up more trouble."

8

KATHARINE was hanging up dish towels. As they flapped in the wind, she saw between them Alice's golden head turn toward her and nestle in careless repose against the top of her cushioned chair.

"Wilbur Newton has been just outrageous to Mary since he came home," Alice said. "I know you'll be so worried about her while we are away that you won't have a good time. I'm willing to give up the trip, Sis."

"But Mary said you'd love Black Mesa in the middle of September," replied Katharine. "The rains are pretty well over and the fall flowers will be in bloom. You're strong enough to make some trips. And you've been so enthusiastic about going."

"I know, but if Mary is in trouble—"

"You don't want to leave her either," accused Katharine.

"We must make up our minds," Alice remonstrated. "If we are to go we must leave on the eighteenth and today is the sixteenth. We've already arranged with Mr. Reynolds to take us. We should give him time to accept other passengers if we change our plans."

"I'll pay him whether we go or not, if you'll only iron out that funny wrinkle over your nose!" cried Katharine.

Alice's face was still too softly girlish to have its wan beauty marred by wrinkles. Katharine wanted to preserve her sister's youth and beauty and have perfect health glorify it again. She received Alice's sudden glance with a smile.

"Suppose I run over to see Mary and let my visit decide for us," she said. "I think the coast is clear. I'd be furious if

106

it wasn't. I'd sooner run into a rattlesnake than Wilbur. His
sister certainly put the finishing touches on his regard for
me. Behold a thoroughly dissolute woman who would not
be running around the desert if she had the common
decency to stay at home. My friend Wilbur, it would seem,
has relegated me to the derelict ragbag with that one
stinging remark. Ah, the terrible ignominy of it!"

Alice laughed. "I'd like to relegate him somewhere, and I
would if he belonged to me."

"Here! Help me out of this awful apron," begged Katharine. "There! Will I do? . . . Have an eye on the road
and if you see my friend Wilbur coming shout, 'Fire! Fire!'
at the top of your voice and I'll come sneaking round the
back way."

With that jocular admonition Katharine left, Alice's wish
for a pleasant visit following after.

It was obvious that Mary was glad to see her friend.
Immediately she laid aside the corduroy breeches she was
mending, and forcing Katharine into Wilbur's chair, drew
up a footstool for herself.

"Oh!" she cried. "I've missed you terribly these past two
days. It's all right for you to come here. I don't think
Wilbur expects I can put you out bodily. But I don't dare
stray to your house. For me, at present, there is no greater
wifely transgression than that. Oh, Katharine, I feel so
bitter! Wilbur is stifling all my better nature. I feel hate
creeping in and I have no defense."

Ostensibly, under Mary's vehement mood rancorous
memories were seething. Katharine's heart went out to her,
but in the tension of the moment she hesitated to offer
sympathy.

"Doesn't your sense of humor help a little, dear?" she
ventured.

"Wilbur has a way of twisting all the humor out of any
situation, though he did accuse me of trying to suffocate
Lenora when I poured water over her to bring her out of
her pretended faint. I really have had it in my heart to
suffocate her since. I'm sure I have. The indignities I
suffered before that girl left! Wilbur says I drove her out.
That isn't true. I fought with myself so hard! Every time
she said, 'We'll have dinner at such and such an hour.
Could you have it ready then? Wilbur wants it on time,'
and a hundred other commands issued to impress me
with my inferiority, I'd try to pretend to myself that I

hadn't heard a word that she said, or I'd silently hum a snatch of one of the dear old familiar hymns—'Rescue the Perishing,' no doubt. It should have been that. To her I presented a smiling exterior. Anyway, I did refuse to do her wash, and that precipitated her flurried departure. That very day she had said to Wilbur that I had the hands of a kitchen slattern, and placed her white ones before him for his approval. Not a half-hour later she descended upon me with her dirty laundry."

"The little fool," cried Katharine. "Her hands are like putty. Yours are graceful and capable and strong."

"It wasn't just vanity that made me rebuke her by refusing to do her personal laundry. My vanity has suffered so many indignities at Wilbur's hands that I doubt if I have any left. Only Lenora's remark about my hands was the straw that broke the camel's back. Thank goodness she's gone now. That's over. Now I have a little chance for diversion."

"Diversion?" Katharine repeated.

"Yes. Mr. MacDonald fired Wilbur yesterday."

Katharine frowned through a minute of abstraction. "I call that bad, Mary. I happen to know Mr. MacDonald has been dissatisfied with Wilbur's service for months and kept him on only because he couldn't get other reliable help. Poor gabby Mrs. MacDonald told me, and she's spread the news. I doubt if Wilbur can get other employment at Taho."

"The reservation trip ended it," Mary declared. "Wilbur was gone almost two weeks and he brought back the scantiest and poorest assortment of stuff Mr. MacDonald ever saw."

"You must tide over this period somehow. Please don't be hurt if I suggest that you let me help with a little money," protested Katharine.

Mary's upturned eyes smiled into hers through a mist of tears. "Thank you, old faithful. Not yet. There's the poultry money. And I'll take a position somewhere—here at Taho, if possible. If not, over at Flaggerston."

"But Wilbur won't stand for that. Don't forget his drivel about family pride. He wouldn't let you take a position as secretary at the Indian school, if you'll remember."

"I've met with his objections again," confessed Mary. "He doesn't know it, but this time they'll be overruled. It's not only that we'll be in need of money. There's the

dreadful monotony of my days. There's my childlessness."
A mild note of anguish crept into Mary's voice. "I would
welcome any occupation. I am really glad that Wilbur lost
his position. All day I have been almost happy about it. I
haven't had such luck in years!"

Katharine was alive to the passionate earnestness of
Mary's avowal. It exalted her that at last determination and
self-confidence had taken root in Mary's soul.

"Then you may be leaving soon?" she asked.

"It might be a matter of two or three weeks. Mrs.
Jenkins is going to Flaggerston before she returns to Leupp
and she's going to look into prospects there and let me
know. She's a splendid woman. She's mastered the art of
always keeping to herself other people's affair whether
they reach her accidentally or intentionally."

"If there's the slightest chance of your going away that
soon, I won't go to Black Mesa," declared Katharine
stoutly.

"By all means go!" protested Mary. "It wouldn't do any
good to stay. You won't want to visit with Wilbur around.
He says he needs a rest. He doesn't intend to look for
employment for a month. That means he'll be home all
day, day after day. He's riding out this afternoon to see
some Indians on a sheep transaction for Mr. Weston. It's
just a lucky accident that he isn't here."

Katharine smiled. "You can't chase me from Taho as
easily as that. At least I can sit on my porch and watch you
pass down the street. And I'll be near should any emergency arise."

There was something unfathomable in Mary's quick
upward glance which followed upon Katharine's words.
The Eastern girl expected immediate opposition to her
suggestion, and she saw it in the wondering depths of
Mary's eyes which begged for understanding.

"I want you to go to Black Mesa for my sake. I want
you to take a message to John Curry," she said.

"If it's imperative, of course I'll go," returned Katharine,
warily concealing her surprise. She would not question
Mary's intention. It was enough that Mary depended on her
now.

"It may seem strange to you, and it may seem inconse-
quential. Just a verbal message. I'd like you to tell John
Curry that if I leave Taho, I will do so of my own volition.
You see, if I go he is bound to hear about it. Tell him I'll be

not much farther away than the outskirts of the desert—
that I remember what he said to me at Oraibi. But tell him
if it's to Flaggerston I finally go, and he comes there on
business, and we should happen to meet, to pass me by with
a greeting and avoid me thereafter. Katharine, I have a
strange divination that he distrusts Wilbur to the extent of
feeling that my safety is in danger, and he might follow me
across the desert thinking, metaphorically speaking, to
snatch me from another cliff. It may be nonsense for me to
feel that way—it may be just because that's what I really
would have him do."

Katharine met the astonishing statement with all the
indifference she could assume. "You mean—" she started,
not knowing how to express the wonder in her mind.

Mary's serious face was cupped in her hands. Not for a
moment had her eyes left her friend's. "I really and truly
mean what I said," she interrupted. "I felt a restfulness and
security in John Curry's presence that I have never known
in all my life before. I feel that his friendship might make
something within me that is now stunted grow. I've been
like a plant born in a dark canyon that once in the year of
its life happened to feel the sun. After that the plant would
struggle harder than ever toward the light, wouldn't it?"

"So nature intended," Katharine responded quietly.

"But I must hide away in my canyon. I must avoid the
sun. I have no choice. And you'll help me, won't you?
You'll go to Black Mesa—you'll tell John Curry?"

Katharine was moved to a complete realization of her
love for Mary. "It's the least that I could do for you," she
said.

Outside the post office an hour later Katharine saw
Wilbur talking with several town retainers who, common
gossip had it, were a nuisance in the community; and she
noted grimly that not one of the familiar figures was that of
an Indian or a sheep dealer.

"Did Mr. Newton just come along?" she asked the
postmistress, who from her window had command of the
porch and the broad thoroughfare beyond, and exercised
the gift of sight most conscientiously.

"He's been here all the afternoon. Too bad he lost his
job. It's likely to make bad feelings between his wife and
Mrs. MacDonald."

"No one knows. But I don't think so," Katharine

averred, her mind running riot with thoughts that would
have startled the postmistress had she been able to read
the girls' mind.

"Of course you know that poor Mrs. Gordon has another
baby, and to me that's worse than Mr. Newton's losing his
job."

Katharine mumbled something about Taho's sudden in-
crease in population and maneuvered a few sidesteps that
removed her from confidential range, after which she suc-
cessfully bolted. Once outside, throwing discretion to the
winds, she approached Wilbur.

"Have you had a busy day?" she asked in a sweet,
disarming manner. "I saw Mary for a moment and she told
me you were off on some sheep business for Mr. Weston."

Newton colored slightly. From the tail of her eyes
Katharine saw the other men were exchanging amused
glances.

"I'm leaving for Black Mesa in a couple of days," she
went boldly on. "I thought you might have some word for
Mr. Weston about the sheep. I'll gladly deliver it. It would
save you writing."

A dead white spread beneath the fading color in Newton's face. "Thank you, Katharine. Yo're shore most ac-
commodating," he drawled. "This sheep business is confidential. It wouldn't be wise even to mention it to Mr.
Weston. My wife's a little indiscreet airing my business
about."

Katharine met his rebuff demurely. "Oh, I'm sorry I
can't facilitate matters for you! I got the impression it was
very important—business that had to be transacted
quickly."

When Katharine reached home she repeated the incident
to Alice.

"But what made you talk to him?" Alice asked. "Were
you really serious about it?"

"I was deadly serious in my purpose. Mary clings to her
faith in Wilbur's honesty. I've suspected it since I first set
eyes on him. I've taken every chance I ever had to embar-
rass him. He has no sheep business for Mr. Weston. That's
his lodge-meeting-tonight excuse to make absences of any
duration he pleases seem plausible. Likely his sheep deal
with Mr. Weston will carry weight for the next month or
more.... Do you know, Alice, I've come to think that

Wilbur Newton will do worse than break Mary's heart? I used to think that he was merely negative, a harmless egotist, as lazy as he was vain, but to me now there is something sinister about the man. I had the strangest feeling as I walked away, a feeling that I would never see him again."

"Oh, come," chided Alice. "You've never been the least bit psychically inclined. You're doing away with him in your mind because he's a burden to Mary."

"I don't mean that he is going to die," corrected Katharine. "Why did you interpret my words so unconditionally, you scamp! It may be that he'll take Mary far away, search pastures new in which to promenade."

Alice met the defense with laughter. "You'd never leave Mary for an instant if you really thought that."

During the time prior to her departure from Taho, Katharine did not encounter Wilbur again. She had tempted Providence by calling on Mary to say good-by, but found her alone as her strange presentiment forebode that she would. Her solicitude for Mary grew, and she begged her, if she could manage it, to send a letter to Black Mesa post with each trip of the mail stage.

It was on the mail stage of the following day, at an hour safely early to escape the surveillance of the late-rising Wilbur, that Alice and Katharine waved good-by to Mary.

"Sure, she's a saint of a woman, she is," Reynolds acclaimed in an Irish accent as broad as his red-mottled face.

Forthwith Katharine acknowledged him as a judge of a good woman.

They rode down the tree-lined avenue of Taho, and circled the mesa, high above the several green acres of Indian farms that beautified the immediate neighborhood of the valley below them. Then the road led away from the rim across the sandy level of the mesa, away from the red country through pearl-sheen and gray. It was an exceedingly sandy stretch. Time and again the wheels of the automobile ground and whirled and barely escaped digging themselves to a stop. The great expanse of free, open country seemed the very top of the world, yet the vast encircling horizon rose grandly above it, bold jagged cliffs, leagues upon leagues of unbroken walls. Black Mesa, the dark haze-obscured buttress to the fore, seemed almost unattainable. Yet it called across the desert miles in its purple loneliness.

"Are we really going somewhere near that mesa?" questioned Alice incredulously.

"Yes, my dear. Black Mesa post is named after that tremendous looming upland. The post is about four miles east of the mesa, isn't it, Mr. Reynolds?"

"About, ma'am," Reynolds agreed after a moment's serious speculation.

"Look! Look! Oh, the darlings," cried Alice, pointing to three jackrabbits which scampered almost from under the wheels into the brush.

"What easy targets they would have been for an Indian youngster!" Katharine said. "The Navaho children hunt them with bows and arrows, even the very little tots. The Indian men do the same, ever since the war, Mary told me, when they were left so impoverished they couldn't afford ammunition for their guns. Few were lucky enough even to retain their guns."

Alice swept the country with her searching gaze. "Don't you love it all!" she exclaimed. "Doesn't it just break your heart with happiness! Such a wonderful sense of freedom it gives me!"

These words made Katharine regard Alice seriously. Her little sister was not given to extravagance of speech. Her soul had been stirred by the incomprehensible call of the desert.

For a while Katharine vied with Alice in a test of observation powers. In this way they called each other's attention to the tenants of the desert, the prairie dogs, rabbits, pack rats, a lone hawk and a wary rattlesnake, and a sly coyote slinking behind a barricade of greasewood bushes. They found the desert a homey place, surprisingly teeming with life.

"This is their home, these hundreds and hundreds of miles of unconquerable country," remarked Alice. "It is their domain, not man's."

They lapsed into silence after a time, through which came the lonely whistle of the sweeps of sand that spread across the trail behind them. Black Mesa loomed ever higher. As they covered the miles between, they rode a gentle downward grade which continually changed the perspective for them. The grade ended abruptly beyond a hill so steep that Alice exclaimed aloud. It took on the aspect of a tremendous sand dune. The wind had covered all traces of a trail.

"It's loikely if this wasn't sand, after tryin' it once we wouldn't have to be a-worryin' no more about payin' rent an' taxes," declared Reynolds. "As it is, you couldn't pitch over if you tried."

Once Katharine felt her heart flutter as the front wheels projected over the ledge, the same sickly feeling that used to come over her when she experienced the highest drop of a roller coaster. Alice clutched her. They clung together, their fear unmitigated by Reynolds' reassuring words. But the wild forward plunge they anticipated did not materialize. The car might have been operated from above by slow-moving pulleys, so gentle was the descent down the precipitous slope.

"There! Wasn't I roight?" asked Reynolds, with a twinkle that betrayed what amusement their discomfiture had afforded him. "Bless yer souls! I'm not blamin' yer fer bein' scared. I was two hours makin' up me moind to do it, the first toime I tried it."

So intent had Katharine been on the terror of the incline that appreciation of the new vista was slow to come. They were in a valley now, more narrowly encompassed than before. Black Mesa, ever elusive, was still remote. New terraces, rocky red steeps, and a yellow range stretched away before them. They rode parallel to the white slope of the plateau they had just left. Greasewood brush grew high and close. The trail showed like a furrow through a green field. Long-eared rabbits, frightened by their approach, bounded quickly to and fro across the road in an effort to reach their shaded coverts. Mounds of red rock sparsely fringed with cedars rose here and there above the plain, and near one, which they passed close by, was a lonely hogan. Chickens scratched around the sand outside the door, and several mules stared at them stupidly, but the Indians were nowhere in sight.

"Good spring round about here somewheres," vouchsafed Reynolds over the stem of an unlit pipe. "But I ain't never looked it up. Them prehistoric fellers that used to live in the caves round about here weren't totin' water any farther than they could help."

Following this comment Reynolds gave himself completely to the business of wheel and pipe. Katharine noticed that Alice was soon far afield in thought. All the joy emanating from the young spirit within lit her delicate features with a sublimity which stirred her elder sister almost to tears. If good health sprang from peace and contentment, Alice's recovery was sure.

Mile upon mile sped away behind them. Presently the trail branched toward the foot of the curving plateau and clung to its shadow for a considerable distance. Whether the great plateau sloped toward the valley at this point, or whether they had been ascending a gradual rise, was hard to tell, but a change of levels was manifest. Another few miles and a very defined ascent confronted them. The car swung up the trail over slopes and into hollows, but continued its gradual climb toward the last ridge, a sand dune, white as had been the terrifying slope by which they had descended the plateau. The wind had molded this dune with the pattern of its action, and left it as rippling and glistening as a breeze-furrowed sea.

"And here's Castle Mesa, our first stop," announced Reynolds.

Whereupon there suddenly hove in view a strange house rising just below the ridge out of billows of sand. It was an octagonal structure built of stone, and it reminded Katharine of an observatory she once had visited in the East.

"Like a lighthouse on a wind-swept shore," exclaimed Alice. "But the sea is only sand. And look! Oh, look, Katharine!"

Katharine's eyes had caught at once the vast panorama of yellow and red ranges and the beetling battlements of the black mesa. Here was sinister solitude; here was barren, bleak beauty; here was the home of the wind and the abode of desolation.

"It's as Mary said it would be," cried Katharine. "Oh, how glad I am that we came!"

On closer approach they saw that the stone house, which stood boldly against the sandy slope, commanded a regal view of the sinister and barren valley. Soon a woman appeared from a doorway and a cheery call reached them.

The woman, tall and comely, with twinkling blue eyes and hair as raven-black as Mary's, grasped their hands in a most cordial welcome.

"Mr. Reynolds brings me the nicest people," she said. "I wish he came this way more often. I don't need to be introduced to you. Think of that!" She nodded to Katharine. "I know by description that you are Miss Winfield. And this young lady, I take it, is your sister." She smiled at Alice then. "She doesn't look a bit like you. Like me, you must be the black sheep of your family."

"And you are Mrs. Shelley?" Katharine asked.

Mrs. Shelley nodded. "That's right. Better come in. You're going to have lunch with me."

Without remonstrance Katharine, followed by Alice, entered by the same door through which Mrs. Shelley had come, and they found themselves in a trader's store, amid shelves of canned goods, print materials, velveteens, cases of candy and Indian jewelry. There were baskets and plaques hanging everywhere, and piles of rugs on the floor.

"Don't mind going through the store, do you?" Mrs. Shelley asked. "Jim, my husband, always says he cut our front door for nothing."

She lifted a hinged section of the counter and directed them to pass through the door beyond. That brought them to a cool adobe room much like a storeroom, where quantities of boxes and rugs were stacked. A shaft of light coming from an outside door revealed a stairway.

"That's the front door," Mrs. Shelley acclaimed with a smile. "You see, it leads directly to the stairs and was intended to isolate our quarters from the store. But I always feel to get the atmosphere of Castle Mesa post, visitors should see the store first."

They mounted the stairs to quarters which drew from Katharine a cry of delight. There was only one room, as large as half the length of the building, which at a glance one could see contained all the utilities essential to the needs of homemaking. In the farthermost corner tied-back cretonne curtains revealed a bed, bureau and a rocking chair, and diagonally opposite was a stove with a crackling fire in it and pots atop from which came appetizing odors. There was a cupboard near by and a sink. Over the sink was a window, and Katharine knew that the view from that window was such as to make a housewife's kitchen tasks seem lighter. Toward the center of the room was a dining room table already set, and several straight-backed chairs stood around it. The remaining area had the atmosphere of a living room, with bookcases, a desk, two couches and low comfortable chairs. There were Indian blankets on the floor and silver-ornamented Indian articles on the walls, and plaques, and some excellent paintings which Mrs. Shelley explained were presented to her by artists who had visited Castle Mesa. The several corners were brightened by tall hand-woven baskets of Hopi design.

A doorway had been cut directly above the door which on the floor below led to the store. It served as a sort of desert French window with a single protective bar across the opening. Through it great broad bands of light sifted, and they drew Katharine to the view it offered. Behind her she heard Alice exclaiming, "What a charming and unique place!" And then Mrs. Shelley, "It's from this door we see the yellow mesa that looks so much like a grand castle. It was an artist, I believe, who named it."

Katharine drank her fill of the rugged, wild glory of Castle Mesa before she accepted an invitation from Mrs. Shelley to tidy up a bit if she pleased before lunch. Alice preceded Katharine to washbasin and mirror, and was helping their hostess serve the delicious luncheon when she, tardy but refreshed, joined them. Reynolds appeared presently accompanied by a man so like Mrs. Shelley in coloring and general aspect that Katharine was surprised to discover that he was Mrs. Shelley's husband and not her brother.

Mrs. Shelley, it developed in their conversation at the table, had been reared in Kansas City, but had not the slightest desire to return or to reside in any other metropolis. She protested that the desert had become part of her and was necessary to her happiness. "When it gets you, it never lets go," she warned them.

"And do you never grow lonesome?" asked Alice.

"Only once in a while in the winter, now that the children are grown up, and away at school after the first week in September. Mr. Shelley has to leave me once in a while when he goes on buying trips, and at such times I usually send for Mother. She lives in California now. I meet more interesting people here in a year, natives and tourists, than I would meet in a lifetime anywhere else. But even without the people the desert still would hold me."

"Even without me, so she doesn't hesitate to tell me," Mr. Shelley interrupted.

Mrs. Shelley laughed the most pleasing laugh Katharine had ever heard. "I always tell Jim not to put me through the third degree about why I never am lonely. I can't explain why I am willing to give up the things that seem so necessary to other people's happiness for the life here. Ask the desert, I say."

"The desert is a sphinx. It won't tell. It's inscrutable. Believe me, I've tried," confessed Katharine.

The two girls were reluctant to leave Castle Mesa and their kind host and hostess. However, they had no alternative but to accept Mr. Reynolds' hint, delivered immediately after lunch was over, that the mail must be moving on.

They rode away with an oft-repeated invitation by Mr. and Mrs. Shelley to come again called in final adieu from the door of the store.

Once they had negotiated the white sandy slope, they were again on the level floor of a valley. They passed a windmill and near by it a pool of discolored water around which some sheep, several cows and two horses were gathered. Then, once more, they were lost in the anything but monotonous isolation of bleak, barren country. The winding trail which they followed cut between Castle Mesa and the gradual rise of ground that stretched on their right as far as the looming bulk of Black Mesa.

"There's the gateway to a whole new country," Katharine said to Alice.

As soon as they had passed through this gateway, there rose before them two great yellow buttes of tremendous height.

"Them's called 'Elephant Legs,'" announced Mr. Reynolds, pointing a stubby forefinger at the great rock formations at the very moment that Katharine was forming the comparison for herself.

To their left, beyond the buttes, ran low bluffs, and between them and Black Mesa was a valley, slowly ascending. Thus confined they rode for miles through stretches of greasewood, until at last the trail climbed high enough to meet a new prospect, where a greater span of country spread before their eyes. Black Mesa completely dominated the northward country. All the other eminences seemed low and regular, so remote were they, save one tall yellow spire in the foreground. Ever the aspect of the country changed, and every mile of the journey offered new sights and thrills for the eyes of the two Eastern girls. They moved into an area of yellow rocks where the trail dipped behind hummocks and rose over small passes, always ascending. Before long they were riding on an upland of

sage where occasional stubby cedars grew. Black Mesa
seemed very close now, even though cedar-crested hills
intervened. The stretch of sage was like a beautiful
garden; green and yellow were the flowering stalks,
purple gray were those bushes now half-dead and those
late to bloom. Between the clumps of sage waved dainty
purple asters and a few black-eyed Susans.

Suddenly, beyond the garden of sagebrush the stage
passengers saw a tremendous blaze of great red, rocky
ramparts of staggering magnitude appear before their startled eyes, just as the car rounded the great jutting wall of
Black Mesa where it turned away to the north. Down
between these ramparts wound a canyon. Katharine scarcely dared to look from the breath-taking reach of the tallest
spire down to the silver stream of water that wound
through the canyon.

With a jerk of his thumb Reynolds indicated the green
country westward. "That valley between them rock mountains is Noname Valley. Just beyond there we come to
Cedar Pass."

First descending, and then climbing, they finally reached
the pass. The country beyond, a level and green valley
dominated by Black Mesa and the great peak of gold,
delighted Katharine's fancy, but it lacked the bewildering
majesty of the country around Cedar Pass.

Ever since they had left Castle Mesa, Alice had been lost
in an enchanted reverie, the lovely light on her face speaking her appreciation more loudly than words.

"Four miles to go," announced Reynolds, after they had
crossed the rain-washed gash in the earth which had been
named for its distance from the Black Mesa post.

Now that they were approaching the end of their journey, Alice was aroused to comment excitedly on the things
she had been led to expect on their arrival. Katharine's own
expectation was disturbed by a flurry of nervous thoughts in
anticipation of her meeting with Curry. She felt that destiny
was using her to pull together the broken threads of Mary's
life, yet what part Curry would play in it she did not know,
and how or when destiny was to take a hand, she could not
tell.

The last four miles seemed the longest stretch of the trip,
which came to an abrupt and unexpected end, when suddenly and without warning from Reynolds they swung off
the main trail down over a ridge and came upon a group of

buildings hidden in what had seemed an uninhabited valley.

Loud blasts from Reynolds' horn enlivened the silence. At once from the low, rambling adobe structures a dozen people, several Indians among them, came running.

Alice grasped Katharine's hand and whispered, "Just like Western townsfolk meeting a stage in pictures of the old days. Isn't it thrilling!"

Katharine noted quickly the barnlike store building from which a sign hung, bearing the name of the post, the wide, green lawn hemmed in by a wire fence, the long, low red-walled house behind it, the cottonwoods with leaves aquiver in action much like her own pulse, and then the people, some of whom she now could identify. There were Mrs. Weston, Mr. Weston, and that harum-scarum cowboy, Beany, who had been at the Snake Dance.

Soon she was among them shaking hands, introducing Alice and in turn being introduced with her to others. Then a tall man in corduroys and gray woolen shirt appeared in the doorway of the post. It was John Curry! She heard his strong pleasant voice, "Well! Well! This sure is great!"

He came to her with hand outstretched and took hers and pressed it in a handshake unmistakably the firmest she had ever known.

"I'm sure glad to see you, Miss Winfield," he said. "And where's the little sister I've heard so much about?"

His eyes lit on Alice with a smile.

"Yes, my sister Alice, I would like you to meet her, Mr. Curry," said Katharine.

Alice acknowledged the introduction in her quiet, dignified way. Katharine saw that Curry was captivated by her sister's gentle smile. Then vaguely, because Mrs. Weston was plying questions thick and fast, she realized that Alice and Curry were engrossed in conversation. Her attention was divided. Her subconscious self kept repeating, "I have a message for you, John Curry, from Mary Newton."

The very richest of Indian silverwork and rugs and baskets lined the walls and floor and corners of the living room, through which, later, the girls passed to their bedroom with its cool, unpainted adobe interior. The clean white of washstand, table, beds and chairs added to the refreshing coolness of this retreat. Navaho rugs and a few pieces of pottery completed Katharine's idea of a perfect desert bedroom.

The Indian maid who had led them there bowed solemnly and left.

"I want to stay here all the rest of my life!" Katharine exclaimed, backing with spread hands to the bed where she relaxed in an abandon of pleasure.

"And I'll stay with you," said Alice. "I like these people very much. That Mr. Curry I could love. He's the only man who ever made me feel that way."

Katharine felt a tremor pass through her. It was as if Alice with that honest declaration had uncovered the one thing she had not told her about Mary. However, she made no comment. She was conscious suddenly of how obvious to everyone was John Curry's complete integrity.

9

THE readiness with which Katharine had agreed to carry Mary's message to John Curry now seemed to fail her in the execution of her promise. She passed four days at the post and three on a trip to Cathedral Valley without Mary Newton's name even being mentioned by either of them. On the eighth day, the day that was to see them break camp in Cathedral Valley, she resolutely determined to break the silence. Katharine and Curry were sitting on a log in a cedar cove when she suddenly determined to take the bull by the horns.

Before her in a clearing burned a cheery fire; pots were heating in the cinders, hooks were warming on the crane. The crackle of the fire sounded close, and there came to her above it the tinkling sound of bells that swung from the halter ropes of the feeding horses. The cowboy cook whistled softly over the potatoes he was peeling. Katharine, pleasantly aware of these things, stared into the fire, as if she could snatch courage from the red-hot bed of coals. Alice came up to her. She had been watching High-Lo hobble the pack mules and was returning flushed, to tell of High-Lo's miraculous escape from a rain of blows from a mule's hoofs.

"There are three of those mules I'd never want to ride," she declared. "But I'm getting very proud of my riding at that. High-Lo says no one would guess I was a tenderfoot."

"Beward of the flattery of a cowboy," Katharine cautioned her with a laugh. "I think High-Lo is smitten with my sister."

Katharine had observed High-Lo's attentiveness. At each

122

camp he had made a bed of cedar boughs for Alice, unwilling to be outdone by John Curry who served Katharine in this way. Such consideration Katharine rather expected from Curry, and she knew he intended to make Alice comfortable too. But handsome, carefree High-Lo was only an apprentice aping his master, and in his deference to Alice he was following a will-o'-the-wisp fancy. Katharine had sensed at once the relationship that existed between John and High-Lo, and Mrs. Weston, always ready in praise of the elder man, had told her the details of their friendship. It was one of her chief delights to discover the many evidences of High-Lo's fierce loyalty.

At supper to which they were summoned with the lusty call, "Come and get it," High-Lo served Alice, and Curry served Katharine. Occasionally Beany would look on with his tongue in his cheek and a mischievous twinkle in his eye and waft some remark to the nearest bystander about one man's success being another man's failure. And after supper when Katharine drew Curry away from the others by boldly suggesting that they climb the mountain behind camp, she felt Beany's eyes upon her and also Alice's, which plainly asked why she should not be invited to go too. When Katharine sauntered past her sister, she was not as serene as she appeared to be.

They climbed around the mound that sheltered camp and over the rocky bluff until they reached a resting place midway up to the top of the great hummock. From this craggy height they could see the tremendous spread of the valley where insurmountable temples and wind-carved domes wore halos of the last low gleams of the sun. Purple shadows were meeting across the darker sage. Over the westward mesa pink, gold and carmine clouds floated through thin, gray-white light, and lower clouds that a short while ago had pushed themselves above the horizon hung high in the heavens like plumes of smoke still tinged with the red of fire. The mellow call of the wind, soughing through the pines below them, made a cheerful sound.

"I wish Mary Newton could be here to enjoy this," said Katharine gently.

John sent a small stone spinning down the rock. Then he spoke up. "I wish so, too."

"Because she would love it," added Katharine.

"And she makes a good companion on the trail," was John's cautious return.

"It's too bad that soon she may have to leave all this."

Immediately John fell into the trap that Katharine had so warily laid. "Leave it? What do you mean, Miss Winfield?"

"She may be going to Flaggerston to accept a position there. Her husband has lost his job."

"But can't he get another? They're usually short of men at Taho. That is, men who have any idea of permanent residence."

"I guess you don't know Mr. Newton very well. Permanent residence or otherwise, no one seems to be anxious to hire him."

"It's rumored he's a lazy cuss. But I didn't think he was so lazy that he'd let his own wife go to work!" exclaimed John.

"Don't misunderstand," Katharine protested. "He doesn't want her to work. She couldn't be around at his beck and call all the time if she did. This is her own idea and she intends to carry it through. He wants a month's vacation, it seems. What kind of heavenly manna he's depending upon for daily bread meanwhile I don't know! They are really very poor, Mr. Curry. Mrs. Newton keeps and sells poultry and eggs, but you know how little profit there is in that in a place like Taho where there is such a plentiful supply."

Katharine looked away to the color-flung west. John sat very still, he too given at the moment to staring at the intensifying hues in the sky.

"He wants a month's vacation, does he?" John said eventually. "I expect that's most convenient to his latest shines."

"What do you mean?" asked Katharine.

He turned about so suddenly that she had no time to withdraw her searching gaze. Curry, she slowly gathered, knew more about Newton than she could have had any reason to believe.

"Miss Winfield, I like you. You're a person to be trusted," John said slowly. "I'm going to tell you something about this man Newton that only High-Lo knows. He's in on a liquor-running deal with Hanley and a couple of women to sell liquor to the Indians on the Navaho Reservation. It's a good money-making racket because most Indians will sell their souls for liquor. That's what the white men have done to them. It used to be pretty bad when just an occasional scrupulous man was the only force operating against it. Then, a number of years back, we passed a state law against selling liquor on Indian reservations. That was before the national prohibition law went through during the war. That state law saved many an Indian from poverty and misery. It's now doubly lawless to sell liquor to Indians. And what's more, it's the cruelest, thievingest thing I know of that a man could do. I've been aching to shadow Hanley and Newton and catch them red-handed. But there's Mrs. Newton. She stands between me and that. To convict Newton would be to expose Ma—, his wife to disgrace."

A chill crept over Katharine as she listened, partly as a result of the gradual withdrawal of warmth from the desert, partly from the incredible information Curry had disclosed.

"Oh, poor Mary! If she ever learned that about Wilbur!" Katharine faltered.

"Do you see what a position I am in?" Curry asked. "I owe it to the Indians to spill that fine gentleman into the penitentiary. I could, easily, if it wasn't for that sad-eyed little girl who'd go down under it. I've thought of things I might do. Go to Taho and pick a fight with Newton, beat him up and when I got him helpless tell him what I know and scare him into giving it up. But he's the kind of hombre who would only make her suffer for that. Why, I could shoot him like I'd shoot a pig with an incurable disease. He isn't any good to himself, let alone to anybody else. He bears watching, I'm telling you. Maybe I better move along to Flaggerston as soon as the season's over here."

Unconsciously he gave to Katharine the moment she was waiting for. "You must not do that," she said. "It won't do any good."

"But it couldn't do any harm just to look the ground over. Suppose someone else got him on this bootleg business? He might involve her. Blast the whole cussed situation, it's just too devilish hard to handle!"

"Mrs. Newton asked me to warn you that should you and she ever meet by chance in Flaggerston to pass her with a greeting and avoid her thereafter. She wanted me to tell you that probably she would be leaving Taho, but she'd keep close to the desert, that she's not forgotten what you said to her at Oraibi."

"That only makes me more anxious to go. It tells me to stay away because she's afraid of Newton. He's giving her plenty of trouble. I can see that."

"But you can't be like a knight of old, go riding by and snatch the princess from the ogre as you snatched her from the mesa rim at Oraibi. You're living in the twentieth century, and the lady in question happens to be the wife of the ogre."

"You mean I'd be taken for a meddler?" muttered John.

"You'd be taken as a man with a too great interest in another man's wife. Can't you see that that would hurt her?"

John flung down his sombrero with an impatient gesture and ran his hand through his hair. "Hurt her! That's the last thing in the world I want to do!" he cried.

"And that's because the interest is there, John Curry. A deeper interest than you have even confessed to yourself!"

Katharine sat breathless, afraid of her daring. The man beside her seemed to stiffen and become silent. Whereupon an uncomfortable fear possessed her that after all she might have been wrong. If he would only speak! Her gaze was fixed on him, but he, unconscious of it, was looking away into the gathering twilight.

"You're very keen, Miss Winfield," he said after a long silence, speaking downward as if she were somewhere on the desert below him instead of by his side. "There is no use pretending to you. I love Mary Newton. It's the kind of a love that makes a man finer for having it. Please believe me. I wouldn't do anything to cheapen it for her or for me. Before this I would no more have thought I would ever fall in love with a married woman than I would of being shot by High-Lo or you. I had no use for a man that I'd suspect of such a thing. Circumstance plays with us strangely sometimes and changes things for us. I never forced myself in Mary Newton's way. The desert threw us together— made us of use to each other. I think I'm stronger for it even if it seems such a hopeless thing to be in love with her. If someone awakens love in you, trying to deny that it's happened doesn't give you back your old freedom of heart. I try to be honest about it and not dislike Newton because he happens to be her husband, but he doesn't try to be worthy of her, and I don't savvy a man like that. She loved him, I'm sure, when she married him. Maybe she loves him now—women are like that. But she doesn't love him for what he is, it's for what she thought he once was. Young marriages are awful mistakes sometimes. I'll never be so lucky as to have a woman like Mary Newton love me, but if I did I'd sure do my best all my life to make her see I appreciated the honor that she was conferring on me. I'd want to keep clean and fine for her. I couldn't do anything dishonorable then—ever!"

At the close of the longest speech he had ever made he turned to Katharine again. The struggle within him was manifest in his face. All the maternal spirit in Katharine yearned to console him.

"I don't condemn you. I feel that if I were a man I'd love Mary, too, regardless," she said. "It's serious for you. But you must remember, it might be dangerous for her. When the man a woman loves fails her as completely as Mary may live to learn Newton has failed her, she's human enough to want to turn to a strong man for protection. It would be a spiritual thing to her—goodness overcoming deceit. And she couldn't help herself. But the world would condemn her. . . . As if human hearts and needs were not holy things!"

"You mean she might come to care for me?" Curry asked, ostensibly disposed to doubt her.

"Why, yes. It's more than possible," returned the Eastern girl, inwardly amazed at the naïve modesty of this man whom even shy Alice proclaimed as so lovable.

"I guess I never thought of that. I just accepted unconsciously that to a woman like Mary Newton marriage closed the way for any other man."

"And so it would, forever, if she had found love and fidelity where she so bountifully had given them. Mary hasn't."

"Yes, I see," John said. "But I think you're wrong about her ever learning to care for me. I can't help feeling that it's only a very small possibility that I may hurt her if I don't stay away. The only reason why I'm going to think you must know best, Miss Winfield, is because you're such a good friend to her."

He looked squarely at Katharine during this declaration. She saw that his face was pale in the dim light of the evening.

"You'll be a good friend to me too, I hope," he continued. "I've had very few girl friends and I've never had a sister. My mother was sort of a sister. She was always very young in looks and spirit, as much of a pal to me as she was a mother. I remember the only binding affection I had ever had for a girl wasn't in the least bit reciprocated, and Mother helped me over that bad time. She died while I was away in the service. It was her going that brought me here from Colorado. On the way over I tied up with High-Lo."

"You'll never leave the desert?" Katharine asked.

"Never for any length of time. I come from a beautiful pastoral country in Colorado and I've been in the Colorado desert time and again, but I love Arizona best, her farm country, her woods, and especially her desert. It's a merciless spell the old desert has. Once it enters your insides you're a goner. I've a lot of cattle in Colorado that run on the same range as my brother's. He looks after mine for part profit. I've often dreamed of getting a big ranch somewhere near Flaggerston, keeping lots of cattle and horses and running a tourist trade, too—taking people out by pack trains from Flaggerston. Mr. Weston's getting on. He says he'll have to give up the post in about four years, and if all went well I'd take that over, too."

"There ought to be good money in it," said Katharine.

"A gold mine if it's done right."

"Perhaps you'd need someone to share in the investment with you," Katharine suggested. "I would, in a minute, and think myself lucky to have the chance. My grandmother left me some money on her death two years ago. It's banked and drawing only low interest. So much sickness dogged our family during those two years that I hadn't the thought or the will to invest it to better advantage."

"This layout would make a good investment, Miss Winfield," John returned promptly. "But it will be a year or more before I can think of the ranch and tourist proposition. I don't want to invest anyone else's money unless I can meet my share of the investment with the same amount."

"Would you give me first consideration when the time does come?"

John agreed, with the first smile he had shown since the serious turn in their conversation.

"Splendid!" exclaimed Katharine. "For then I'd always have an excuse for visiting Arizona. Otherwise my people would never understand it. As soon as Alice gets well, spending her summers here in the North and her winters in the South—I guess near Phoenix or Tucson—I'll have to go back East. Then I'll have a terrible time convincing my

Europe-commuting family and friends that the West is a place for anyone other than invalids or hobos. I think I'll have to start a reform, a sort of See-America-First campaign."

A silence fell between them. The wind, fresh and cool, grew stronger as night descended over the valley. It moaned through a sea of boughs like the ocean spending itself upon a lonely shore. Over all was a cloud-ridden sky. Here and there in a patch of purple-blue lone stars shone down upon the gray monuments and mesas. These cathedrals of God's silent hand, these wonderful rocky slopes, these ledges and benches where the wind spent its force, these caves and crags that echoed with the solemn hymns of desolation, these sage-choked plains, grim, gray, engulfed in the shadows of night, were endeared to Katharine forever. For bound by them she had been permitted to share the burdens of two friends.

"We had better go," Katharine reluctantly suggested. "The descent will be difficult in the dark."

John rose to accompany her. He led the way, care for her welfare in every movement. As they reached the gentler grade that led around the knoll to camp, the boughs of the cedars seemed edged with red reflected from the roaring campfire. Then from the shadows beyond the firelight they saw Stub and caught his voice recounting one of High-Lo's escapades. They could see High-Lo's face showing part irritation, part good humor, and Alice's, as she gravely chided Stub for telling tales.

Katharine felt unduly self-conscious as she stepped into the firelight.

The party had ridden almost thirty miles that day, something of a strain for Alice who began to droop soon in heavy-eyed weariness. Bed had a sweet comforting call for all of them. When the girls were snug under their blankets, Alice reached for Katharine's hand, and from the silence that followed Katharine knew that she was formulating some thought difficult to express.

"Could you really live here forever?" Alice asked after a while. "At Black Mesa or Taho?"

"I would gladly, if I were surrounded by people I love."

"That's necessary, of course," agreed Alice. Another silence hung between them, then she added very solemnly,

"You know, Katharine, I think you like John Curry awfully well, yourself."

"Of course I do, silly. Everybody does," Katharine replied, keenly aware of the drift of Alice's questioning. "And I'm sure he must have a sweetheart tucked away somewhere in Arizona."

Alice said no more. Her hand relaxed from its hold on Katharine. In a short time the girl was sleeping.

But Katharine stared for a long time into the blue sky above her, where the sight of countless other spheres made so trifling the destinies of individuals on the small earth she knew.

"Yet we do matter," she told herself, resolutely dismissing the dangerous thought Alice had stimulated. "People's struggles and heartbreaks must be for some good end."

The wind moaned fitfully. She found herself slipping gently into unconsciousness, and soon she was dreaming of a ranch near Flaggerston where Mary presided with the contentment of a saint come into her own, and John Curry, a confused combination of himself and High-Lo, seemed rightful lord of the establishment.

10

By late afternoon of the next day John was leading his pack train back to the post. The girls, riding fast, had preceded him, and came out with Mrs. Weston on his return, bright and smiling, in the dainty costumes they wore so well, looking more like persons who had stayed at home than like worn travelers.

"We trust you had a fine trip, Mr. Curry. We're glad to see you home again," Katharine called gaily to him.

John turned sidewise in his saddle and met Katharine's laughter. "You've sure shaken the dust. No one would believe you had ever belonged to this outfit. I call you thoroughbreds—that's what!"

It was satisfying to John to be home again, to see Mrs. Weston, mother to the last man of them, bustling around with an inquiring word for each boy's welfare. Manifestly she missed the boys and anticipated their return as if indeed they were her own sons.

"High-Lo behaved himself?" she asked John. To conceal her conversation she pretended to be engrossed with Nugget whose nose she was patting.

"You bet! He'll be expecting me to write him a pass to heaven soon."

"Bless the boy! He's a caution! Keeps everyone in hot water when he's around. But when he's gone I miss him. Between him and Magdaline I've felt as if I had an orphan asylum on my hands."

Magdaline! John had not given her a thought for days. Memory of his recent talk with her stirred a feeling of apprehension within him.

"She's come back?" he asked.

131

"No. Not yet. And she's not at Sage Springs. Her father came into the store yesterday. He knows nothing about her and doesn't seem to care much. 'Maybe with white friends,' he said. We're none of us responsible for her, of course, but she is such a pretty little thing and so obviously unhappy that I'm afraid."

Though Mrs. Weston did not particularize, John grasped the significance of her words. Almost immediately he said, "There are times when I'm afraid Magdaline may run wild. Still, she had a bigger field here. And some of the boys wouldn't have needed much encouragement to help her cut loose. She's attractive, and some of the boys are pretty raw material. Maybe she's gone off somewhere just as High-Lo does to nurse a grievance. Anyway, that's what I'm trying to think."

High-Lo, coming upon them, broke in with a sly, "What's that about me?"

John gave him a lusty poke in the ribs. "I was telling Mrs. Weston that if you weren't such a lazy cuss we'd have these animals watered and in the corral long before dark."

"Huh! And who's boss of this outfit?" High-Lo retorted in fine scorn.

"That shuts me up," said John. "Guess you'll have to excuse me for the present, Mrs. Weston."

While the boys were in the midst of their work, the mail stage arrived, which occasion almost precipitated a strike among them, for it was a matter of great moment to hail newcomers and to stand around while the mail was being sorted, speculating on the chance of a word from home. High-Lo, who had never once received a letter during his employment at Black Mesa, was usually the most expectant of all. Yet despite all the protests and High-Lo's vociferous appeal, John remained obdurate. Horses and mules came first. The boys had to put in a hard half-hour's work before they were free.

The mail, it developed, was light, and there were no newcomers. Mr. Weston remarked to John over the counter in the post that the season for tourist trade was about over. As usual High-Lo's ever-anticipated letter failed to materialize, and John, coming from the store with him, smiled at the familiar words, "Strange that I don't hear from nobody!"

"Miss Winfield got a letter," added High-Lo. "Golly!

Must of been a love letter." With a swing of his sombrero he indicated Katharine, who in marked preoccupation was walking slowly down the path from the house, tapping a letter thoughtfully against her lips.

John stepped forward to open the gate for her. "Coming out, Miss Winfield?"

She started ever so slightly and then said, "Oh, yes, thank you. I was coming out. In fact I was about to look you up. Can you give me a minute?"

High-Lo wheeled off at once. "I'll see if them saddles is hung up," he called back.

Distress was so apparent in Katharine's face that John was immediately disturbed. "Bad news, Miss Winfield?" he asked.

"News concerning Mary Newton. You'll understand everything better if you read it for yourself. I'll tell her someday that I let you read it. Get off by yourself somewhere. . . . Here!" She thrust the letter into his hands. "I'm going up on the ridge. Join me there soon."

She moved away. John, standing where she had left him, weighed her request. Such a precious thing to hold in his hand—a letter from Mary Newton! Dare he read the intimate thoughts she had entrusted to Miss Winfield? It did not seem logical that the girl who yesterday had warned him against indiscretion would press him to read this letter without considering the fitness of such an act. He recalled her troubled look and it decided for him.

In the toolshed, locked against possible interruption, he opened the precious document and his eye slipped quickly over the salutation to the content:

I do not know how to tell you what has happened. I cannot think it is true. Wilbur has left me, deserted me. Judging from the note he left he will never return.

Two days ago the question of my accepting a position came up again. I had heard from Mrs. Jenkins that a photographer in Flaggerston wanted someone to keep his books and receive his patrons and wished me to consider the offer, so I approached Wilbur. He was as unyielding as flint. I talked to him suggesting to him that we both try to make our lives count. You know what to me would make my life worth having lived. But I did not mention children, knowing too well his dislike for them. Under the circumstances it would be wrong for me to contemplate motherhood. But I tried to make him see if we shouldered the wheel together, lived carefully and saved our money, that perhaps in five years we could start in the cattle business on a small scale and develop a ranch. I admitted I felt his discontent, and tried to make him see that despite it we must weather life together and try to find some measure of happiness.

It was hopeless the way he met my poor little pleas. He said marriage was a poor game at its best and made a slave of a man, that he didn't intend to have me trying to hand out advice to him as if I were the smarter of the two. I listened to him, as he revealed the smallness of his nature, until I thought that I just couldn't bear it. But I was patient and conciliatory. After all, Katharine, Wilbur is the product of foolish vain parents, and perhaps when we were first married I was too indulgent. I was so anxious for approval and so hungry for love. Had I been older and wiser I might have not encouraged in him traits that I did not recognize then as his faults.

That was our last talk. He punished me with one of his gloomy silences, and meanwhile I hesitated to write to Flaggerston. On the afternoon of the following day, when I returned from trading eggs at the post, Wilbur was gone. I found his note which said that he wanted his independence as much as I did and was taking it for good, and now I was free to attract men again, and might even go into partnership with the photographer I was so interested in. He took with him the few bits of jewelry he had given me before our marriage and emptied my change box, too, and left me with the rent unpaid. I would not tell you these miserable details if it were not that in the telling I can smother the regrets that arise to assail me, the something that once was love, and comes like a disturbing presence now that I am alone.

You may think at once that I will surely leave Taho because of these present developments. But I know I shall stay. I can't leave, Katharine, I am desert-bound. A horizon line of mesas confines my world. I want no other. I can find peace on the desert. There is much to do here. I will try to get employment in the Indian Service. After your winter in the South, perhaps you and Alice will come back to Taho and board with me. Such anticipation would be balm to my chastened spirit.

Do you think, Katharine, that I failed Wilbur? Think over everything you know, and then tell me, dear. And don't let your personal prejudice or anything that I have said affect your judgment. Try to view as objectively as you can my situation with all your keen perception.

I await your return hungrily, but I beg you not to let this letter speed it. I wanted you to hear the word from me before rumor spreads the suspicion that's sure to arise. It may be best for me to satisfy inquiring minds with the truth.

Think of me a little. Pray for me with your eyes to the mighty hills, and in the quiet of evening when all Nature is listening.

A fierce, burning anger possessed John. He was seeing straight to the core of Mary's problem and what he saw was torturing to him. A terrible desire crowded through his mind to find Newton, to choke him half to death, to drag him at a horse's heels back to the girl he had deserted. "Why are laws made against killing such a man?" he demanded of himself. But instantly he felt rebuked by eyes of patient forbearance. Mary was a woman who would not understand justice meted out in deadly passion. He ground the letter in his hand as if it had been Newton writhing under his strength; then seeing what he had done, he grew quiet and thrust the crumpled sheets into his pocket, unlocked the door, and with giant strides mounted the ridge.

Katharine was there waiting for him.

"I thought you would never come," she breathed. "The dinner gong will ring any moment. Alice will be looking for me."

"I had to read slowly because I couldn't believe what I read. Putting it straight, it's hell, Miss Winfield. I'd like to catch that scamp and drag him back to her. She's hurt— terribly hurt by this final indignity. You'll go back to her pretty soon, won't you? She was feeling brave when she wrote this letter. It may be different now."

"I've decided to go back with Mr. Reynolds in the morning," Katharine returned. Her eyes narrowed thoughtfully. John felt them boring into his very mind. With a feeling part curiosity part dread, he waited for whatever else it was that she had to say. "I wonder, does Mary realize this may change everything for her?" she went on. "This may make her a free woman. Do you recall that Wilbur Newton suggested that himself?"

John felt himself ardently considering the idea. Yet for a moment he was puzzled. "Free woman? What do you mean?"

"She's a resident of a state that realizes the folly of keeping embarrassed and lonely forever a good woman whose scamp of a husband has deserted her."

"Maybe she'll divorce him, you mean?"

"Exactly."

The thought of Mary freed from Newton gave rise to a wild, incoherent hope in John, but the wave of emotion subsided when it met his better judgment.

"Somehow to most of us divorce is an ugly thing," he said. "I always see the green mud of a pigsty when it's mentioned. It strikes me as something that Mary Newton can't walk through."

"It's the misuse of the law and the cheap scandal that usually accompanies divorces that makes people abhor divorce and would make Mary shrink from it," returned Katharine. "I know such a thought hasn't entered Mary's mind. No doubt, spiritually speaking, she's trimming a lamp to set in the window of her soul for Wilbur. That's very noble, Mr. John Curry, and my view may seem materialistic, but at rock bottom it's not. Mary could give great happiness to a man like you, help you to a fullness of development, bear you beautiful strong children, and train them as children upon whom will depend the future of our country. Is there anything more noble than that? Should her life be wasted at the whim of a man who has deliberately broken the vows of legal contract that bind them? To me it is like the old barbaric custom in India of burning a widow on the bier of her dead husband. To be dead morally and spiritually, as Wilbur Newton is, is greater alienation from a woman like Mary than physical death would be."

True as Katharine's words sounded, they were not entirely convincing to John. Still, Katharine had hopes for him. She was a loyal friend. She would break down every barrier in the way of his happiness. There was within the girl an impatience to destroy evil and accomplish good. Altruistic desires, however, did not change circumstances. Curry felt that he understood Mary even better than Katharine did. Yet he fought to submerge in his consciousness the cry that he might be mistaken, that Mary would welcome freedom, sue as early as possible for a divorce, and give him the right to try to win her. Deep within his soul, however, he knew that such notions were false.

They stood there in awkward silence. John, conscious of Katharine's desire for corroboration, hated to destroy her confidence, but felt that he must do so.

"Newton may come back. This may be a trick to make her give in to him about earning her living."

Katharine shook her head. "Are you forgetting Wilbur's new business? Couldn't it happen that he found it uncomfortable to have a wife who might grow suspicious of his desert journeys? I understand the man so much better since you told me about his machinations with Hanley."

That was something to consider and John acknowledged the reasonableness of what the Eastern girl had said.

"And that brings up something else," Katharine went on. "Ought Mary not be told the truth about Wilbur?"

"No!" returned John decisively. "Why hurt her further? She's suffered enough."

"But it would help to make her see the light. She'd understand your desire for a closer friendship."

John flushed. "That's it. I don't want to win Mary Newton's regard that way. I don't want her to be given that kind of a comparison to judge me by. As you said yesterday, she might want to turn to me. Because then she'd sure know that he had failed her and I naturally would appear in a more favorable light. No, don't kick him for my benefit. I'd want her to care as if Wilbur Newton had never existed."

"Yes, yes. Of course," Katharine said quickly. "Stupid of me not to realize you'd feel that way. I'm overanxious."

"And I'm hard put to know what to think or do," John replied. "I could be selfish enough to go to Taho with you."

"You mustn't."

"I know it," John assented, miserably.

As he spoke the dinner gong rang in high irritation. Katharine heard it with a frown. "How soon will your season end?" she asked without making any move to go.

"It's about over now. Two weeks more is all Mr. Weston will be needing me."

"What did you intend to do then?"

"Usually I go back to Colorado. This fall for a while I'd like to keep my eye on Hanley's operations. A little later I may find someone who will want sheep herded over to Colorado. That would give me an excuse for waiting around."

"And you want an excuse just for Hanley?"

At once John saw that Katharine had misunderstood him. "Yes. Just for Hanley. I don't need an excuse for Mary. I wouldn't leave the country without seeing her, and maybe when I do, I won't leave at all."

This Katharine received with a nod of approval. "Let me know when you are coming. I think it would be best for you to see Mary at my place. You'll be my guest. Not hers. Less chance for gossip."

Gratitude which he could not adequately express welled in John's breast. "You're sure making good on the friendship promise," he said.

Further word was halted by a reminder from Katharine that the dinner gong had rung and she must be going. John sensed that she would prefer to return to the post unaccompanied, so immediately found urgent reasons why he must look over the stock in the corral before he ate. He was rewarded with a smile more expressive of appreciation than words could be.

When Katharine told Alice that they were going to leave with Mr. Reynolds the next morning, she was grieved by the look of disappointment and challenge she met in her sister's eyes. At the time Alice was about to start for the living room. Instantly she lost her interest there. Professing fatigue, she slipped into a chair and fell into a stubborn contemplation of the Indian rug at her feet. Katharine recalled then that Alice had met her with a reproachful look when she arrived late at table, which had made her embarrassingly conscious that Curry's was the only other vacant place. And it had been at her that Alice looked when ten minutes later Curry had appeared. Whatever was

Alice thinking? Better that she knew the truth than dwell on morbid fancies! Katharine drew her sister's eyes to hers with the appeal, "Dear little sister, I can make you understand."

Alice listened without comment. By turns she appeared startled, sad and shocked. That her alarm over the disclosure of John and Mary's mutual interest was greater than her distress over Wilbur's desertion she made plain by her immediate protest. "But, Sis, Mary is married. Mr. Curry can't change that."

The remark irritated Katharine. "No. But Wilbur has altered conditions somewhat. So could the law."

Alice was quick to reply. "I don't like it. It's so—well —sort of common—Wilbur's leaving Mary, and Mary's—"

"Mary's what!" demanded Katharine brusquely.

"Oh, Mary's—" Again the girl found herself at a loss for words.

"The world met in my sister!" thought Katharine with a sigh. Aloud she said, "And Mary's terrible unhappiness. Of course, dear, you realize that."

But the appeal excited no sympathy in Alice. Her eyes were cold, her chin firm. Katharine found herself speaking almost too indignantly as she explained in detail Mary's misery, John Curry's fineness, and the peculiar circumstances that had thrown John and Mary together.

"You must not be too quick to judge the situation," Katharine concluded. "There is much to be considered."

There were tears in Alice's eyes then. "I love Mary. You know I do," she faltered. "And maybe my feeling against her caring for John isn't altogether fair. I'll get over it after a while."

Alice's tears came so fast that Katharine was worried about having excited her so. Was there more behind these tears than the affairs of Mary and Curry? She asked Alice about it, chafing the small cold hands, eloquent in their listlessness.

"Just—a little—something else," Alice hesitantly admitted between her sobs.

Memory of what Alice said the evening she had first met Curry stabbed Katharine. She could only murmur when she tried to voice her thoughts.

"Do you care for John Curry yourself? Is it that which makes the difference?"

Alice shook her head in violent negation. "Something else."

With her fear banished, Katharine readily divined that the very slightness of Alice's reason made confession of it difficult. She did not press her further.

Cries of protest sounded in the living room when Katharine announced her intention of leaving in the morning. The Westons' concern gave her comforting appreciation of how greatly she and Alice had endeared themselves to the household staff and guests at the post.

"It's shore hard on us," said Mr. Weston, "but if it's necessary for you to go to Taho at once, there's no way of changing it. So long as you promise to come back next year, we won't try to hold you now."

High-Lo and Beany did not accept affairs so philosophically. Their features grew long. As the other boys sauntered in, they passed along the unwelcome news, like brothers in misery seeking the sympathy of all their comrades. Thereafter, every time anyone came through the guest hall a battery of eyes was turned on the doorway. With amusement rising above her distress, Katharine recognized the homage they were paying to Alice. When after an anxious hour of waiting the sight of Alice did brighten their horizon, it was evident that the boys found in the girl's unsmiling face consolation for their own dejection. What did it matter that they were mistaken about the cause of her sadness?

Morning found the boys spick-and-span and shaved, but low in their minds. Chief mourners at the burial of their dead hopes, they gathered around the mail stage, funereal in aspect.

"No wonder those boys take this so bad," Mr. Weston said to Katharine as they watched John carry out the baggage. "You're the last roses of summer. No more young lady tourists this year."

"It's Alice," murmured Katharine. "She's a whole bouquet to every one of them."

And it was Alice about whom they clustered, her comfort for which they had concern. Katharine smiled as she watched the leave-taking.

Many messages were given to Katharine in the flurry of good-bys. The cowboys, led by High-Lo, threatened to visit Taho soon. John, handing Katharine to her place in the car, said, "I'll be riding in to Taho myself. Don't forget. Say nothing to her about it. I don't want to run the risk of being told to stay away."

Then they were off. They could hear shouts and see waving sombreros behind them at the post as the stage mounted the ridge. A few of the boys leaped to their horses and tore alongside making the crest ahead of the car. A few shots were fired into the air in greeting and farewell as the horsemen shouted their last good-bys. The stage turned with the trail. Katharine looked back to see the boys slowly disappear under the ridge; then she sank back, happiness and pain struggling in her breast.

Alice and Katharine at once gave themselves over to the desert silence. They met and passed familiar places: Four Mile Wash, Cedar Pass, Noname Valley, the cool plains of flowering sage, the hogan by the great red mound of rock. And to watch each speed by was like saying good-by to a loved friend. Then followed the great towering elephant legs and the ramifications of Castle Mesa, the mighty and stupendous fortress!

Mrs. Shelley waved a greeting from the tall door-window of her home. Katharine could imagine Bluebeard hiding his wives in such a place as this, hear the last one crying fearsomely from that very watchtower, "Sister Ann, Sister Ann, do you see someone coming?" But the Mr. and Mrs. Bluebeard of Castle Mesa were as happy and kindly a couple as ever lived.

Again the girls enjoyed a most hospitable reception. Katharine, wishing to know the Shelleys better, invited them to visit her at Taho. They parted happily.

As soon as the sand slope obscured the hospitable Castle Mesa post, Katharine beheld the white bank of the plateau sloping above them. Somehow the once remote place seemed not very far from Taho now. In a short time they reached the great dunelike sand mountain. Not until it loomed before them did either Katharine or Alice realize that while descent had been so thrilling, ascent must be impossible. Mr. Reynolds expressed wonder that they had not thought of that long ago, and grumbled about the extra three miles added to the home journey. But Katharine was well-content. She had ceased to think. She gave herself wholly to the sensorial appeal of the desert. Time sped, and likewise the car. Too soon Taho came into view.

"Straight ter your house?" asked Reynolds.

"No," replied Katharine. "Mrs. Newton's house please.

Then on your way back to the post office please drop our baggage over the gate."

"I'll see it safe to the porch, Ma'am. No bother at all."

They came then to Mary's house. Katharine pressed some money into Reynolds' hand, requesting him to keep the change. Then with Alice following, she hurried up the walk that led to Mary's porch. A moment later Mary appeared in response to her knock.

11

You! Oh, Katharine!" This salutation, voiced with a hungry cry, was sweet reward to Katharine for coming at once to her friend's side. Mary swayed ever so slightly when Alice stepped beside her sister in the doorway.

"You both gave up your visit for me?" Mary went on. "How good of you! It's selfish of me to be glad! Come in. I'm all alone."

Her last words sounded a bit forlorn and her voice was sad as she spoke them. Yet her serenity was as gallant as ever. Mary could meet life stanchly. Her eyes said so, and so did her bearing.

Alice broke through Katharine's meditation with a call from the door through which Katharine had already passed.

"I'm not coming in, thank you, Mary. Just wanted to say hello. Tomorrow I will. You and Katharine ought to talk alone. Give me the key, Sis, I'll run over to the house."

Katharine blessed her sister silently.

"But you must both have supper with me," Mary protested.

"Indeed not! You'll have your supper with us. While you and Katharine chat I'll get busy. Come over in about an hour."

Katharine squeezed Alice's hand as she slipped the key into it.

"We'll be over promptly," she said. "Mary loves a Spanish omelet, remember?"

"I do remember a few things," Alice shot back in retort.

The screen door closed with a click. The two girls faced each other, and Alice was forgotten.

"So my letter brought you!" said Mary, as seating herself before Katharine she contemplated her with a look that was almost adoring.

Then the Eastern girl knew that under her friend's calm exterior there was a desire to relieve her heart.

"Got it and came just as quickly as I could. I knew the sooner you could talk to someone who understands, the better for you. I am here to help if I can. Pour it out, old dear."

The merest shadow of a smile passed over Mary's face.

"Well, he's gone," she said. "It's not a bluff this time. He won't come back. He's taken everything. At first I was so dazed I didn't think of his trunk. That's gone too. I found it missing after I wrote you. Billy Horton, one of the cowboys, came in yesterday to apologize because he let Wilbur transfer the trunk to his shanty. Wilbur had told him to send it to Flaggerston with the first car out, and to express it collect to his mother's home in Texas. Billy said he wasn't smart enough to see there was something irregular about Wilbur's request. That came to him after Wilbur left. He said he'd turn the trunk over to me. But what do I want with it? Why should I hold it?"

"That would be very foolish," agreed Katharine.

"So I thought. Billy was very good to tell me about the trunk. Indirectly he was informing me where Wilbur had gone."

"You think then he has gone to Texas?" Katharine inquired.

"Perhaps not straightway. But that's the only place that seems ever to have been home to him. They understand him there."

To Katharine's way of thinking, only blind affection would prevent anyone from seeing Wilbur as he really was. Great pity for Mary consumed her.

"Understand him?" she said. "I wonder! How can they when they are cut from the same cloth, a very drab-looking cloth at that! What depth of real understanding could Lenora have?"

For a moment Mary said nothing. Then she leaned forward, swept by a gust of passion that flashed in her eyes.

"Oh, Katharine! Do you see what a failure I have been? How, why, where I've been remiss is so hard for me to discover. I only know sort of helplessly that I *have* failed. God knows I tried to make Wilbur happy. Yet circumstances were against me right from the start. I'm trying hard to be fair. It can't be all Wilbur's fault that our lives were without accord. Am I one of those people who can't see herself as she really is? Can't hold a mirror to my soul? I married Wilbur. I was sure that I loved him then. But our period of adjustment covered years instead of months, and never did we truly adapt ourselves. Is it too late, Katharine? Is there something I can still do to make good?"

"Do you love Wilbur now?" asked Katharine.

"There! It's a relief to have you ask that. I've tried so hard to be honest with myself about it. I think I do. But it is a love that is largely pity. And Katharine, I never wanted to love a man that way. It's like the love of the strong for the weak. Maybe it's altogether maternal. I don't know. I only know there is something. Surely, though, not the thing most women crave. Instead of being protected and cared for, when I married Wilbur, I had to become his protector against the world—the people who recognized him as a man whose future was behind him, who saw his monstrous vanity. It was I who had to do all the nurturing of what little love there was. I had even to think for him without making him aware that I was doing so, letting him accept my ideas as originally his own. I had to steer him from mistakes—meet his debts. I was the one to take all the responsibility. I was forced against my nature to be independent. My dependence upon Wilbur had only the substance of his blind reasoning. . . . What will happen to him now?"

Katharine struggled against the provocation to tell poor wretched Mary the truth about Wilbur and to hurt her beyond the point of a woman's ability to bear suffering, in the hope that the truth would forever purge her heart of any feeling for the man; but John Curry seemed present to stay her, as indeed he must have been, knowing her first hours in Taho would be with Mary; and her conscience, reminding her of her promise to him, likewise silenced her.

"Rest assured, he will act independent of you," Katharine said. "And may what he does break him! Breaking a man, Mary, is often the best way for him and the world to discover of what stuff he is made. And who knows? You may prosper if Wilbur does launch into some mad thing. As far as you are concerned it might prove a good investment rather than a loss."

Plainly, Mary was puzzled. "Aren't you speaking rather vaguely?" she asked.

Katharine smiled. "I speak conditionally. Perhaps that is why I seem vague. While you are facing so uncertain a future, there is little to do but make conjectures. I call leaving you Wilbur's first big misstep as concerns his own well-being. You were the one good influence he had to cling to. Aren't you willing to admit to yourself that your marraige was a misalliance?"

Despite Katharine's tenderness of voice, Mary flinched under her words.

"It was a misalliance," she admitted. "But I backed it with a vow sacred in the eyes of God."

"Yes, of course." It was so easy to agree to the sacredness of marriage, yet hypocritical to pretend faith in the letter of the law, so Katharine could not drop the matter there. "Mary, why was marriage instituted?" she went on.

"To propagate the race, I suppose. And as a protection for children, the family and the state.... As a protection for love perhaps."

"Propagate the race! Did Wilbur want children? Protect the family! Whose family? The husband's? Protection for love! Why, Mary, the only protection for love is love itself. As for Wilbur, I think he is incapable of loving anyone except himself."

"Still, I'm sure he must have loved me once. I'm reminded of the old adage about love going out of the window when poverty comes in the door. That was the trouble with Wilbur.... If only I had had money!"

Katharine frowned upon this. "Had you some money, then perhaps Wilbur would have found more binding the vow that is sacred in the eyes of God! Is that the idea? I don't mean to be sacrilegious, but I think God would rather not be connected with so materialistic a proposition as that."

Tears welled in Mary's eyes and one fell on her hands which in their tight clasp gave evidence of her distress. Then she looked up with a gesture of self-command, manifestly summoning the will to dry her tears.

"Dear ever-logical Katharine," she said, "can't you see that I am fighting these all too evident truths—that the more I am convinced, the harder I must fight? I married Wilbur. I am one-half of the contract. I am trying to keep my end."

"You mean there is no condition under which you would break it?"

"I think that usually chickens come home to roost, so I must wait."

"And that's final," said Katharine more to herself than to Mary.

Mary made no comment. Her silence was her affirmation.

"Then you have not thought of securing your freedom?" Katharine asked. "In Arizona if a man deserts his wife and does not return within a year the wife on presentment of appeal will be granted a decree of divorce almost at once and without any sensational publicity. I learned this when Mother was studying up on a speech in favor of more liberal national divorce laws that she was to deliver to the Women's Federation, and I am glad Arizona is fearless in this regard."

"I will wait for Wilbur."

Mary's voice lost all its softness. Such hard, cool tones did not spring from pain or passion. Calm, resolute in her intention, she gave her answer not as a challenge but as an immutable verdict. Only through pretense could Katharine reopen the subject now.

"If you can speak so surely, then you must love Wilbur more than you admit. You want to believe that he will come back."

"I do. But it is not because I can't live without him. It's because there is protection against myself in having Wilbur. There is a self that I can govern only by a sense of duty as his wife. That self is the unsatisfied woman in me. That self is to blame for my interest in John Curry. I didn't want to be interested in him! Oh, you do understand me, don't you, Katharine? There was no intentional disloyalty. Taking my interest on its surface value, it is absurd. There can be no genuine depth of feeling. Why, you could count on one hand the times I have seen Mr. Curry!"

For a moment Katharine hung back from a bog of thought on which to venture was perilous indeed. But she plunged through, because Mary was waiting there on the other side, and she might be able to help her.

"How often you have seen Mr. Curry has nothing to do with your feeling for him. You can't measure it that way. I always have maintained that I would recognize the man I could love the very first time I should see him. And it happened that way. He seemed the composite of all the finest men I ever knew. I had recognized him, though the truth about love dawned slowly."

"*You*—love—someone?" Mary faltered.

"Someone who does not love me—who cares for someone else."

Mary spoke. "I am sorry, Katharine. I wonder why you are denied him? I wonder if there is a reason for such things? You with your bravery make me feel like a coward."

Katharine smiled down the pain that assailed her. "I can look across the boundaries of the Elysian fields and find a good measure of content. I can find happiness in other people's happiness. I mentioned this because you begged the authority of time to support your argument. Truth is, there is no argument. You like John Curry very much. I like him myself. So does Alice like him. We should see more of him."

At the moment Mary's face was a study. "We?" she blurted out.

"You—I—Alice. Yes! Don't look at me as if I were the tempter himself. Satisfy yourself about John Curry. Find out if you do care. If you don't—there's Alice. It would not take much association with Curry for Alice to find a genuine attachment there. He seemed to find her attractive."

Mary reddened. "He would, naturally. She is so beautiful—a gentle flower of gold—and he is so strong and tall. They would make a handsome couple. I hope for Alice's sake that you two, at least, see more of him. Like you I've looked over forbidden fields so long I'd almost be afraid to enter even had I the right."

"I hope he comes this way soon," added Katharine.

She hated such subterfuge. Mary was too guileless to suspect her, so guileless that the shot had gone home straight and sure, making her wound evident. Now was the way clear for Curry's visit. Now would the planned event betray no malice of design.

"You gave Mr. Curry my message?"

"I did. Also I gave him your letter to read. I wanted to make him feel murderous."

Mary leaned close. Her eyes glistened. "And did he?"

"Yes. But he contemplated only half-murder. He wanted to drag Wilbur back to you."

"Back to me!"

Katharine replied with a quiet yes which disguised her elated feeling of triumph. To outgeneral Mary in the aggressive maneuvers she was waging for Curry was particularly gratifying; to strip away Mary's defenses was to reach the truth. Mary did care, deeply, dearly, though she would not admit it now, even to herself.

12

BECAUSE John was on his way to Mary, it made little difference that the sky was overcast with gray clouds threatening unseasonable rain. The sky of his mind was aflood with sunshine. The wheel that trembled under his fingers as the car sped along obeyed an unconscious guidance. Restless High-Lo, who swayed in the seat beside him, was burdened with speech of which, bit by bit, he relieved himself, much to John's discomfort.

"Say, are you takin' me to jail or just to Taho? An' what's the rush an' silence about?" he asked. "Ain't you got a few words for a condemned man?"

"Just not feeling talkative," replied John.

"Thanks for the information. If there's any more such onexpected news, you better shock me now while I'm strong enough to stand it. I thought you'd swallered your tongue. There's things I'd like to know about. For instance —what's the idea of sellin' your car? When do you expect I'll ever get to ride another, 'less it's a truck?"

"Got to have cash. Want to bank it till its working time is due. Have a friend who may need it anytime. Get the most you can for me in Flaggerston. I'll give you a percentage."

"Keep your percentage!" blazed High-Lo. "What interests me is that you're tryin' to keep some other cuss like me out of trouble an' you've not been tellin' me anything about him. Call that square? What gets me is who would you sell this car for? What have I been missin'? You know, John, anytime you want me to keep right on hittin' a trail, you tell me."

"Jealous! That was what he was!" thought John. Aloud,

he continued: "The day will never come when our trails part, son, unless you tie me at some crossroads in order to escape. This won't affect you any, High-Lo. It's something that your friendship has helped me to do. I'll tell you about it when the time's right."

"Riddles!" ejaculated High-Lo in fine scorn. "Well, I'm trustin' you. If I wasn't I'd run away with your damn car to make you follow me."

Dust, like smoke, curled past them. The last time at the wheel of the old car that had given such faithful service! Under other circumstances, John might have suffered regret. As it was, the prospect of service gave him the courage to part with it. "All for Mary!" the whirring motor seemed to say.

"Then you're shakin' me in Taho, shore? Not thinkin' of comin' on?" High-Lo cut in.

"Right. And you're to go straight off. I want you back in Taho soon. No stalling in Flaggerston. Quick business and business only."

"Ye-ah!" drawled High-Lo.

They reached Taho trading post at a time of late afternoon when inactivity marked a waning day. A lone burro stood in the road sleepily observing the car. The pendulum-like wagging of this lop-eared creature's tail ticked off the dead moments outside the quiet post.

There John and High-Lo parted. The car left as it had come, unheralded by the natives, and John to all appearances had dropped from the blue void above him.

Strange that there should be only a matter of hours now between him and Mary when, unknowing, Mary moved in the little white house that gleamed through the trees up the road. "Call at eight," Miss Winfield had written. Three hours to wait! No, two hours and fifty minutes. He would give himself ten minutes to walk leisurely up the road. Two hours among the Indians down at the farms. A half-hour coming and going. Twenty minutes to clean up at MacDonald's house. He'd shave again. Maybe he'd gather some information about Hanley among the Hopis. Hopi John was so proud of his English that he'd tell anything just to use it.

Hopi John did have things to tell. Hanley had recently passed through Taho on his way to Flaggerston and, rumor was current, to Phoenix later. Sheep business again! Always sheep business! Following some deals at the farms intoxicated Indians came to blows in the village. Excellent sheep business! John cursed the man roundly. Hanley came alone and left alone, according to Hopi John's report. Winter would drive a man such as he south. His insidious operations would be renewed in the spring. Would he meet Newton in Phoenix? The Blakely girls lived in Phoenix. Nice party!

While climbing the long road back to the mesa in the twilight, John considered these things, yet came to no decision as to a plan for himself regarding Hanley. The girl who lived up the road in the house that gleamed through the trees would be the one to decide all things for him now.

Through MacDonald's courtesy, John was refreshed with a bath and shave, and the dust of desert travel removed from his clothes.

"You may think you're fussin' up for a dance, but there ain't none that I've heard of," said MacDonald. "Or maybe it's them new young schoolteachers. The one from New York sure is mighty purty."

"I never was a teacher's pet," John returned. "It would be a new experience. I'm half-afraid to try."

MacDonald laughed and forgot to pry further into his guest's affairs. "Just lift the latch and walk in when your courtin's over," he finished.

The dark leafiness of cottonwoods and poplars shaded the footpath John followed, and he liked this escort of darkness because he felt color beat into his face from the high pulse of his heart. His cold, trembling hands did not seem to belong to him. He thrust them into his pockets out of sight.

"Four houses below Mary's," he said to himself.

He had better count down. Still, there was no need of counting. A flare of light burst from all the windows of one house, beacons of welcome. He looked beyond, far down to the white house where Mary lived. It was somewhat like her—white, still, gently present through enveloping shadows. Suddenly he was in a yellow haze of light and his hand irresolutely reached for a gate. Now had come the occasion which unnerved him. But desire was greater than his fear. The gate closed behind him. He was on the walk ... the steps . . . in dark silhouette against the light. Before he could knock, Katharine appeared.

The pressure of her hand and a few words quietly spoken

were but fleeting incidents. A vision of Mary caught over Katharine's shoulder stayed his thoughts—Mary, arranging purple asters in a bowl with an unfeigned concentration, and a grace of action which thrilled his hungry heart.

She saw him presently. Perhaps it was only the glow from the rose shade of the lamp that lit her face. Then she smiled.

He had crossed the threshold. He had her slim white hand in his and she was saying, "Katharine said we were to receive a caller. I never dreamed it would be someone from Black Mesa. You've come far."

"I didn't feel the miles," said John, happily. "I left and I arrived. It was that quick."

"And your work at the post is over for the season, I suppose," came a voice from a remote corner.

Alice was reclining on a couch, half-lost between high piles of gay-colored Indian cushions.

"All over, Queen Alice," John replied. "And I am the envoy of a dozen lovesick cowboys come to tell you that their affectionate remembrances precede them here."

Alice frowned on him haughtily. "Be yourself, Mr. John Curry," she said. "You sound like a sofa-warmer when you talk like that—not at all like a cowboy. It's unbecoming."

With her light words Alice put John at his ease. It was no longer strange to be there. The presence of friends, the revival of pleasant associations gave him confidence. It was Mary who seemed suddenly abashed. Katharine led the conversation to Black Mesa activities and drew Mary into an argument about the use of horses for pack animals, defending, as John knew, something she did not really credit, in order to draw reproach from Mary.

"Burros, and burros only, should be used," Mary maintained and thus a flood of conversation grew from small currents of thought, Mary contributing volubly to its content, eyes aglow, cheeks flaming, lithe body giving force to the intent of her words.

What they talked about mattered little to John. He was floating down a river of words only because it carried him along with Mary. Time played havoc with him. It halted in its flight, it seemed, till the ticking of a clock through a brief silence reminded him that some occasions slipped too quickly into the past—that time was relentless and favored happy hours least.

Alice and Katharine served lemonade, and delicious squares of cinnamon-covered toast, and cookies which Katharine said Mary had made.

"Not since Mother's going has anyone given me things as good as this toast and the cookies," said John. "I hate having the Black Mesa boys miss anything like this, but I warn you, if you'd feed it to them once, they'd pitch their bed-rolls out back of your house and never go home this winter."

"I'd cook all day for them," declared Mary. "I can see them like little boys, with fingers in the cookie tin. They'd never find it empty if they were my family."

A faint rumble of thunder sounded as Mary spoke, and Alice, who hated electrical storms, looked disturbed.

"We can't be going to have a real storm at this time of year!" she protested.

"Looked rarin' much like it this afternoon," John averred. "I thought it would give sooner or later."

The leaves of the cottonwoods rustled, a jagged fork of lightning rent the sky, thunder rolled and echoed and rolled. Then plashing drops of rain streaked across the window. They multiplied fast and soon a great wave of rain came sweeping over the mesa, drumming on the housetop with a hurried beat.

"My windows!" Mary ejaculated. "Open! Every one of them! I'll have to go."

"Goodness, yes!" said Katharine. "That paper house of yours will float in no time. Mr. Curry, you'll have to take Mary over. I'll get an umbrella."

She was at a little cupboard. Beside the umbrella she tossed out a coat. "Make her wear that, too."

John helped Mary into the raincoat while Katharine opened the door for them, holding it against the wind which would have flung it wide. The light of one lamp blew out. Alice called from over the other which she was lowering, "Shocking! You're being sent home. Fine hostess my sister is!"

"Thanks for a great time," called John. "I'm staying on, and would like to rustle some horses to take you ladies riding some day."

His voice was lost in a clap of thunder.

Once outside, John, placing himself against the rain, felt Mary leaning slightly against his other side. The rain sang all around them like the rush of surf. The umbrella swung and sagged under the weight of the steady wind. John wanted to turn it to the wind and let it go to roll like tumbleweed down the unobstructed avenue, so he could lift Mary in his arms and run with her to shelter; but he clung stoutly to the slender-handled thing, hating its resistance and likewise his own.

Soon they stood at Mary's door laughing, shaking off the raindrops, watching, for a moment, the stream that poured off the umbrella tip.

The rain and the wind beat upon them. The wind flung the door from Mary's hand and drove them forward with it. It took all John's strength to force it shut. Then he struck a match and Mary lit the lamp.

"If you'll please close these front windows," Mary directed. "The curtains are soaked already. I'll take care of the others."

She was panting heavily when she returned to him, and dropped to a chair near the door.

"Won't you please sit down?" she said. "This storm is terrific. You never could make the post now. You'd get drenched. Better wait a while."

John thought of the times and times when he had ridden all night in the rain. It was unpleasant, and it did mess a fellow's clothes, and—his last thought conscientiously accepted as the vital one—he did not want to leave Mary. He blessed the rain. He hoped it would continue and with it her hospitality.

"Thank you, I will sit down a while," he said.

There was a chair near the table where he stood, a great, comfortable-looking chair with arms spread invitingly. He was about to sit in it when a cry from Mary checked him.

"No! Not there, please! . . . Draw up the rocker if you will."

Her alarmed tone was baffling. Had he committed some social error? If she had wished to sit in the armchair herself, certainly she would not have corrected him that way. Nevertheless, he reddened.

"I'm sorry," he said.

"It's waiting for someone—that chair," Mary went on. "I just couldn't bear seeing you sit in it because—"

She stopped there, her face the color of the flaming Indian paintbrush. She was radiantly beautiful. She had shed her calm.

Though John was eager to hear her reason, he would not urge her to go on. He said nothing.

"Perhaps—you understand," she added weakly.

"I'll not even think about it. I know you are in trouble. I want to help you, Mrs. Newton, in any way you will let me."

Fluttering eyelids lifted and Mary looked at him again.

"I'm so used to seeing Mr. Newton in that chair that he seems present this minute. Isn't it ridiculous to think of you as sitting on him had you taken it? Yet that's how I would have felt. That just came to me now. Perhaps what I say sounds irrational. Does living alone make people queer?"

"I'd advise you not to live alone for long out in this desert country," John warned her. "Take in some reliable woman to board with you until the Winfield ladies return in the spring."

"I'd like to. Not that I'm afraid to be alone. Government positions pay so little, and I want to meet certain obligations and later save some money. I'm not getting any younger!"

One could think only of youth in Mary's presence. The thought burned on John's tongue, but he did not voice it.

"Take in an Indian girl if you can't rent. Do it for company's sake," he suggested. "I sort of wish you'd promise me to do that because I might be going away some this winter, and I'd be worrying sure. I hate to think of you alone while it's possible your husband might return. Don't be hurt by my saying this. Sometimes wife-deserters come back changed—that is, harder than before, especially men who hit a trail for the desert. They often pick up a grievance out there."

"But Mr. Newton went to Texas. He sent his trunk there," said Mary.

John felt that Mary was sadly mistaken about her husband's destination. A flash of lightning and a break of thunder followed after her words angrily. It saved him from remarking on what she had just said. Indeed, her momentary attitude of concentration on something removed from their immediate presence showed that she expected no comment.

"Do you intend to make Taho your headquarters this winter?" she asked presently.

As brief a time as an hour ago John had made that very

decision, so with conscience free he said, "I've been making plans to do so."

"And not go to your brother's ranch in Colorado as you usually do?"

Again a deafening roar! But it could not have been the interrupting clap of thunder that made Mary's eyes widen with fear. The muscles in John's mouth tightened. How much she reminded him now of the terror-stricken girl he had rescued from the cliff edge! His blood raced with his thoughts.

"Not go!" he repeated.

"But you must!" she pleaded. Her voice pleaded, her great luminous brown eyes pleaded, and her hands turned outward in her lap, fingers half-curled.

"And why must I go?" asked John, now hopelessly baffled.

"Your—your cattle," stammered Mary.

He laughed, but he was not amused. Mary was so obviously avoiding the issue.

"The cattle get along without me for eight months. They can stand it once for a full twelve. It's the mavericks I like to look over. They are the new-borns, you know. They arrive during my absence. They can't miss me if they've never seen me."

"There's your brother! He depends upon your coming, I'm sure!"

It was disturbing to have Mary look away, talk at him and not to him. He could not reach the cause of her distress unless she trusted him. Again he tried to treat her evasions lightly.

"On the ranch I'm just another hired man. By staying away I'll help Colorado's army of the unemployed."

"And here in Arizona you plan to help me, you think," Mary concluded in a low tone.

John waited for her to look at him before he replied. But she continued to stare at her fingers, and she spoke again without lifting her eyes.

"Staying here won't help me, Mr. Curry. You must go."

Something stirred in John's mind, linking this occasion with the predictions Katharine had made. Yet he received her words incredulously. "If my motive were selfish, I wouldn't be staying on. I swear I wouldn't."

She met his eyes at last, and hers burned with a strange

light. She seemed to sway toward him. Her breath and voice appeared almost to embrace him.

"You must go, John, because I wanted you to come. I've repeated to myself daily a catechism of deceit. 'I don't want to see him,' I would say, and tried to make myself believe it. Before, when you were about to sit in Wilbur's chair, I cried out. My catechism again—I did not want you there. Truth is, I did want you there, with all my heart, as I have seen you in a dream, crushing Wilbur's insistent image out of sight."

She rose, pushing her chair back violently. John watched her move from him. Shock, joy, and a nameless longing emerged through turbulent waves of thought. He felt the fire of her courage entering him. He, too, rose. He strode toward the window. The width of the room was between them. When he turned she stood expectant, her head inclined attentively.

"Thank you for being so frank," John said. "The truth is best and easiest met. I've been wanting to come to you. Ever since one day on the desert when it came to me that you were dearer to me than anyone on earth. You are. If Newton had been the finest fellow in the world I couldn't change what I feel, and I wouldn't feel I was hurting him any. It's no sin to love a woman, whatever her connection, if you have reverence for her and for honor. And for that reason, if Newton were any kind of a worthy chap, I wouldn't be here now. He didn't make you happy, and now he's cut and run. What's wrong, then, if I want to help you honorably—asking nothing, expecting nothing except the permission to serve?"

"No, not wrong!" Mary shook her head as if to emphasize her denial. "I don't mean it would be wrong. You'd be honorable and keep it free from scandal. But if I saw you continually, if what I feel strengthens and then Wilbur comes back——"

She finished with a hopeless gesture.

"You'd feel you had willfully put me between you and him," John supplemented.

"I would know that I had."

John saw then his own naïveté. Mary was right.

"And if he should never come back—this year, next year, the year following?"

"Then I would know he will never return."

"And my banishment would end?"

"Banishment!" she echoed in confused haste. "That is an unkind word. It suggests that you have offended me. Believe me that you haven't! I see you as someone big, splendid, and true, far stronger than I am and almost incapable of wrong. I was not suggesting that you go out of my life altogether. I wouldn't want that. I want you to go on with your own life as you would have before this crisis came into mine. Go to Colorado. That is what you originally planned. When you return to the reservation, if you come through Taho, visit me as you would your other friends."

John grasped at once this less harsh sentence which was being so graciously given. "I'm very likely to come through Taho," he said. "I can think this minute of a dozen things that make it imperative."

Mary advanced to the pool of light that spread between them. "You will take us riding before you leave for Colorado?" she asked.

"Gladly. I can't leave for several days. Have to wait for my pal, High-Lo."

John suddenly found that he had nothing more to say. So much that boiled in his mind was inhibited by the obligation Mary had imposed upon him. Moreover, he was conscious now that they were alone in her house, that the hour was late, that a storm, completely forgotten, still raged outside. And Mary, manifestly, had gone adrift in her thoughts and could not reach him again. He knew he must go, and ventured to remark upon it.

"It's still raining," Mary replied.

That was the thing for her to say under the circumstances. It sounded too conventional, and she seemed ashamed of the implied insincerity for she quickly added, "Still, you must go—if only because I must not want you to stay."

So he left, his hand warmed by the touch of hers. He resisted her insistence that he take Katharine's umbrella. He forgot about the discomfort of soaked clothing. He wanted the feel of rain in his face. Snug in the depth of his pocket his right hand retained its gift. The outside world was dark. The rain stung him. Clouds still emitted lightning. Thunder reverberated through the blackness which closed with a rush on each flash of illumination. Halfway to the post he cut through an alfalfa field toward the open desert. The naked wasteland, vast, imperturbable, ignored the elements that flayed it.

The riding excursion materialized as John promised it would, and he had Mary's smiles again. As they rode he watched Katharine's furtive glances at every mention of Colorado. When the day ended and Mary said, "I'll look for your return in the spring," he accepted his dismissal quietly. He would not see her again until spring, unless they met by chance during the day or two that he remained in Taho. He was pressed by restlessness to put out for Colorado at once, but High-Lo had not returned.

That evening he called on Katharine. Alice, weary from the afternoon's strenuous ride, had retired early, a circumstance which John found favorable. He had come to talk about Mary. Katharine accepted his news tolerantly.

"We must try to believe that Mary's judgment is best," she advised him. "I've changed my opinions a bit. I'm afraid of Wilbur Newton. He gets white-mad and white-mean and unreasonable about nothing. And if we're wrong about his carrying on further with Hanley, and he should return, he'd act the offended one and he'd make her pay. For the present it may be well for you to disappear. What Mary plans for herself six months from now, a slacker husband will have little right to question."

"Your talking like that makes me stand going some better than I thought I would," John confessed. "Yet I do get skeerish when I think you'll be leaving soon. But I know how it is. Alice is your first consideration."

"Yes."

"Then comes Mary."

"Yes."

"And you couldn't coax her down to Phoenix with you?"

"No. She ought to be here in case Wilbur comes back."

"Sure enough. . . . Can you beat that for law? She'd be the one who deserted if she were to be gone when he comes back. Looks like she can't leave if she wants to."

"She can't. But she's never thought of it that way. And you're right about divorce. I doubt if she'd ever consider it."

"Newton's likely got that figured. What a yellow dog he

is! ... Come to think of it, I don't know what made me suggest Phoenix. He may be there. Hanley's on his way."

Katharine nodded assent.

"I've made up my mind to one thing," John confided. "I'll lay off Newton's dirty work on the reservation provided he doesn't come back and mistreat her. That would be my cue. I'd land him behind bars, and she'd be safe. Safe to get away. And she'd go, too, if I had to kidnap her to show her the sense of it."

He carried this thought away with him. He honestly wished Newton would recover from his present deterioration, if from that Mary could glean some happiness, but if the fool was headed for complete destruction, he would save Mary from being dragged along with the man to whom she was married.

As soon as he reached his room he wrote a letter to his aunt in Texas, asking her to deposit so many dollars—he left a space for the amount—in some bank in San Antonio, to take out a draft for a Mrs. Wilbur Newton for the amount deposited, and to send the draft to her address—Taho, via Flaggerston, Arizona.

13

MARY found winter days busy times, but she found winter evenings lonely. No one applied for the room she advertised at the trading post and post office, so she communed with a silent house whenever she was home. Anywhere else Mary could not have endured such complete isolation. But Taho held her. She was bound. She could not leave. Sometimes alone in the silent rooms she felt she must flee from her loneliness, but whenever the suggestion came, it passed as quickly as it had appeared. There would come a sudden whiff of sage and snow, the low, barking cry of a coyote, or the restless whistle of wind that whipped along the ground, and the idea of leaving the desert would be forgotten.

The memory of what had happened in September was with her always. Wilbur's chair never ceased to remind her. She never sat there. She wanted to destroy it. She examined with an open mind her reticence to obey the desire and discovered that as long as she let the chair remain in its place, she had objective proof that John and she, there in her home, had justified their friendship.

Snows had come early. Yet between the frequent storms were days like spring, unseasonably warm. At the school grounds the Indian children wallowed through rivulets of sluggish water whenever they moved from building to building. They loved such places, looked for them rather than avoided them. Then they would become a fretful lot, cheeks swollen, eyes inflamed, and faces screwed time and again for violent sneezes. Headaches were reported. The infirmary would become a busy place.

Then word came that Mrs. MacDonald had been taken violently ill with influenza, and by the next week the disease was a matter of such grave concern that Mrs. Gordon's baby had died of it. The school doctor looked with alarm at the copper-hued youngsters who came to him labeled "Infirmary Cases." Day after day cards were filled with such notations as: "Watch for Influenza Symptoms, Mild Case Influenza, Malignant Case Influenza." And the nurse told one of her schoolteacher friends that the doctor was worried, and soon all Taho knew.

By Christmas the town was under a virtual quarantine. Not that one had been ordered from headquarters. But people were driven by fear to confine their immediate families and shut out the malady if they could. The register of nine at the white children's school had a blank placed beside it for attendance, and the teacher substituted for a sick teacher in the Indian school. The church Christmas party was canceled, likewise the Indian school holiday festival.

On Christmas Eve fresh snow covered the mud wash of the last storm and fell steadily for a night and a day. Not a soul ventured on the broad avenue that was Taho. Not even an Indian or a stray dog tracked the covering of snow. All Christmas day Mary kept logs burning in the open grate of the living room. She was indebted to Billy Horton for the wood and for killing the chickens she had set to simmer on the kitchen stove preparing a broth to be sent tomorrow to the infirmary. She thought of Billy's kindness as she sewed small woolen nightgowns which she had cut from a light blanket. They, too, were for the infirmary. Each time she rose to stir the broth or feed the fire she cleared a place on the frosted window and looked out on the cold and shrouded town which lay empty and desolate. It was the loneliest Christmas day she ever had passed.

Late in the afternoon she began to look for lights from the houses down the avenue. Evening would be cheerier, she hoped. To give a feeling of comfort to other lonely souls, she lit her lamps early and scoured the frost from the windows so the light would shine brightly through. Snow was heaped everywhere. It burdened the cottonwood trees and every fence and post bore its load of white. Presently between the laden branches Mary saw yellow patches gleam. They were the infirmary lights. One after another they appeared. Mary imagined the nurse making the rounds with her electric torch. There were lights from every window; rooms never before occupied were in use now. She was reminded that yesterday she had dug up several cots from the school storeroom for the doctor who was loudly deploring their lack of equipment.

Mary was preparing her evening meal when a knock on the front door startled her. She was expecting no one, for the night already was completely dark.

"Who is it?" she called against the wind which howled through the keyhole.

"Dr. Kellogg."

Assured by the familiar voice, she opened the door, and the doctor entered, tracking snow with him. Normally he appeared a thin wiry man, but in the big bearskin coat he seemed almost rotund. Mary wished the worried look he wore could be removed with the coat.

"Merry Christmas," he said with not the slightest change in expression, and added immediately, "Are you busy?"

"Not very. Preparing a meal. Perhaps you'll join me."

"No, no! Thank you! Wondered if you'd help me out at the hospital. The nurse is down with the flu now. It was bad enough to have only one nurse for forty kids. No nurse at all is terrible."

"Certainly I'll help," said Mary.

The doctor eyed her critically for a minute. "You've not got the sniffles, backache, headache, pain in your limbs or sore eyes, have you?"

"Not a thing."

"Then don't get them, and you'll do. I'll trot along. Come when you can. I mean, come as quickly as you can."

He let in more snow and a great gust of wind before he closed the door behind him.

"Poor fellow," thought Mary. "He's hardly equal to it."

She shortened her preparations for supper and poured the savory chicken soup into jars to cool. Then she donned rubber boots and a close-fitting cap and brought her very familiar but somewhat threadbare coat from the closet. Turning down the lamp, she sallied forth into the storm. Barring the friendly gleam of lights across the snow, Taho seemed even colder now that the blue shadow of night had descended. Remote houses became spectral things, seeming to sway beyond the intercepting fall of whirling snowflakes. A mass of snow slipped from the slanted roof of the new government building and struck a drift below with a soft thud. The wind shook the curtain of snow and tore at

Mary's cheek. She followed the deep footprints Dr. Kellogg had made. She saw where his coat had dragged, building piles of snow along the way.

Mary reached the infirmary and entered without knocking. It was a frame building, as drear and drab within as the schoolhouses. An odor of coal oil was prevalent. Lamps needed trimming. She would attend to that presently.

The doctor hailed her with, "Think I'm losing a case upstairs. Pneumonia's set in. Girl. Indian. Such a poor-looking little thing. Comes from Sage Springs. God, but I hanker for the city at times like this. A real hospital, the right equipment, sufficient help. Above all, efficiency. Before Miss Lange came here to nurse I was sent an empty-headed girl who hadn't completed even a probation term. I set her to labeling medicines and she labeled them all wrong. Had to destroy a lot of medicine for fear she'd use it before I could straighten things out. She might have killed someone. She might be responsible for casualties now through this curtailing of supplies. We were short enough without that. I made out an order for more, but you know the red tape involved in spending money here. It's awful. I'm running short of everything."

Mary gasped. "Have you taken the matter up with the government agent, or the missionary, or the school?"

"It's up for consideration. Everything's 'up for consideration'—supplies, new quarters, extra nurse. But it's action, not consideration, I need."

"Can't you order things from Flaggerston yourself?"

"Yes. With cash on delivery. I've bought things, myself, as much as I can afford. I'm supporting a family back East."

Mary knew how little he could save from his meager salary. "How much of an expenditure would cover your present needs?" she asked.

"Oh, there's so much! Hot-water bags, ice bags, medicines, blankets, towels—everything! Three hundred dollars would be slim."

"And five hundred?"

"A fortune."

"Maybe I can let you have it?"

Now the doctor gasped. "Have it? What do you mean? Who on this reservation owns that much money unless it's MacDonald?"

"I have a draft for that amount."

"But where'd you expect to get it back from?"

"I'm not thinking of getting it back."

"And that, I reckon, is all you own. You with a husband who's—" The doctor stumbled over another word and then murmured, "I beg your pardon."

"You haven't offended me," Mary returned quickly.

"You mean to give that money for these poor beggars. Come now, you were just a little too impulsive, weren't you? Suppose you help out with a hundred."

"I want them to have it all."

"You're—you're too good. You're—you're not natural," sputtered the doctor. "I shouldn't let you do it, but I can't help it for the kids' sake." Then he groaned, "Oh, but I wish I had it before this storm came on. Wires are down. We can't telegraph an order, and who'd try to take a car out in this snow?"

"Bill Horton will. He's a lad with a heart. All I'll have to do is tell him the situation here."

"It was an inspiration, a sure-enough heaven-sent inspiration, my going to you tonight," the doctor declared. "I was desperate. 'Who'll help?' I asked myself. There were faces that turned away from me as quickly as I spoke. But I saw you clear as spring water. And I went to you straightway."

"Well, put me to work," said Mary. "And between your labors manage somehow to make out a list of the things you need."

"God! This *is* Christmas!" said Dr. Kellogg.

His words thrilled Mary. Her forlorn day became suddenly a very happy one.

"I'll put you up with Joy," added the doctor, strictly professional again. "We'll try to pull her through."

Joy! What a name for the unhappy isolated little creature into whose room Mary was ushered. She was an eight-year-old mite with a body too frail for such a burden of pain. How pitifully she fought to breathe, plunging her hands upward like one drowning!

Mary thought of Katharine's description of Alice's struggle—how oxygen tanks rushed into service helped her through. Oxygen tanks. Oxygen. She shivered in the cold, for the two windows were open top and bottom. Joy needed all this air. She must fight for the precious oxygen, poor child. And meanwhile her body must be kept warm. So bricks had to be reheated and hot-water bags refilled between periods when Mary chafed the rebellious hands. Now and then, through the night, the doctor came in and gave the child hypodermic injections. His visits were brief and he had few words.

After midnight the wind lulled, the snow ceased. An occasional cry sounded from the other rooms, and the sound of coughing. Joy still labored and fought. She uttered sibilant words, staccato cries cut short by the succeeding struggles to breathe. Mary's own breath came heavily, an unconscious reaction of her effort to help. She felt no need for sleep. The child's fight had become her fight, and unbroken vigilance was the only way to victory.

It was six o'clock in the morning when Dr. Kellogg pronounced hope. "She may come through," he said. "And it's you she can thank. . . . Sure you're not feeling stuffy yourself? No pains in your back, head, limbs? Eyes not sore?" He quoted these symptoms mechanically.

"I'm as fit as I was last night."

"Good. Two things for you to do this morning. See this Horton fellow and then get some sleep. List's ready."

"I don't need sleep," Mary protested. "A cup of coffee will set me right for the day."

"Not for the day. Only until I get someone to take your place."

"Oh, no, doctor! Joy's mine to pull through now!"

"And then who'll pull you through?"

"Why, the will to help her, of course."

"That sounds all right, but I believe in exercising care."

"And meanwhile take no precautions yourself!"

"I'm a doctor."

"And I've accepted a nurse's place."

With the night's triumph scored in her favor, Mary went to the government mess where she could have breakfast and see Billy Horton at the same time. At first Billy received her request that he drive to Flaggerston as a joke, but when he was convinced of her earnestness and heard the cause for which she was pleading he capitulated without further ado. She went then to fetch the draft. It was in her change box where it had lain for seven long weeks. She had intended never to cash it while its origin remained a mystery, nor would she, had this emergency not pressed her. It represented five hundred dollars deposited in her name in a San Antonio bank. It had arrived in a typewritten envelope with a San Antonio cancellation stamp, but no word or address to explain it. At first she had thought her relatives from Texas had sent it. "If so—why?" she asked herself. They knew nothing of her financial difficulties. Furthermore, they were not given to generosity, and a generous act undeclared would be a breach of their ethics. She could neither reject nor accept it on the assumption that it came from them. The thought that Wilbur might have sent the draft presented itself tardily. It did not seem consistent that Wilbur, who was selfish, who had deserted her, taking with him what money was in the change box and her jewelry, who had no money nor the credit to borrow it, had turned benefactor.

"Texas . . . Texas!" she would repeat to herself, trying to stir associations that might reveal a clue. And taking the chance of having a letter to her father intercepted by her stepmother as others had been, she wrote asking him in what state was the copper mine in which he had taken shares for her when she was a child. She knew the mine operations had been suspended years ago, and, as far as she knew, never reopened. An answer that the mine was in New Mexico satisfied her that so far she was more in the dark than ever as to the identity of her benefactor.

While the mystery was yet unsolved, she would not, could not, let the money remain idle in the San Antonio bank when there was a crying need for it in Taho. She hurried to Billy, eager to make her act irrevocable.

Indomitable will and several cups of strong coffee kept Mary at Joy's bedside through the day, and she would have resisted the fatigue that crept over her toward evening had Dr. Kellogg not said Joy would live, and convinced her his faith had nothing to do with his insistence that she accept relief.

A schoolteacher named Miss Hills took Mary's place. Not only had the girl slept during the day to fortify herself for the night, but before reporting, thoughtful of all that Mary had undergone, she had arranged with neighbors to have Mary's house warm for her return. Tears came to Mary's eyes when she found what had been done. There was a certain sweetness in being so deadly tired. She slept twelve hours. At eight she was on duty again. Joy lifted a feeble hand to greet her.

Several new cases came in that day. Doctor Kellogg grew anxious about Billy Horton. They looked for him hourly, but Billy did not arrive until the morning of the next day. He appeared to have been through a Homeric struggle. When Mary tried to thank him, he turned away shamefaced and said, "You mustn't be handin' me too much credit, Mrs. Newton."

"Why, you—you've done everything!" declared Mary.

"You picked me to ask to go because I've been doin' little jobs for you, didn't you?" Billy asked.

Mary was puzzled. "Yes. That was what made me think of you."

"An' you might have been wonderin' about my sudden interest, an' thinkin' it was that trunk business I was tryin' to square."

"No. That never occurred to me. I've thought of you as a fine upstanding lad who understood my difficulties."

"And there's where in the beginning you got me a little wrong. I was asked to help you, so it's only square I shouldn't take too much credit."

"Asked to help me?" echoed Mary.

A more vivid red mounted the boy's windburned face. "Yes. John Curry asked me and offered to pay me, and I like to throwed him for that. He asked me to do chores for you and make myself generally handy."

Mary's cheeks burned in their turn.

"That was thoughtful of Mr. Curry," she said, very self-conscious and fighting it. "And ever so good of you."

"What gets me," Billy went on penitently, "is that I had to be asked. I'd have wanted to do it, you see, if I'd been smart enough to figure you'd be needin' a man. I'm not smart like John."

"You are brave," Mary interrupted.

"But that doesn't get me over havin' to be asked. I'd like to do somethin' on my own, somethin' that would square me. . . . Say, if Newton comes back, an' you don't want him, I'll beat him up for you."

If the boy were not so valiantly serious, Mary would have been amused. As it was, her breath left her and her thoughts whirled dizzily. When words were again at her command she said, "I don't think it will be necessary to beat Mr. Newton up. He won't come back."

Her last remark she uttered with conviction and she repeated it to herself, "He won't come back!"

For John Curry, who loved her hopelessly and had to go away at her request, she was suddenly lonely, terribly overwhelmingly lonely. Long hours this loneliness persisted.

She would have conquered in the end if Miss Hills that evening had not come in upon her while she was occupied with Joy and said, "You ought to have a child of your own, Mrs. Newton. You'd make a wonderful mother. I hope you'll marry again, once you get your divorce from that husband of yours."

"I—I haven't planned to divorce Mr. Newton," Mary returned, on the defensive at once.

"But you must! Heavens! Don't you suppose he wants it? Men don't leave a girl like you unless there's another woman in view."

The words struck Mary with the sting of a lash. The very unexpectedness of the remark made its import seem more monstrous to her. Wilbur's wanting a divorce . . . . Another woman in view! Was the moral view of marriage so completely lost that a young girl of good character viewed her situation so lightly? Was there no longer any sacred regard for the marriage relation? Was it all hypocrisy?

"Perhaps to some men marriage is a loss of independence, and they marry without taking that into consideration," Mary said, suddenly reminded of Wilbur's own words.

"And loss of their independence merely means a bridle to check them from having affairs with other women. Independence? Nonsense! Who is really truly independent in this world? Independence stopped when man quit supplying all his needs by his own labors. The poor word is rather sadly hackneyed these days."

"I guess you're right there," Mary concluded, then fled from further discussion.

But she could not flee from anxiety so easily. Hadn't Wilbur intimated that the photographer in Flaggerston whom she had never seen could take his place? He had not mentioned love. Freedom, to have affairs with other men as Miss Hills would put it, he had basely insinuated was a thing she desired. She was married to him then, and divorce had never been mentioned between them. And why should she want a divorce unless to marry again? She shuddered as the thought came to her that she did not want Wilbur to return. Was she not part of the same great hypocrisy? Was that not proof that her own ideals were false, that she was struggling for a belief in the traditions of her fathers rather

than receiving intolerantly anything that threatened to destroy them? And there was her love for John. As he had
said of himself, she could not change it. All the defenses
that she had built around her with evasions and arguments
were threatened now. She had a baffled feeling that constancy to a single ideal was being demanded of her, and
that fate was leading her blindfolded to make the choice.

Through the days that followed, Mary fostered all her
reserve energy to meet the demands on her strength that
the long hours at the hospital called for. She had little
leisure to think of other things.

The influenza epidemic spread through Taho like fire
down a sage plain. It raged in the Indian village, too.
Contagion was most prevalent among the men. The schools
were closed. Fewer and fewer were the people who attended government mess. All the inhabitants of Taho were
numbered either among the sick or the nursing. Mary faced
the day when Billy Horton, too, succumbed to the pes-
tilence. That created a grave situation. Billy had taken the
place of the cook at the government mess which supplied
food for the hospital patients. Someone had to take charge
there, and with no one else ready to assume the responsibility, Mary stepped in. She had no idea of the demands it
entailed. When she struggled with knife and saw against a
resisting quarter of beef, when with the aid of a stout stick
she had to enforce her request that an Indian lad kill
chickens for her, she was astounded by the proofs of her
efficacy.

In spite of the added duties she found time each evening
to rub with liniment forty and more chests and backs.
Through this faithful service to the children she earned
from them the title, "Grease-mother."

After the epidemic began to wane, there came a morning
when Mary did not report at the hospital. While trying to
dress at the usual hour dizziness overcame her. She rested a
while trying to recover, but the bed seemed to turn round
beneath her, and even when she closed her eyes it did not
cease circling. She felt deathly sick. Three hours she lay
with limbs as stiff as if they had been clamped in irons, and
with a strange buzzing in her ears. Mrs. Gordon called. In
high alarm she went for the doctor who came at once.

"Exhaustion!" he declared.

Mary, looking at him, thought hazily that he might have

been judging his own malady. Yet with a feeling of relief she gave herself over to the tired man's care.

A week later Mary was about again. The doctor, more wan than ever, was still at his duties with machine-like constancy.

"Two deaths in all," he told her. "And no more malignant cases."

"Then Joy has really recovered? No relapse?" asked Mary. She had feared all along that kindness had colored truth in the answers she had received to her inquiries about Joy.

"She recovered. But she shouldn't go back to school this year. Live outdoors. Sleep outdoors. I'm afraid of her lungs, and she has a slight gland infection."

"Why can't she come to live with me?" asked Mary, suddenly impressed with the idea. "I'm off all day Saturday and Sunday, and away only six hours on other days. My neighbor would gladly keep an eye on her during my absence. And Joy's such a good little thing, perfectly reliable, Miss Hills tells me."

"That would be the best thing in the world for her!" Dr. Kellogg exclaimed. "Lord! You certainly ought to be able to take care of one after what you've done with forty!"

The government agent's approval of the plan was promptly received, and Joy's well-loved grease-mother became her foster mother.

News of Mary's gift to the hospital had long since circulated about Taho. Mary gathered that it had been received incredulously by some, who accepted it later only on the strength of a belief that she had sacrificed an inheritance; but whatever misgivings had arisen, all opinions tended finally to canonize her and to consign Wilbur to a greater depth of degradation for having left a woman so virtuous as she. Mary had not foreseen such a result of her generosity, nor yet the word that went abroad when she adopted Joy.... "Poor girl! You see, she's wanted children all the time!"

14

PATCHES of green showing through the melting snows of the Colorado uplands began to attract cattle from the valleys where they had grazed during the winter months, and to scatter them hither and yon over the vast area of their summer range. The lowing of cattle, so intimate during the tedious season of snows, now carrying from afar on a breeze laden with the scent of spring, seemed to hold a note of farewell for John. He had had enough of Colorado. He had come here against his own desire. There was a hunger in his heart and a restlessness in his soul that nothing could appease. His eyes turned longingly toward Arizona. He wanted to turn his horse's head that way and give him free rein. He was riding home from Cleland with the mail, with the realization that he would have to repeat the journey several times before he could conscientiously leave his brother's ranch. He saw in the distance High-Lo coming to meet him, accompanied by a rider on a mount that seemed somewhat familiar. He tortured his memory until he recognized the horse as one Beany rode in Arizona and then he knew that the slim, straight figure in the saddle was none other than Beany himself.

"Yea, Cowboy!" yelled the rider in a voice that cleared all shadow of doubt. "How are you ridin' these days?"

"Managing to stick on!" John called in response.

They came up then, wheeling their horses about, one on each side of John.

"Just back from Black Mesa?" asked John.

"Yep," returned Beany. "And it shore was lonely holdin' that post alone for the winter."

"Folks away long?" John followed.

"You're talkin'! Went to Phoenix for Christmas and come back only a week ago. Guess they was scared of the flu. It shore hit the reservation awful hard—particular down around Taho. Three deaths down there."

John's heart began to thump. "Deaths? Who?"

"Lord! I ain't the local undertaker. How d'you expect me to know?" asked Beany.

"Didn't any word get through to Black Mesa?"

High-Lo chuckled and intercepted Beany's answer by saying, "He wants you to tell him that them that died with the flu was Texans."

"Wal, I can't give names," said Beany. "If what I got was true there was a baby, an Indian kid and a kind of youngish woman."

"White woman?" asked John, legs and arms gone suddenly numb.

Beany slid over hard in one stirrup and peered into John's face. "Say, are you takin' the census?"

A hideous fear made John vehement. "Answer me, you fool."

Beany took offense. "Someone's been feedin' you pepper or bad liquor!... Yes, it's a white woman. Not been there long. Tuberculosis case and took the flu quick. Wife of one of the government men."

John gave a great expulsion of breath. A burning heat within him suddenly lost its fire. He felt the reins slipping through his fingers and retrieved them.

"By golly, John!" High-Lo ejaculated. "Bet you were thinkin' of Miss Alice Winfield. But they were to leave late November. Good they got out."

"Say! That reminds me!" Beany broke in. "Mrs. Weston saw them Winfield girls pretty much in Phoenix, an' she run into the Blakely girls there, too, goin' it pretty strong with Hanley. They say Hanley's part Mormon. He's like to want 'em both."

"Anybody seen anythin' of Handsome?" asked High-Lo.

"Handsome?"

"Sure. That splinter of a would-be cow-rider called Willy Newton."

"Oh! Wilbur Newton! Hain't seen him, but I've heard some. He's opened a small post in that deserted adobe buildin' at Sage Springs."

John caught a significant wink and nod from High-Lo.

"On what, I'd like to know?" queried High-Lo.

"Borrowed funds, I'm guessin'. And if he can go any other way but broke, I'll give him my horse, and the saddle thrown in."

"Any idea where he gets his supplies from?" asked John.

"Gallup, I guess. Over the Luckachuca Mountains. Some thinks that's easier than through Flaggerston. Course I don't know, never bein' over that way. I'm just figurin' 'cause nothin' comes through by way of Black Mesa."

Again High-Lo winked and nodded.

"I heard Hanley would be in Colorado some time this winter," lied John in an attempt to lure Beany into telling some more that he might know and yet appear not too interested. "Did Pop Weston mention his leaving Phoenix early?"

Beany screwed his face into a reflective knot, then untwined it. "Come to think of it, yes. Seems though, speakin' of Gallup, that it was there Pop Weston said he'd went."

John did not dare look at High-Lo, for the lad had burst into a whistling of the long-neglected refrain written to immortalize the old sow.

"Gettin' back to Newton," said Beany, riding closer to John as their suddenly obsessed companion led off the road onto the sage flat, "ain't he got a wife? I thought so. Leastways I heard some fellers talkin' about how she was downright pretty."

"She's red-headed and freckle-faced," announced High-Lo between the last and first phrase of his endless tune.

"She's not," said John, off guard at the moment. And recovering: "You never saw her. You don't know what she looks like."

"Oh, don't I! You're the one who never saw her. She's as red-headed an' freckled as a woman can be. Newton did it. Made her change color like that. She was dark afore she married him. Then one time she come home late, an' he bein' such a mean cuss locked her out for the night not carin' that it was rainin'. An' bein' left out in the rain like that she rusted. An' she ain't been the same girl since. . . . O-h-h-h-h—"

John knew what was coming. He heard the first word and note before it fell.

"The old sow woke up in the mornin', and one of her pigs was dead," wailed High-Lo.

Beany grinned from ear to ear. "The damn fool!" he drawled. "But say, what d'you make of it? Newton livin' at Sage Springs alone?"

A night shared with Beany kept John and High-Lo apart. However, early the next morning after Beany had left for Cleland they strolled toward the corral together and relieved their minds of a number of thoughts they shared.

"Of course, you got it," High-Lo remarked. "Newton's post is financed by Hanley, the post bein' a cover for their real business."

John nodded.

"An' they're dumb fools if they think they can get by with that. I reckon when we're on our way to Black Mesa I can use that roll of bobwire I toted along. It's hangin' in the barn."

John anticipated this reaction from High-Lo and knew he would be hard to handle.

"Don't be too anxious. Give them plenty of rope to hang themselves with."

"Hang themselves, nothin'! I'm goin' to be there for the dance. Why the delay? You wouldn't go through Sage Springs an' tip yer hat to that feller!"

"No. I'd tip a gun if I gave in to myself."

"Wal? Doesn't that settle things?"

"No. We're going to Black Mesa by way of Taho."

High-Lo looked at John in mild contempt. "Taho? A hundred and twenty miles out of our way? Are you gettin' awful fond of ridin'?"

"No, but that's the way we're going," John replied.

High-Lo halted, thrust his hands into his pockets and rocked gently on his heels. "That's the way *you're* goin', John. I'm goin' by way of Sage Springs. I'm so sick of nothin' happenin' that I could bust an' run. You ain't goin' to spoil my party. Of course, if you've turned yellow—"

John swung around, his right hand itching. "Take that back, High-Lo."

"Mebbe I will!"

"No! Take it back now."

"Wal, then I'll say, 'if you've turned sick,' instead. You've shore turned su'thin'! Did you think I wasn't wonderin' none why you didn't foller this up last fall, why you didn't try follerin' up Newton like you said we would when we quit Pop Weston, why you've cut me short every time I've mentioned Hanley to you? What d'you expect me to be thinkin'?"

The time had come when John could no longer deceive High-Lo. The boy was asking for the truth and he ought to have it. "If I mix in this affair I can't do it without betraying the woman I love," he said unsteadily.

High-Lo's jaw fell and his eyes widened to their limit. Then his lips met in a thin line and his eyes narrowed. He studied John a minute. Presently he said, "The woman you love?"

"Yes. She's Wilbur Newton's wife."

High-Lo blinked as if in anticipation of a blow he stood to take.

"Don't look at me that way, pal," begged John. "My love's honest—as honest as heaven. You've got to believe me. Let me tell you about it. Not here. We can't stand here. Come on over to the corral."

He walked away without looking back, and it was a full minute before he heard High-Lo plodding behind him. He observed that the boy took care not to catch up. When they reached the corral High-Lo still kept his distance, squatting on his heels about twenty feet from where John stood. He snapped a piece of brush and started drawing designs with it in the sand. John moved closer, and though High-Lo's silence disturbed him, he ignored it, and began his confession starting with the day he first saw Mary. Soon the stick with which High-Lo played ceased moving, and shortly it fell to the ground. John perceived him capitulating slowly to the thrill and romance of the narrative. He was listening intently for all that his head was averted. So John went on, becoming lost in his own recital. Suddenly it was over. He had explained how Mary had sent him away. There was nothing more to tell.

High-Lo looked up. He stared at John in frank amazement. "An' this has been happenin' to you," he muttered, "an' you not tellin' me till now?"

"But you understand that, don't you?" John pleaded.

"Mebbe. You see, I ain't never been in love. Sure, I've been mixed up with women when I was drunk, but I never had the thing that's hurtin' you so hard. What you've told me make me see red an' hate it all. Hate it all! Do you hear me?"

High-Lo's face moved convulsively as he brought his long speech to its passionate close. John was grieved to see the boy so shaken.

"There's nothing come between us. Don't feel that way. I need you more than ever. You've saved my life—my self-respect. I'm sure if you hadn't come to Colorado I'd have gone back to Taho like a weak fool. You've been my backbone. God! How I needed you!"

"You've got me wrong," returned High-Lo. "I'd hate anythin' that hurt you. That's the trouble. It is hurtin' you—you who'd give your guts for anyone else. No. Don't get the idee I'm jealous. Not of any woman."

John fell prey to emotions that made speech difficult. "And you'll stick by me?"

A scoffing snort was High-Lo's only response. There was fire in his eye. He sat deep in thought for a long moment. Then he cried, "I got it!"

"What?"

"All your strange cuttin' up. Sellin' the car, talkin' about stayin' over in Taho an' then not stayin' . . . lots of things! An' you thought it was her died in Taho. . . . Here's a bit of advice. Hang on to that five hundred. She'll be needin' it. An hombre like him will have to have a fancy funeral."

"What do you mean?" John asked tersely.

"This!" High-Lo shot back immediately. "All my life I've knowed that someday I'd do suthin' big. All my life I knew that suthin' not reg'lar was goin' to happen to me. It's come. I have to shoot a man. An' I can do it like I was shootin' a hydrophobia skunk. Conscience just that clear."

"Newton?" blazed John.

"My, but you're smart," drawled High-Lo. "That's my man. I'll shoot him tryin' to stop me from stoppin' him sellin' booze to the Indians. See? He's a dead man. I'm a hero. You're a bridegroom."

"But you can't shoot Newton!"

"Oh, yes, I can! My arm ain't paralyzed. I'm leavin' you mucho pronto for Sage Springs. You'll still be in Colorado when I'm seein' my party over the trail."

High-Lo sprang to his feet and stalked off.

"High-Lo!" called John.

No answer.

"High-Lo!"

Still no answer. The boy's head was thrown back stubbornly as he swung along.

John drew his gun. "High-Lo, I'll shoot you in the heel if you don't come back!"

John might have saved his words. He shot into the air which proved another waste of effort. He fired the gun again. Then High-Lo turned.

"That girl has sure set you crazy!" he yelled back. "Pack your gun. You might need it to poke between me an' a sheriff." With that he broke into a run. John, furious at him, started in full pursuit. As he passed the sheepshed he caught sight of an old lasso rope dropped carelessly over the fence. He snatched it and swung the rope to a good-size loop. Then he renewed his pursuit. His arm swept wide, the rope circling, and in another moment High-Lo was checked with a startling jerk, and his hands were bound to his sides. He pulled back fiercely against the taut rope, his eyes blazing.

"Sorry!" said John yanking him closer. "You've got to listen to me when my affairs are at stake. When you get an idea of your own you're worse than a pack mule."

Though the indignity of his position made High-Lo fume with wrath, he seemed to grasp that John was in deadly earnest and in no way attempting to make a fool of him.

"Well!" he stormed.

"I said I needed you to help me, but you'll only ruin things if you don't let my opinions count," John protested. "You or no other man is going to have blood on his hands for me. I never could face Mary Newton if you did such a thing. Don't act in the heat of your passions. Cool off. Think clearly. Then act. It happens that Mrs. Newton says she will see me this spring. All winter I've been haunted with the thought that Newton had come back. Now I know he hasn't. I'm pretty sure he never will. I can go to her free and happy. I know she doesn't want him back. I have a place in her life even if it is small. Don't take it away from me!"

High-Lo's head dropped. He scrunched the sand lightly with the toe of his boot. "I'm the fool. I thought you was. Hang close to me, John. I'll try. I wouldn't shoot Newton now even if the sheriff hung him up for me for target practice." He freed himself of the rope and tossed it away with a grin. "Shot at and hog-tied all in one day! That's better than dyin' by inches in a place where nothin' happens."

The days passed uneventfully. They slipped into weeks. High-Lo grew more restless. John, counting each sun, blessed it for passing. There came the time when he could wait no longer. What if he had to put in a month of unemployment when he reached Arizona? He must see Mary. He went to his brother and told him he was leaving and taking High-Lo with him. His brother expressed no surprise. Rather he agreed that he should go, saying that he felt the time was at hand when John ought to sell out his interests because only habit, grown from a faithfulness to family ties, kept him in Colorado.

High-Lo maintained that he had been waiting for word to go every time John opened his mouth to speak during the past few weeks, and every morning had packed his roll in readiness.

They were off without loss of time. For John their exodus was attended by all the palpitant hope and anticipation of the pilgrim of old to the promised land. Eight days they traveled, sometimes making trading posts at night, more often sleeping in the open and faring on Indian corn and jerked mutton. On the ninth day they climbed the broad back of the mesa behind Taho and saw the town in the far distance, a green oasis in a waste of sand.

15

ONE afternoon in April Mary stood in the road in front of the house straining her eyes beneath her hand, wondering anxiously if from an impenetrable cloud of dust the mail stage would emerge. But the dust was being stirred by approaching mounted Indians. In her disappointment, she was conscious of Joy's black eyes contemplating her smilingly. Like a stray brownie hesitating for a moment in the world of reality the child seemed, a little elf who did not understand, so accepted happily any circumstance that presented itself to her.

"No come?" she said.

" 'It has not come?' " corrected Mary.

"It has not come?" Joy repeated with her unfailing good nature.

"No, dear. But when it comes there'll be a letter on it telling us Aunt Katharine and Aunt Alice will be here soon. I'm sure of that."

"Will Aunt Katharine send Joy for school?" Joy's gleaming white teeth showed as she finished in a smile. But the smile did not mean that she wanted to go back to school. She asked the question often in this disarmingly happy manner. Mary had come to recognize the smile as faith that her answer would be the desired one.

"No, Aunt Katharine will not send Joy *to* school."

"*To* school," Joy said in devout contrition. She walked closer to Mary. "Maybe soon Joy be white girl," she announced.

"White girl?" repeated Mary, off guard. Time and again she had been confronted with this announcement. It was an obsession with Joy that she might some day turn white, and her strange little soul seemed to burn incessantly with the longing.

"Yes. See? Joy make white here." She lifted her arm and pointed to a scar for inspection. "Then Joy don't go to Indian school."

"Joy never will be a little white girl," Mary said gently.

Tolerance for Mary's misunderstanding glowed from Joy's great dark eyes. "In Sunday school Joy sing, 'Wash her, be whiter than snow.' Joy wash and wash and wash. Joy's white here." She fingered the scar triumphantly.

Thought Mary: " 'Wash me and I shall be whiter than snow!' "

It was disconcerting to have to cope with Joy's rebellion against her natural state. She could not compromise with the yearning in order to appease the child. Quietly, insistently she had met it with denial. Now she wondered sadly if she were harming Joy by her devotion. The life she led, the care and love she received as the ward of a white woman, were estranging her from the people of her own race and removing her far from the colorless life of the children who lived in the dormitories. Had she the means, she would educate Joy, send her to college, train her to preserve the best that her race had transmitted to her, to accept the best that the philosophy and art and religion of the white people could give her, develop her to be a help to the women of her own race, who were being sacrificed to an age of change which was crushing their old faiths and customs without adequate substitution. Lacking the resources, she might be cruel and not kind to Joy as she so heartfully desired to be. The little one had quickly won her love. Never had she received such obedience, patience, appreciation from a white child! Nor were her reactions the mere submission of an obtuse, negative individual. Joy was bright. Her inquiring mind dug into many matters Mary had to avoid. She recognized circumvention and repudiated it. Her thirst to learn was so great that Mary feared that she was destined to suffer because of it.

Though the urge of a generous impulse alone had led Mary to adopt Joy, the arrangement had reverted to her own good in the way of self-preservation. Joy had become her refuge from loneliness. Try as she scrupulously did, she could not keep John Curry from her thoughts; yet she continued her losing fight. Feeling deep down in her soul the hypocrisy of her act, Mary placed a picture of Wilbur on the mantle over the fireplace. "My husband," she would say to herself each morning early, and again each night with as much punctuality and as little feeling as did Joy when she said, "Our Father which art in heaven." She was merely watering the ground where a flower had been uprooted, trying to make herself believe there would be a reblossoming. For what she thought was her own self-protection, she practiced this self-deceit. And now with April come she still denied the flutterings of her heart, telling herself that her anticipation of spring had to do only with Katharine's return.

Would Katharine find her changed? she wondered. The wonder developed into fear which made Mary realize that she was not sincerely herself. It was the detection of her hypocrisy that she feared. Was she a coward only because she would not see the truth? Always she put the thought from her as quickly as she could. Going deeper and deeper into the intricacies of thought where Joy's remark had thrust her, she discovered that the only way she could maintain her peace of mind was to forget everything except the present moment. So she proposed a race to the steps, and this time allowed Joy to win.

As they entered the front door Billy came in the back way with an armful of kindling wood.

"Saw you out there," he said. "Didn't knock. How'd you get in so fast?"

"Joy and I had a race," said Mary.

Billy deposited his load in the woodbox with no trace of his usual celerity. He even picked up the tiny slivers he had scattered, going down on his knees to do so.

"Any word of anythin' on the reservation out Black Mesa way or Sage Springs?" he asked, devoting himself sedulously to the minute flecks of wood.

"Had a letter from Mrs. Shelley last week and she said the Westons have been back almost a month."

"Other folks have come back, too," said Billy.

"No doubt everybody's getting ready for the summer," returned Mary.

"Folks have come that we weren't expectin' back," Billy went on. He quit his painstaking job with this remark and walked toward the front door, his back to Mary when he spoke again. "Newton's out on the desert somewhere," he said.

Mary stared at Billy's stalwart form, silenced by the

shock his words had carried; and the words became transformed into the tall, lanky form of Wilbur effacing Billy there in the doorway. Wilbur near! Wilbur back—perhaps coming to her now! Returning in the spring! But she knew that it was not Wilbur she had expected!

A sudden awareness of Joy tugging at her skirt and the child's words, "What's matter, Mudder?" brought Mary's mind back to the present.

"On the reservation—you mean?" she said haltingly, while to Joy she gave a smile which was meant to reassure her.

"Yes."

"Just come?" Mary pursued.

"Looks that way."

"In other words, you don't know for sure?"

Billy swung around, his hands in his pockets for defense. He seemed to be holding himself back from a dash to safety. "A feller gets news from Indians and cowboys without knowin' who handed it on to who, an' you take the main idee for truth. All I'd want to make a trade on is that right now Newton's somewheres back toward the border. It's somethin' I thought you'd like to know."

"Yes. Thank you."

"That's all, Ma'am. An' I'm around, Ma'am, when you're needin' me." His hand was on the screen door, holding it part way open. "Don't think I'm presumin'," he continued, "if I give you a little advice, me bein' a kid an' all. I'd keep away from Castle Mesa an' Black Mesa. That is—don't go out sort of meetin' him. Men that come back like to come the full way alone. An' remember, if he does come, an' you don't want him, I'm willin' to help make things hot for him." As he spoke his face cleared from embarrassment to candor. Before Mary could reply, he was gone.

"What's matter, Mudder?" Joy asked again.

"Something Joy wouldn't understand, dear," Mary hastened to say, shutting her mind against the thought that the child might be taken from her soon. "Run out and watch for the stage. Mother will let you get the mail if you're good."

That promise was enough. Joy scampered to the gate at once. Mary sank down into the nearest chiar and clung to the sides, as if by so doing she could steady her reeling thoughts. Fate at last was destroying all of her little deceits, forcing a decision which she was not yet ready to make. Wilbur might come any time! All she had believed to the contrary was mere wishful thinking. She was Wilbur's wife. Wilbur was not the type of man Miss Hills had described. He was vain, weak, negative, but he was not unfaithful. He was returning, but she did not know from where. All she knew was that he had not spent the winter on the reservation. His pride would never allow him to stay where people could point a finger of scorn at him. Mary believed in his pride; it was the only forceful thing about him, the thing that had deceived her into believing that she loved him. Love! Poor defiled word! Poor misquoted symbol! Must she go on inhibiting forever the secret desire of her heart? Life with Wilbur would have as little delight as a purposeless journey over the sands of a vast, colorless desert. She pictured sadly the long procession of the years to come. She had not moved when Joy called in that the stage had arrived and she reminded Mary of her promise.

"Watch till you see Mr. MacDonald go over," Mary advised the eager little girl. "He waits till the mail is distributed. You may go then."

Mary tried, by throwing herself busily into her household tasks, to drive from her mind the dread thought of Wilbur's return, but mechanical duties called for so little concentration that her mind could not shift its harassing burden. The future loomed too dark for her to withdraw the present from its shadow.

How long Joy was gone Mary had no idea. In truth, it took the child's return to remind Mary of her absence and the letters in her hand of her errand. Joy presented the letters proudly.

"Two, Mudder! . . . From Aunt Katharine?"

"One's from Aunt Katharine," Mary replied. "The other from New York. H'm! I wonder—"

She slipped the official-looking envelope into her apron pocket and went into the living room. Joy stood by her chair as she perused the letter from Katharine. Short and to the point, it told Mary to expect them that same week. "Next mail stage," thought Mary.

Joy was delighted with the news, and begged for permission to hold the letter. She examined solemnly the signs that were carriers of such pleasant words. Mary meanwhile opened the other communication. A lawyer, obviously her father's lawyer, was giving her firsthand the distressing news that her father had suddenly passed away, and that she, joint heir with her stepmother to his estate, had been willed ten thousand dollars, a check for which was enclosed.

Mary was too stunned at first to grasp the truth. She had to reread the letter, to examine the check that was attached with a clip to the typewritten sheet.

"Father! . . . Dead!" she said aloud.

"What, Mudder?" asked Joy.

Mary did not reply. Sorrow swept over her for the hard lovelessness of the man to whom she had been only a circumstance of marriage, who tolerated her as a moderately just man tolerates discomforts he has brought upon himself. There had been no abiding love between them. There was nothing from which grief for his partner to her birth could spring. In unemotional regard he had made this settlement on her. She wished sorrowfully that she had known so she could have thanked him before he died. He had said to her once when she thanked him for a Christmas gift, "I can't stop anniversaries from coming." She wondered if he would have met her now with, "I can't stop death overtaking me."

Ten thousand dollars! It was a fortune to her now. It was wealth. It was power. Ten thousand dollars! To have had it while her father lived—to have had it when Wilbur needed it most! Might it have changed things? . . . "She's holding out on you, tricky Northerner!" Terrible, scathing words that came from the past to torment her! That was what Wilbur had wanted—money!

"Joy, darling, perhaps I can make you happy yet," Mary cried. "Perhaps all my dark days are behind me now. This may be the beginning of better things." A taste of salt was on her lips. She was weeping and had not known it. She was crying, yet she did not understand the reason for her tears.

"Yes, Mudder," said Joy obediently. She came to Mary, alarmed by her distress and worked her way into her lap. This simple token of sympathy was what Mary needed; she accepted it greedily, hugging Joy to her as she repeated between her sobs those alluring promises.

That night, shortly after Joy had been put to bed, Mary heard a heavy step upon the porch followed by a knock. Billy never knocked. Would Wilbur knock if he returned? The very thought of Wilbur paralyzed her. She wanted to

call, "Come in," but her voice failed her. She rose hesita-
tingly. If, when she opened the door, she should find Wilbur
facing her, she knew she would swoon; she could feel all
sense of reality slipping away from her now. She made the
door; the knob evaded her, but on the second attempt she
held on more firmly and the door yielded. Then a cry
escaped her. It was John Curry she saw, eager, expectant.
Surely someone outside of herself was listening to his
words, the girl she was yesterday, perhaps, surely not Mary
Newton of today who in a hysteria of dread and fear was
waiting for her husband to return. She could only nod as
she backed away, inviting him with her eyes to enter. She
steadied herself against the table where he came to take her
hands and press them hard in his.

"Didn't expect to come through this early," she heard
him say. "Couldn't wait. No other excuse. Haven't you
some word for me?"

"I'm—I'm glad to see you," Mary murmured. "I'm
afraid to be so glad." She raised her eyes imploringly. "Why
did I ever tell you to come by in the spring? I've been
cheating us both with my expectations. I've been a creature
without strength or decision. Perhaps that is why I am
being brought to task at the eleventh hour."

John's face bent down to hers. "I don't understand."

She saw what he said in his eyes. His face, so beautiful in
its rugged strength, was very close. She wanted to caress it.
She wanted him to draw closer, she wanted to draw closer
to him, to lift her lips for his kisses. She clung to the table
with hands that were still numb from his clasp and fought
down the mad desire.

"Wilbur's come back to the reservation," she said, deliv-
ering the announcement in tones as final as her words.

"Wilbur never left the reservation," John returned quietly.

Mary weighed his remark. It had no meaning. Words—
that was all—just words. She felt lightheaded. Her feet
were on the ground but she seemed to have to pull at her
mind to hold herself steady. "You must be wrong. He went
away, but he's reconsidered. He's on his way back to me
now."

John was looking at her gravely, tenderly, trying perhaps
to read what was taking place behind her imploring eyes.

"Do you *want* to think that," he asked, "or do you prefer
the truth?"

"Why? Is there something that you know?" parried Mary, conscious that her question was superfluous.

"Wilbur Newton never left the reservation. He's opened a post at Sage Springs."

Mary smiled wryly. "That's awfully strange! Opened a post at Sage Springs? He has no money. No credit. How could he finance a post? Tell me, did you see him at Sage Springs?"

"No, but Beany told me about it. You remember Beany from the Snake Dance trip? And MacDonald knows. He says he wasn't spreading it because it would be known in Taho soon enough."

"And Billy knows. That's what he wouldn't tell," said Mary. "He is sparing me. He is kind." While she spoke she was searching her mind, which rejected and accepted alternately the news Curry had brought and the others substantiated. There was the matter of money. "How could he finance a post?" she repeated to herself. Groping through obscurity, she came upon the idea that Wilbur might have inherited some money of which she knew nothing. It could have happened, as had the unforseen good fortune which that day had visited her. Besides there was that five-hundred-dollar draft from Texas coming soon after he had left her. He might have taken her change and jewelry because he had no ready cash.

She presented the idea to John. "Perhaps Wilbur has money. Perhaps I was mistaken about his resources."

Mary sat down then. She had to from sheer weakness. John remained standing. "I received a draft for five hundred dollars in November," she went on. "It came from Texas. Just a draft. No word. I scoffed at the idea that he had sent it. Now I feel that he must have sent it."

Because she was looking at John so intently, she saw the confusion which overcame him as she spoke, the way he drew his glance from her as she replied in a tone that was unconvincing, "Anything's possible."

In a flash of divination she realized the truth. John Curry was her benefactor! The realization overwhelmed her with exasperation for her stupidity. "Anything is possible but that, is what you mean," she said bitterly.

"I don't understand," he exclaimed, more embarrassed than before.

Mary forced him to look at her. And when their eyes

met squarely she returned, "Only this minute it came to me that you sent that draft."

It seemed at first that he would deny it, but at last with a smile and a nod he confessed. "If you knew how I wanted to help, you wouldn't hold a little thing like that against me. It's awkward sometimes when one needs money. I've known what it means. If ever a day of need came to you, I wanted you to have a little reserve at hand."

Mary looked down at her hands for a moment. Then she spoke. "I did need it, not for myself, but for the sick children in the hospital during the influenza epidemic. I cashed the draft. I gave it all away."

"It was yours to do with as you pleased."

"No, no! It wasn't, but I was desperate for the sake of the children."

Curry strode to the window, then he turned, and coming back to the place he had abandoned he drew up a chair.

"Mary, if the need was so urgent, I would have wanted to help. You did it for me. You've made me very happy. You must forgive my blundering ways. Perhaps I am stupid compared to the men you knew in the East; perhaps I'm a fool when it comes to knowing the right thing to do, but you must not be hurt by that. Just try to forgive my blundering ways."

He was condemning himself. Mary could not stand that. His deed of mistaken kindness had been one of love. She longed to tell him that she understood, but she could only say, "I'm not hurt. In fact, there's no harm done. I can return the money. I have money now. Today I received word that my father died leaving me a comfortable legacy."

"I can't stop here," she told herself. "I am only hurting him more." So she floundered recklessly on. "If I had this money long ago things might have been different. And now, who knows, it may not be too late. Wilbur might return if I let him know about it."

She was filling in time—words, words, words! But when they echoed in her ears, out of their seeming emptiness came a suggestion. Why not send for Wilbur? If money did not bring him back nothing could, and she would know that he had gone from her life forever. The waiting, the fear, the uncertainty would end. She would have to give Wilbur his chance. It was best to force his intentions; if he returned she would resign herself to her lot, and if he did not come—and her longing for John spoke passionately from her heart, Pray God he won't"—then there might be happiness for her in the days to come. She was conscious that as she meditated, John was staring at her sharply.

"You would let him know about it?" he asked incredulously.

Mary faced him. "Yes. I want him to know at once. The sooner the better. I want to see how much he cares. . . . You've always declared you wanted to help me. Now is your chance." Her voice rose hysterically. "Take a letter to Wilbur for me. It will be safe in your keeping. I know it will get to him. I want to be sure that it gets to him."

John sprang to his feet. "Are you crazy? Are you going to buy that man back?"

How horrible it sounded! Yet it was true. She was trying to buy him back in the hope that she would find she was rid of him forever. No more uncertainty, no more fear! "Yes, since you put it so cruelly," she said. "If he can be bought, and my purpose is—"

She stopped. John was laughing without mirth. He towered over her, eyes ablaze, lips drawn, a scornful John she had never seen before. "Oh, he'll be bought all right. You'll have him back. Husbands—so much per head for the keeping! My God! *You!* And here I've held you in the same reverence I had for my mother. She wouldn't violate her soul and body that way. Buy back a man whose love is dead, who, God knows, cares only for such bribes as you're willing to hold out to him now! You're Mary, are you? My Mary who was with me throughout the lonely watches on the desert, who lived in everything beautiful I saw, who seemed so near perfection that I almost worshiped her! Indeed I am a fool, a blundering fool. . . . My mistake was only that I made you something that you never were."

A numbness possessed Mary. Her powers of speech and movement were gone. She was like a person who had witnessed a harrowing play and was waiting for some chance for a happy ending although the final curtain had fallen.

"Write your letter," the outraged man went on, breaking through her silence. "I'll take it to him. I don't go back on my word. If you think that's the best thing I can do for you, I'll do it."

"It will be the last thing," Mary heard herself say, in a voice that was little more than a whisper.

CAPTIVES OF THE DESERT 191

"Very well! I'll go. I'll send someone for the letter. I wish you whatever it is you want."

He had snatched his hat, yet still stood towering before her.

She rose to her feet unsteadily. Her head was high and her blazing eyes gave him no quarter for his angry outburst. But restrained beneath the agony of her resentment was the agony of longing.

He hesitated. He was breathing as if from the effort of violent physical exercise. His eyes were shot with pain. Suddenly he was close upon her, enveloping her in his powerful arms, gathering her in a close embrace. His face loomed over hers, his eyes like darts of flame were burning into hers. She felt her strength give way to his, and flutteringly shut him from her sight. Then came his kisses, hard, demanding, again and again and again. She swayed as he thrust her from him.

"I've taken *my* payment beforehand," he cried hoarsely. "And now you'll never see me again."

She watched him, a blurred object moving toward the door. Then the door slammed. He was gone.

Mary felt the floor sway beneath her. The walls were spinning round. When she reached for the table it seemed to move from her. The flame that had swept over John had consumed her too, with all its devastating power. She called his name, but her anguished cry was wasted on the empty room.

There was no break in the violence that possessed John. He strode down the avenue grinding the sand as he went, his sense of outraged love growing far beyond the bounds of reason. He, who had always been master of his passions, always had obeyed them, now he was their captive. He went straightway to the room at MacDonald's which he shared with High-Lo. He found the room in grand disarray and High-Lo at the mirror shaving. He flung himself face down on the bed.

"Pack up! We're moving!" he mumbled.

High-Lo pirouetted, razor suspended in action. "My God! What's happened to you? Did you get the go-by?"

"I'm going after Newton," John returned. "I'm to send him back to his wife. She's been left some money and she wants me to bring him a letter telling him all about it. The money'll fetch him. She knows it."

High-Lo flung the razor down, and forgetting the lather on his face came over to John. "Do you mean that straight?"

"It's true. It's knocked me for a loop." Unable to relax, Curry moved to a sitting position. "It means the end of things for me here. I couldn't stay. I'll deliver the letter and then we'll go to Mexico."

"Mañana land—where there's nothin' to do till tomorrer every day of your life 'cept watch that someone doesn't spike you in the back." High-Lo laughed a little grimly. "John, you sure you want to go down there? Doesn't seem like a place for a man of your ambition."

"We might make some money in the cattle business," said Curry, and he rose wearily and began to pace up and down like a lion in too small a cage. "Guess I'm loco, talking about packing tonight," he said after a while. "Forgot I didn't get the letter. Go ahead. Shave. Go to your dance. You'll have to get the letter for me in the morning."

"Dance be damned! Think I'm goin' to a dance, do you, when you're feelin' like hell? Why don't you let me go over an' talk Mrs. Newton out of this thing? Lordy, I can't imagine anyone wantin' Newton back after he left without a by-your-leave. Sure she's not up to payin' him to stay away? Sure you got the straight of it?"

John halted. "Please keep away from Mrs. Newton. You'll see her tomorrow morning. And I'm trusting you to say only one thing when you see her—that you'd like that letter Mr. Curry is to deliver for her." He reached for High-Lo's arm and swung him around so they stood face to face. "I told you some time ago that Mary Newton was the woman I loved. I was deluding myself then. She isn't. I never knew her till tonight. I must have been loco. I don't want to hear her name again. That's why I'm clearing out."

High-Lo's hand fell heavily on John's shoulder. "Look-a-here, old man. Mebbe I don't understand all that's happened. But I know you're shore kiddin' yourself now. This stuff about not lovin' her is all wrong. Don't I know I can make you mad as blazes an' have you cussin' me to hell an' back, an' all the time you don't mean it? Don't I know that there ain't a thing I could do that you wouldn't be over-lookin' soon, no matter how bad it was? Do you think you can make me think that it's different with this poor girl that got herself hitched to Newton? You're lovin' her so damn hard this minute that you're knocked clear out of yourself."

Moved by the boy's earnestness, John turned away. Suppose what High-Lo said were true? It took but a moment's thought to repudiate the suggestion, and the fierce wrath to possess him again. Why had he forced his embraces if not to show her that he no longer cared?

"You don't get it," he cried vehemently. "She's buying back a man who doesn't love her. She's going to live with him. My God! Don't you know what marriage means?"

"I reckon I do. An' it's because you love her that you're tormentin' yourself. An' what kind of a wizard do you think you are anyway to be understandin' women? Maybe she loves this damn fancy cowboy."

High-Lo's final words were staggering to John. "You may be right," he said. "She may love Newton after all, but—God—to want to buy him back, after he left her flat!"

On the morning of the next day John rode ahead out of town while High-Lo called on Mary Newton. It was the second time he had come to Taho to stay, only to leave abruptly! He thought grimly how in one moment a man's world could fall in ashes about him, and every prospect change. The desert was a forbidding, desolate place, as unyielding as life itself. It was the burial ground of his hopes. Better to seal off the past quickly. His back to Taho! God! Why were the stars out of reach?

Time seemed interminable before High-Lo appeared.

"Kind of funny the way she took it when I asked her for the letter," High-Lo said. "It wasn't writ. She kind of balked a little at first, an' then set down to the job. Say, she'd be wonderful pretty if she had some color. She's awful sad-lookin'. Have you ever seen her smile?"

High-Lo handed John the letter with a labored breath that might have been a sigh.

John had no answer for him. He said to himself, pocketing the letter, "The order for my execution."

16

ON the evening of the second day John and High-Lo rode
up to Black Mesa post. It seemed deserted, no horses nor
cowboys about, no Indians idling near the door. Attracted
by a light, they went into the store where they took Mr.
Weston by surprise.

"Thought you were in Colorado!" he exclaimed. "What's
the mattter? Sheriff drive this kid out?"

"It was a hankerin' for a holiday that drove us," said
High-Lo. "We're not lookin' for work. We're on our way to
God-knows-where."

Weston looked from one to the other. "Not pullin' out
for good?" he asked in dismay.

John, grasping that High-Lo depended on him to reply,
said, "There's Hicks to take my place if we keep heading
south. It's almost sure we'll not be back."

"Oh, come now, ain't you satisfied here!" ejaculated Mr.
Weston. "Wages unsatisfactory? You ought to know you
were in for a raise. I'd be treed without you. Hicks is good,
but he's not in your class. Can't hear of it, John." Mr.
Weston spat his tobacco with a gesture of finality.

John stared through the trading post door over the
legions of miles that beckoned him. "Got the wanderlust,
partner. I'd like to stay for old times' sake, but you couldn't
get ten per cent efficiency out of me if I did."

"You're ailin'!" declared Weston. "I'm not takin' you
serious. What you need is some of Ma's home cookin'." He
went to the door and called, "Hey, Ma! Fix up for John
and High-Lo. They've come to stay."

Mrs. Weston's voice carried across the yard, "It's sure

fine to have my boys home. Glad they didn't wait the month. Bring them in right away."

"Better be moving over," was Weston's laconic comment after John had exhausted his protests.

High-Lo lifted his pack to comply. "Things dead right now, are they?" he asked.

"Indians not buyin' so well. They sure dug themselves in while I was away, accordin' to Beany. It don't seem that Sage Springs post should hurt me any. But something's wrong."

"Bad winter? Indians had the flu up this way?" John queried.

"No. Flu didn't get this far."

"Heard about it and were scared, I'll bet," John added.

"I don't know!" Weston replied speculatively. "Can't get to the bottom of it. Remember Magdaline? She's here. Come in a couple of days ago. Seemed to have gotten around this part of the reservation a lot this winter. Talked to her about the loss of trade and she says in the funniest way, 'You don't keep the right sort of stuff, Hosteen Weston.' Then she wouldn't say nothin' more. Newton can't have in any better stock than I have. I've always treated the Indians fair. But he's sure tradin' in on rugs an' silver, an' even sheep, awful fast."

What was a mystery to Weston was plain as day to John. Liquor brought the trade. Magdaline was enough Indian to keep their wretched secret. Her scorn for the white man, he figured, must have increased a hundredfold.

Mr. Weston had forgotten his impulse to go at once to the house. "Could you size the situation up if I sent you over to Sage Springs?" he asked, biting off a fresh chew of tobacco.

Before High-Lo could admit that they had intended to go there, John quickly replied that they would ride out in the morning.

"Newton's hard to get talkin'—not over sociable," Weston explained.

"See if you can get a meal from him. Jolly him up about the place. Make him wag that stiff tongue of his. You can pretend I sent you over to see Magdaline's uncle. He's promised rugs to me this long while. But don't say nothin' to Hosteen Athlata about Magdaline's bein' sick. She's in a bad way. Looks husky enough. But she fainted yestiddy an' sure scared hell out of the missus. She's hankerin' to go to

Flaggerston now, right when the missus would be glad for company. She'd make a good hand for the summer. But if she's made up her mind there's none of us can hold her. Now maybe a word from you, John——"

John accepted the recommendation with a roar. "No, sir! Don't count on me!" And thinking it best to change the scene as well as the subject of conversation, he led the way out of the post.

Nothing Weston had said could have prepared John for the shock he received when he saw Magdaline. Attired in Navaho garb which she had vowed never to assume, her figure showed such ample development from the slim creature of a half-year ago that John at first could not believe it was she. And her face, once the register of every emotion that swayed her, now was somber, masklike. If she was surprised or pleased to see him, she concealed the fact. She offered her hand and said, "I hope you are well."

John replied awkwardly that he was. He was wishing as he spoke that the Magdaline of old could be restored to displace this strange aloof creature, barren of the fire of youth. Had the walls of her canyons crushed her as she feared they would? Was this the manifestation of her doom?

"High-Lo still grows," she said with only a nod for him.

She did not join the boys at the table where Mrs. Weston had laid a meal of vegetable stew and coffee and a pie of generous proportions, yet John felt her eyes upon him as they passed into the dining room.

He encountered her later on the ridge where he wandered, the victim of a strange restlessness. They met suddenly behind a hillock against which she was crouching.

John exclaimed aloud, and she shrank from him as if his cry had been a blow.

"You frightened me," John said. "I thought you had gone to your room. So did Mrs. Weston."

"It is better here," she said, "but even the desert stifles me now."

"You are not well, I hear, Magdaline. Is something troubling you? Is it because you are still so unhappy?"

"It is nothing to you," she retorted, turning away. "I go away tomorrow to Flaggerston."

"So Mrs. Weston tells me. She's sorry. She thinks you are in no fit condition to travel."

She made an impatient gesture. "I understand my condition. I will be well traveling slowly. I am saying good-by to
the hills as I go and mocking the prayer rocks of my people
for the last time."

"You don't mean—you're so sick—that you feel you—"
He spoke stammeringly and could not finish.

"I am going away forever. You mean death? No. I think
it must be good to die. Then you do not stifle like I have
been for weeks. Your breath and your mind go out like
fire. Then you are cool ash without flame. But I cannot die
now. I am two fires . . . a baby. And I am not married."

"My God!" muttered John.

Magdaline raised the masklike oval of her face to him. It
was very dark, very stolid there in the shadow, and her eyes
were listless, much like blackened glass.

"Yes. It is terrible. I cannot help that I have done what is
done. Sand cannot help moving when a great wind blows
behind it. I have been just as helpless as the sand. But I am
thinking after it is done. That is what is terrible. The poor
baby that does not ask to be born is going to have a spirit
that will make it suffer. I have wished myself never to have
been born. Sometimes I think I can save it by killing
it—killing us both. That would not be like dying."

More alarming than her words was her lack of emotion.
It was as if she had lost the power to feel, had become
insensible to everything and everyone.

"That seems the easiest way when hope is gone," John
said after a minute's reflection. "But has hope gone entirely?" He was questioning himself as well as Magdaline.
"Going through life is something like riding a deep canyon
where the light seldom shines. It is a strange canyon with
unexpected turns and insurmountable walls and cross-
canyons, boxed completely from the light. I suppose when
we hit the closing wall of one of these box canyons it looks
like the end and we want to beat our life out there.
Sometimes by accident, sometimes by design, we feel our
way out into the place where the light comes through at
times, and we go on down that way because farther on
there may be a way out into that light. Don't you want to
struggle on a little longer, Magdaline? I'm boxed in at
present myself, in a canyon as dark as hell, but I'm feeling
around for the way out."

The girl stirred a little from her apathy. "You, John
Curry, who are so good? I do not understand."

"I'm more deserving of trouble than you, Magdaline. It is only your own kindness that makes you see me so good. The worst in me is seething right now." He paused a minute, reflecting on her case. "Why do you go to Flaggerston?" he asked after his brief silence. "Why not stay in Taho? Dr. Kellogg will take care of you."

"I have a little sister in Taho at school. She must not know what is to happen. No one must know here in the desert because—" A feeble note of feeling had come into her voice, and she turned away.

"Because?" John encouraged her gently.

She looked at him imperturbable once more. "Do not ask me."

Another silence fell between them, which she presently broke.

"In Flaggerston I have a friend. She married a Mexican who works on the railroad. I can go to her and she will not tell. Then maybe the missionary will send me back to Riverside or to Los Angeles. I will be a servant for white people. Maybe another box canyon, Mr. John."

John was deeply disturbed. "You'll need money. You can't leave the desert penniless, face your trouble without funds."

She lifted her arms. "There are my bracelets. I will sell them when it is necessary."

"What they'd bring won't last long. Let me help you."

"Why?"

"Because we're both looking for the light, Magdaline."

She shrugged her shoulder slightly, giving him a faint reminder of her former self.

"I'm leaving early tomorrow morning," he went on. "You say you will leave tomorrow. God knows when I'll be in Flaggerston again. If you don't make up your mind by morning to let me help, perhaps I never can. Will you tell me by morning?"

"I will not be able to look at you in the light of day. I do not mind the darkness. It hides us both."

"Then let me make up your mind for you. After you are in Flaggerston a while, call at the post office for a letter. There'll be money in it." John took a small purse from his pocket and counted out fifteen dollars. "Meanwhile take this."

Magdaline pushed it back into his hand. "I should have

said before I have fifty dollars. Someone who knows gave it to me."

"I thought no one knew."

"One other must know besides me," she said significantly. "I told him. He can't marry me. So I got paid. Fifty dollars instead of marriage."

"You need better protection than that," John said, with the fire of hate for the unnamed man leaping through his blood. "Look for the letter in Flaggerston."

"You, too, are in trouble. I cannot help *you*," she said stubbornly.

The subject having so firmly been closed, John suggested that Magdaline return with him to the house. "You should," he insisted. "It will be very cold here presently."

"I won't feel it," was her response. "Go yourself. Walk as you would if you had not found me here. I will return when the house is dark."

Her command gave him no alternative, so he left. His desire to walk, he found, was gone. Magdaline seemed to fill the desert by her presence and crowded him out. He joined the others and spent the evening listening to Mr. Weston's tales of the late eighties.

That night John lay awake hours after High-Lo had, in rapturous exhaustion, flung his arms wide and found immediate repose. He could not reconcile himself to the fact that the last lap of his journey to Sage Springs would terminate within another day. Mary came to him, Newton came to him, Magdaline came to him; and when he finally did fall asleep, he dreamed of all three and of the Indian who had wronged Magdaline, and Newton appeared serving liquor to them all, and Mary drank, too, while she rocked an Indian baby on her knees. He woke in a horror of fatigue.

While they were dressing, John cautioned High-Lo to pack light for the trip, as they might have to pack blankets on their return to Black Mesa. They would not have to linger for information. Once the letter was delivered, he could tell Weston that Newton no longer would be a menace to his trade, for Newton soon would be gone.

"What I'm packin' goes on me," replied High-Lo.

Looking his way, John saw him buckling on his cartridge belt. "You won't need that," he cautioned.

"Never take a long ride without it," High-Lo rejoined. "Snakes in this country. Once a couple of the varmints cut my horse up some. But it's not real rattlers I'm afraid of. I'm packin' against the day when I meet one that don't give me warnin'!"

They built a fire and cooked their own breakfast. Before they had finished, Weston came in half-dressed and rubbing sleep from his eyes. He went out to the corral with them. It was not yet dawn, only cold, blue-gray light and lusterless stars.

"You're sure takin' my wishes hard," Weston protested. "Didn't mean for you to get out this early."

"Want to ride in this afternoon," said High-Lo. "Gives us time to look things over and get our invitation for the night."

John said, "We'll spend about ten minutes at Sage Springs, and we'll sleep on the desert tonight. Which side of Sage Springs will we find Magdaline's uncle?"

"Ten miles to the north from the post near some of them worked-out prehistoric caves. Messy-lookin' hogan. Worst around. But his wife sure can weave blankets."

They rode away from the rift in the sky where day was breaking. The horses, glad to quicken their blood, broke into a steady trot. Black Mesa valley was bathed in amber light. Through it a lavender haze showed over the corrugated ramparts of the mesa, and ahead blue peaks were overlaid with a sheath of gold; and circling the horizon came a wave of pink that soon receded under the full blaze of sunlight.

"An' you're thinkin' of leavin' it," High-Lo ejaculated.

"The sun rises other places," said John. He was thinking of the legions of unexplored miles in the heart of Mexico.

"But not like it rises on Arizona. I'd rather be buried here than livin' most places. You sure you want to go away down there? Sure you want to give that letter to Newton today?"

"It's what *she* wants that counts with me."

"She don't know what she wants. She's afraid of what she wants, bein' such a nice girl. 'Cause on the outside, folks not understandin', it don't look so good. What's more, there's no girl takin' an Indian kid to raise who ain't tryin' hard to do right about things."

John hitched to one side of his saddle. "What's that about an Indian kid?"

"Sure. She's got a kid around the house. Kid calls her

Ma. MacDonald was tellin' me she saved the kid dyin' in the hospital an' then takes her home to cure well an' is keepin' her."

Strangely John felt himself driven to talk about Mary, even though to think kindly of her would be his downfall. "I thought I asked you not to mention Mrs. Newton again," he said.

"My memory never was much good," High-Lo returned blandly. "One thing sticks. That's what Hanley done to me an' my horse. If I'm seein' you through your fool business, I reckon it's up to you to see me through mine. I want Hanley. I'm not exactly hankerin' to kill him. Want to beat him up good an' wrap him in his own bobwire. I don't leave for Mexico till that's done."

"That may mean waiting around a month. I'd have to go on without you."

"What's a month? Want Hanley to go on breakin' down the Navahos an' makin' 'em poor on liquor? If you think Mrs. Newton ain't worth savin' from her husband, is she worth savin' from what he's done? Is it worth hurtin' the Indians who've been mighty damn decent to you?"

John's irritability increased. Truth driven home was not pleasant to him in his present mood. "Go your own way if you're not satisfied with mine," he muttered.

"Not while you need lookin' after," High-Lo returned. "I was always dependent on you. Now things is changed."

Down into canyons and washes, up over rocky ridges, through cedars and junipers they rode, sometimes in single file, sometimes together, the sun mounting higher and taking away the chill of morning.

17

FROM five directions trails led to Sage Springs post. Not an Indian was in sight along them, a strange coincidence, considering that it was late afternoon when trade should have reached its height.

Business is poor everywhere, thought John.

The adobe shack, once the home of a visionary oil prospector, was small for its present use. A poorly lettered sign above the door jutted on either side beyond the width of the shack like a windmill fan. The prospector, favoring alike the distance to the spring and his well, had built the shack halfway between them. So it stood barren, forlorn, against the leaning wall of a low mesa. It was almost forbidding, as if disease lurked menacingly behind its door. From a distance the door appeared closed. Riding closer, John saw that it was. Moreover, it was barred.

"What do you make of it?" asked High-Lo.

"Don't know. Indians not coming, it looks queer. Wonder if he's away?"

They rode up and peered in the windows. The place was deserted yet neat enough inside, with what scant provisions were visible arrayed on counter and shelves. Rugs, draped over a wire, cut off a corner of the one-room shack. Newton's private quarters, no doubt.

"That's a piece of bad luck for you!" said John in disgust.

"Maybe he's not far off," High-Lo suggested.

"See what we can find out from the Indians over at the Springs. They may know something."

They wheeled their horses and rode a mile down the

mesa and around a promontory that hid a green oasis from
view. Several hogans were clustered around cornfields and
in the shade of cottonwoods. A pinto pony, ears up,
watched their coming. A dog barked at them from the edge
of a field. That brought an Indian to the door of the
nearest hogan. He was a young fellow whom John recognized as a returned schoolboy. He waited to be approached.

John rode up to him. "Can you tell me if Newton's likely
to be back to the post today? It seems to be shut up."

"It is," said the boy. "Hosteen Newton's gone away."

"How long is he gone?"

"Yesterday."

"When will he be back?"

"Maybe so after the Indian dance."

"Dance?" repeated John. "We haven't heard of any
dance down at Black Mesa."

"Indians don't tell. Don't want Hosteen Weston to come.
Don't want any white people."

"How is it Newton's going?" John rejoined.

The boy grunted disdainfully.

"They like his whisky—eh?" John went on.

His remark drew keen attention from the boy.

"You come for whisky?"

John tried to avoid a direct answer. "Like some yourself?" he asked.

High-Lo drew up alongside.

Scornfully the Indian continued to look at both question-
er and newcomer.

"No! Pete is no fool. Pete hate the whisky because it
make his father foolish. Where go the sheep, one today and
one tomorrow? Pay for whisky! Hosteen Newton get rich.
Pete's father get poor. Maybe you got money for pay for
whisky."

"We don't want whisky," said John. "We want to stop
Newton selling it."

The Indian fixed a penetrating gaze upon him. "Stop
Hosteen Newton? How you stop him?"

"Make him go away."

"Then come other man."

"What other man?" asked John, reaching to uncover the
intrigue suggested by the boy.

"Pete don't know him. Pete see him two time with
Hosteen Newton."

"Here?"

"No. Far away in canyon."

"Never see him here?"

"No."

"Ever see him alone anywhere?"

"Once far away in canyon."

"Same canyon?"

"Yes."

"When?"

"Last moon. Other dance."

"Was this other man at the dance?"

"No."

"Big man, is he? This way big?" John described girth and an expansive abdomen. "Bowlegged like some of the cowboys. Legs so?" John desdcribed circular lines with his fingers.

"Yes."

"I know the man. We'll send him away too."

"Most Indians want Hosteen Newton to stay. Like Hosteen Newton for sell them whisky. Damn fool Indians!"

"You bet!" broke in High-Lo. Aside to John he said, "Plain what's goin' on here. They've been operatin' right along. Let me nail Hanley if he's around. Can't you see what he's doin' to these poor beggars, an' keepin' under cover all the time? Newton's the tool!"

"When's this Indian dance coming off?" resumed John.

"Maybe four days, five days. Indians come long way."

"I see," John reflected aloud. "They've only begun to gather."

"Can you take us to the canyon where you saw Newton and this man?" he asked.

"You find him, you send him away?"

"We'll chase them both, Pete!"

The boy gave a grunt of satisfaction. "Maybe take gun?"

"No, leave your gun home."

The Indian disappeared into the hogan for a moment, returned with a rope, and strode off for the pony.

"We shore walked into it!" ejaculated High-Lo. "If we can't find 'em before the dance, we'll find Newton, anyway, at the dance. Hanley won't be far away. Makin' tracks for Gallup, I reckon. Newton we can get shore and quick. Hanley we'll follow."

"In either instance, no shooting!"

"Unless someone draws. That makes it different," High-Lo said.

They took their horses to water in a pool below the spring where presently the Indian, Pete, joined them.

"We go long way around mesa," he said, a sweeping movement of his arm directing them to wheel their horses northward. Then he pointed somewhere close to the direction of the post and added, "That way Indians go to dance. I will show you how to hide from them."

A whip cracked. Pinto and rider shot past John and High-Lo, demonstrating the pace they must follow, and though their horses were tired they had to be pushed, for Pete was head of the outfit. He kept close under the promontory wall where they were safest from detection, holding his horse to the lope at which he had started. After a long while he reined in. Then John and High-Lo caught up.

"When dark come we cross valley," he said as they rode alongside. "Moon come soon. We cross valley before moon come. Camp in mouth of canyon. Nobody see you. Water, too. Maybe little feed."

It was gratifying to John that Pete had some thought for the horses. According to what he said, they would have to hurry to reach the crossing point before dark, and then, if possible, push right on without a stop. John studied the prospect. He was mistaken about the uplands opposite. They did not meet this mesa. The queer winding of the promontory they had followed had deceived him from a distance. They led five miles on, to the westward, almost parallel to the other mesa. Ten miles at least separated them. The Indian knew his country and would expedite travel for them. They kept their horses moving fast. After a while shadows began to creep upward and outward; the sun was setting. Gold light and red light merged into amber and violet, then faded to gray. Fragrance of sage and cedar freshened on a breeze. The air grew so cold that the heat of a fast-driven horse became desirable.

When they met the valley trail John insisted that they rest their horses a while. However, on the strength of the Indian's prediction that it took a couple of hours to cross the lonesome expanse of desert, they cut the rest time short.

The moon rose before they reached the mesa, but they escaped its aisle of light in the shadow not yet encroached upon. Before them loomed another wall above which arched the sky with its field of stars.

The shadowy forms of horse and Indian moving ahead beckoned the two white men onward. Suddenly the two were lost to sight. They had gone around an escarpment which John soon realized formed an apron-like turn to the mouth of a canyon. Rounding it, he came onto a bench thick with cedars, and then he saw that there were two levels; below where a narrow ribbon of water glistened was the basin. Pete had dismounted. Manifestly this was to be their camp site.

The Indian gathered wood for a fire while John and High-Lo unpacked and unsaddled the horses. What they needed for comfort was a roaring fire, but for concealment's sake they built only a small one against the windward wall of a cave. Frugal provisions made necessary a light meal. Luckily the urge to sleep was stronger than the urge to eat. When at last John stretched out, his saddle pillowed under his head, a blanket drawn close around him, he sank quickly into the perfect oblivion of sleep.

With morning came reality. He was on a hunt for Newton to deliver a letter. Yesterday at this time he had thought the mission would be over by nightfall. He felt as if his courage were waning and imagined with melancholy satisfaction that he was as uncertain in purpose as Mary.

They dispatched camp tasks quickly and got an early start. John and High-Lo rode at some distance behind the Indian, who went slowly up the canyon, looking for tracks. As they progressed, the canyon floor widened, the yellow walls rose higher, the notched corners grew denser with sage and cedar.

"If we don't find them up here," said High-Lo, "we'll move right along to the dance. Newton'll be there, shore."

John did not feel sure of anything except that he wanted to get the business over as quickly as possible and hurry away. Instinctively he kept studying the sandy trail and the bare patches of ground for tracks. Several times the Indian led down into the deep wash, crossed the thin strip of water with its treacherous quicksand bottom, and up slopes of soft red earth where the horses labored.

They arrived at length at the opening of the canyon, a wide impressive level, where several other canyons intersected with the main one. These great red gates in the walls yawned mysteriously. The soft gray sage flats and the clumps of green-gray cedars on the slopes began to give color and charm to the bare main canyon.

About the center of this oval the Indian ran across a single track, coming from the west. It turned into one of the intersecting canyons. The track was fresh, and the depth of the impression it made in the sand attested to a heavily burdened horse.

This canyon was narrow and deep, high-walled and curving, and it was choked with sections of fallen cliff and patches of oak and cedar groves. A dry stream bed wound tortuously through the canyon; here and there holes in the smooth rock bottom showed the green gleam of water.

John saw several old horse tracks, of different sizes, made at varying times. They had been made by Indian horses. John thought it best to hold their Indian guide with them and to proceed cautiously. The nature of the trail was such that hoofs made no noise. It would be best to surprise Hanley and Newton, and even then he did not anticipate a cordial welcome. They had selected one of the wildest canyons John had ever seen—something quite unexpected, considering its entrance to the main canyon.

They rode for another mile, under beetling walls, through thick green groves, around sharp corners of the canyon wall, along the brink of a deep sandy wash. Once the Indian raised a quick hand implying he had detected something. But he rode on without comment. Soon after that John's keen nose caught a hint of cedar smoke in the dry air of the canyon. Then they rode round a corner of the wall into a small beautiful glade, backed by a precipitous cliff, under a shelf of which showed camp and fire, horses in the shade, and two men suddenly transfixed in an attitude of surprise.

Hanley had been in the act of opening a bottle of liquor. He bristled. He glared. Newton turned as white as a sheet, and edged behind Hanley, toward the horses.

"That'll be about close enough," called Hanley, harshly, when John and his companions reached the center of the small glade. "What'n hell do you want?"

"I want to see Newton, and I've got a little straight talk for you," replied John, bluntly, as his quick gaze took in the evidence of the damning guilt of the hidden camp.

"Wal, he doesn't want to see you, an' I'm not hearin' any kind of your talk," returned Hanley, sullenly.

"You'll both have to," said John calmly.

"Get out of here!" bellowed Hanley, savagely.

John rode ahead of his companions, finding it hard to comply with the rigid rules he had set for himself. This was decidedly not the way to meet a man like Hanley. But Newton, slinking still farther toward the horses, roused only his contempt.

"Hold on, Newton," called Curry, his voice hard and cutting from the restraint he was putting upon himself. And as he halted, and swung his leg around to dismount, he saw Hanley furiously level a gun and yell. John dodged even before he saw the spurt of flame. The heavy bullet hit him high in the shoulder, staggering him so that, as his horse plunged and wheeled, he could not regain his stirrup. The horse leaped into a run, carrying John while he swayed out of the saddle. Then he fell heavily to the ground.

He sat up in time to see the Indian disappear frantically down into the wash. Heavy shots drew John's attention toward the camp. High-Lo's horse was running into the brush, while High-Lo stood out in the open, a smoking gun in his hand. The shooting had ceased. John got to his feet, putting an instinctive hand on the hot wet wound in his shoulder. Then he saw Hanley stagger out from the shelter of the cliff and fall face forward on the sand.

High-Lo strode forward, looked down on Hanley a moment, then turned to run toward John. Manifestly he was overjoyed to see him on his feet.

"John! Lordy, I hope you ain't hurt bad," he exclaimed, and began to tear John's shirt from his shoulder. He ran a finger into the wound. "Not deep. Didn't get the bone. You're lucky. That damn skunk. He let you walk right up to him. . . . John, I told you what Hanley was. . . . Wal, whatever he *was*, he ain't now!"

"Did you kill him?" asked John.

"I shore did. An' I'm sorry I didn't before he plugged you. . . . John, let's go up by the camp an' I'll wash an' tie up this bullet hole, best I can. But you ought to get back to the post pronto an' have it dressed proper."

"Newton beat it, didn't he!"

"Guess he's miles away buryin' himself in dust. The yellow dog!"

"And I'm stuck with that letter," said John. Using his left hand he drew it out to satisfy himself of its presence.

"Blood on it now," remarked High-Lo.

John's thumbprint showed in red.

"I can't deliver it in person, that's sure," John declared. "Newton'll never let me get within talking distance. Say, what became of the Indian?"

A rustle in the brush answered John's question. Pete slipped through, looking about cautiously.

"You say no gun!" he protested.

"Well, I wasn't figuring very good," said John. "I guess you're the hombre with the sense in this outfit, High-Lo. I must be getting softening of the brain."

"You'll have worse if we don't get out of here."

"But the letter!" John persisted. Then after a moment's rumination he said, "Pete can take it. It's the letter, Pete, that will send Newton away from Sage Springs to Taho where he belongs. There's ten dollars in it for you when you get back to your hogan. Call for it at Black Mesa. I'll leave it with Weston. Newton's got to be back in Taho before you get it. Sabe?"

"No gun!" said Pete.

High-Lo laughed. "Gun? Didn't you see Newton bolt like a scared calf? Run him down till he's tired. Then he'll stand still and moo at you. Take Hanley's gun. See it there? An' throw it away if you find you don't need it."

"Pete go now. Maybe quick catch him."

He picked up the gun, kicked the soles of Hanley's boots with a grunt of satisfaction, then mounted and rode away.

It took only a cursory study of the camp to show why the men had been struck with fear. The seat from which Newton had sprung in such haste was a partly opened case of liquor. Hanley had laid out an array of bottles. It began to dawn on John that they had diluted and rebottled the stuff, thus cheating the Indians two ways.

"All ready for the dance," said John.

High-Lo relieved himself of a few extravagant expletives as he set about to wash John's wound.

The shoulder burned with a savage heat, and John winced under the treatment. As soon as that duty was done, High-Lo ripped open the case of liquor and smashed the bottles.

"I'm sure cured of the stuff if I can do this," he said with a sheepish grin. "No Indians goin' to get the d.t.'s on this. Let the layout explain Mr. Hanley's finish if anyone gets too curious. Bet the Indians won't go talkin' none."

John's mind was wandering from the scene. "She'll never know about this," he was thinking. "Pete'll get him. He'll go back. It's all over. Now for Black Mesa. Then Mexico."

They were back at Black Mesa again with a story of a scuffle with Newton and assurance for Weston that the Sage Springs trade would not longer corrupt his. They made light of the shooting incident, mentioning a pal of Newton's but giving no name.

Thirty-six hours of pain and mental stress conspired to make John hopelessly wretched. He was hungry, yet when he touched food it nauseated him. His wound throbbed, yet he pretended it bothered him very little. Everyone wanted to do something for him. He was ashamed that he resented their interest. His irritation was greater than his will to resist it. His blood boiled without relief.

High-Lo, he noticed, would not let him out of his sight. With an effort to appear as well as he claimed to be, John sat in the living room with a book open before him. Pete, Newton, Mary were living and moving on the black spotted page.... Newton had the letter.... Mary was bringing him back.... A couple of days and he'd be there. Suppose she already had regretted sending for him? He scoffed at the idea and fell to thinking about Mexico. Desert, cactus, heat. That's all Mexico meant while his wound throbbed so. "God!" he ejaculated to himself trying to conquer a strange dizziness.

He heard Mrs. Weston. "Magdaline left a letter for you, John. Better give it to you before I forget."

The letter was near at hand in the table drawer. "There!" she said, tossing it on his book. "Magdaline always worshiped you, John. Poor child! Nobody can do anything with her. I tried my best. The way she went smack back to being Indian was a caution. But that didn't last. Now she wants the cities again. She'll never be satisfied."

Magdaline! He thought of the felicitousness of the name. Then contrary to an impulse not to bother with the letter at the moment, he slashed it open. Her writing to him irritated him. Then he remembered that he had asked her for her address. This was more than an address; it was a lengthy letter. He scanned it. She reminded him of their talk, particularly of his comparison of life to a canyon, saying she could feel her way to the light if only someone strong like John could help her. He was so wise and brave. She was so foolish and cowardly. She had faith, she confessed, in nothing but him. Would he who believed in God pray for her who believed only in him? Maybe then the power she could not comprehend would help her.

She gave no address.

"Poor girl! Poor Magdaline!" he said to himself. "She thinks I'm wise and brave. I was really preaching to myself when I talked to her. She gave no address! What is she going to do? She's an exile, too. Both of us are exiles. Wonder where she is? Wonder why she didn't leave her address. Who'll take care of her? God! The men who will lay in wait! Nothing but an Indian, that's what they'll think. Maggots! She needs affection. She needs protection. I'm the only one she believes in. Why can't I help her? Why am I looking around for something to do to distract me when the job's right here—here riding the same saddle. She's an exile, too. I could take her away. Marry her, of course. Who cares in Mexico? Squaw man? What of it? Intelligent, educated woman. Nothing compared to Mary Newton's sacrifice. So she was going right on out leaving no address, was she?"

His head throbbed. His blood beat through fevered veins. He got up and went out and High-Lo followed him.

"You look like the devil. Why don't you go to bed?" High-Lo protested.

"I will presently. Got to get some sleep. We're off tomorrow."

"You're off all right now—in the head!"

"I've got to get to Flaggerston and find Magdaline."

John felt High-Lo's arm gently embracing his left shoulder.

"You're right plucky, John. But a little fever's got you an' you ought to give in to it. You forget we're goin' to Mexico, old man. A feller'd think you had gurgled some of that stuff we found yesterday."

Feeling High-Lo turning him, John resisted forcefully.

"Hold on a bit. Let me tell you what's on my mind. Then I'll go to bed. . . . When we came through here a few days ago Magdaline told me she was in trouble. A baby. See? She's desperate. It would break your heart to hear her. I might have done more to help her when she was here last summer if I wasn't so set on my own affairs. I was the one person she poured her heart out to. I saw her walking right straight for trouble and never stopped her. She didn't understand herself. But I understood her and I should have been more kind. I feel sort of to blame. I was short, I remember. She said she loved me. Told me straight. She writes that she still loves me. I'm going to look her up in Flaggerston and marry her. There will be three of us going to Mexico."

High-Lo's arm fell away. "I've had crazy ideas in my time," he said, "but none like that. You're more than sittin' in my place, I'll say! You're not goin' to marry Magdaline! You're plumb crazy!"

Dizziness returned to John. "Oh, yes, I am," he said in a voice more weak than calm.

He felt his way unsteadily back into the living room. Mrs. Weston looked up as he entered. "Bed for mine," he said, summoning a little cheeriness to his voice. "Good night, folks."

Hearing High-Lo's footsteps behind him he quickened his pace down the hall. Once in his room he quickly shut the door and turned the key to lock it. The handle was shaken ferociously and there followed a bang on the door.

"Let me in," called High-Lo. "I want to dress that wound."

"It was dressed an hour ago," John returned.

"Three hours ago! It needs another. Let me in."

John sank down on a chair wearily. "No use to bang, High-Lo. I want to be left alone. Go to bed yourself. See you in the morning."

The more High-Lo swore, coaxed, pleaded, the more John's determination against letting him in grew. High-Lo was carrying his role of guardian too far. After all, he was only a kid.

By the time John had struggled out of his clothes, High-Lo's arguments and patience were exhausted. His good night was a rain of blows on the door followed by the sound of retreating footsteps. Satisfied that the boy had given up, John got into bed.

He awakened before dawn with the memory of interrupted sleep, of the ride of the day before, of High-Lo's dismay last night. What was it about? Events returned in order. Magdaline! Strange he had forgotten! Why, he had decided to marry her! At first he was alarmed at the thought. Three of them going to Mexico—two of them exiled! Three not going if High-Lo knew it! Well, he must not know. The only way to outwit him was to go to Flaggerston without him.

John was out of bed in a flash. Pain drummed in his shoulder. He dressed stealthily, using his one free hand. Once he was dressed, he brought up a chair to the high window to enable him to climb out. He struck his wound in his descent, which brought an involuntary cry to his lips. Dogs barked. Fortunately for him, they had barked once before during the night and even more violently.

Supported by his knees and one arm he crawled below the windows to the front of the house. There he straightened and strode swiftly away. The dogs came to him, tails wagging. They followed him to the corral where he saddled one of Mr. Weston's horses, downing the voice that reminded him that such a taken-for-granted loan came close to horse-stealing. His own horse was worn. He could not make the trip. John planned to ride hard.

The morning was cold. John's mount answered promptly to the spur. He seemed to feel the desperation that possessed his rider. They were only a few miles from the pass when the sun came up, but from there on the journey was to be retarded by many an upward climb. During the ride to the pass John suffered no indecision of purpose. The flight was the thing. He had pledged himself to a cause and he would take what came. He could not turn back now!

He measured the trip in his mind. He would camp beyond Castle Mesa that night, many miles beyond Taho the next night, and reach Flaggerston by noon the next day. His horse's hoofs beat, his wound beat, his heart beat. His mind no longer planned; it was blank to thought. He was conscious only of sounds and feelings and the passing scene: the beat, beat, beat—of hoofs, wound, heart—the miles, miles, miles—mountains, valleys, walls.

18

THE day after Katharine and Alice had arrived, Mary awoke with a feeling that she must fly from them. Alone with Katharine the night before she had been unable to confide in her friend the recent harrowing events, and her failure she accepted as a judgment against herself which Katharine would surely comprehend. The letter was on its way to Wilbur. Revocation now was impossible. If she tried to look fearlessly at the future she was conscious only of pretense, conscious that she was false to the man she loved, to the man she had married and to herself. John's denunciation had left its deadly mark. She told herself that she must forget him, but the frequency with which she repeated the injunction was proof to her honest self that she could not. She did love him. Yet Wilbur was coming—perhaps today. "No, no!" she cried fiercely, cringing before the impending event.

When she called Joy to dress, the child, with eyes of love, saw at once that she was not herself. "Mudder sick! Poor Mudder!" she said. Then she whispered innocently, "Mudder not so glad she was Aunt Katharine come?"

It was obvious that Joy was glad Aunt Katharine had come. Anyone who could produce so fair a vision as Alice was to Joy a generous friend, and that fate was most beneficent which had brought both gift and giver as companions to her home.

That day was destined to be full for Joy; when Mary went to work she was left in care of Alice and Katharine. Mary's day, on the contrary, was long and wearisome. Time and again her conscience smote her because she should have warned the girls that Wilbur might appear at

any time, and not have led them to believe that they were
to continue with her. She hurried home straightway at the
close of her working hours.

From a distance Mary descried a figure on the porch
step, and thinking it was Katharine she hurried along. A
nearer view disclosed an Indian girl as alert and motionless
as a statue. She rose as Mary turned in at the gate.

Mary was impressed with the sadness of the girl's face.
"Young enough to be a schoolgirl," she said to herself. She
smiled and nodded to her visitor.

"Are you Mrs. Newton who takes care of my sister
Joy?" the girl asked.

"I am Mrs. Newton," replied Mary. "I understood Joy
had a sister. You're from Sage Springs, are you?"

"Yes."

"You've come to see Joy—not to take her from me, I
hope."

The girl gave a quaint gesture of denial with swift
eloquent fingers. "I shall not take her home. I came to
thank you for your kindness to her. I learned about it in the
village. The Indians think you are very wonderful. At Sage
Springs we would have known late if she had died, without
knowing even that she was sick, they tell me. I was much
surprised to find she was not at the school."

"Did you knock? Is there no one in?" asked Mary.

"No one answered when I knocked."

"Won't you come in now? Joy must be away on a walk
with friends who are visiting me. You look tired. If you
arrived today, I don't wonder. That's a long trip. Perhaps
you'll have some tea with me."

"Thank you," said the girl.

She followed Mary into the house.

"You'll be comfortable there," said Mary, designating
Wilbur's armchair.

The girl gave Mary a scarcely perceptible smile as she
took the proffered place.

"And what is your name?" asked Mary.

"Magdaline," came the reply.

"That's a beautiful name," said Mary and added to
herself that there was something infinitely sad about it, like
her face.

"You have been to school," Mary went on to the girl. "I
know because you speak so well."

"In Taho and in Riverside."

"And you came back to the desert to stay?"

"I was sent back. Now I am leaving for good. I go to Flaggerston on the mail stage tonight. That is why I came to see Joy. I may never see her again."

There was no regret nor sorrow manifest in her colorless voice.

"You are going far?" inquired Mary.

"Yes. Exactly where I do not know. California some-place maybe, after—after a while."

"But you can always write to Joy. If your parents consent I will adopt her legally. That is—I want to." Mary thought suddenly of Wilbur to whom children were a nuisance, and involuntarily her eyes strayed to his picture. When she looked at Magdaline again she saw that the girl had followed the direction of her glance and was contemplating the picture, too. Suddenly it seemed that the girl was staring like some wild creature of the woods startled in flight by the sound of a shot. The girl rose and swiftly sped to the mantel. Her action amazed Mary.

She snatched the picture and extended it in a shaking hand.

"Who is this?" she demanded hoarsely.

"Mr. Newton," Mary replied more alarmed than before.

Magdaline accepted the reply with a defiant toss of her head and a sound, half laugh and half cry. "What is he to you?"

Mary felt as if she had been thrown into a whirling eddy where on each turn Wilbur's face flashed by her. "My husband," she said through trembling lips.

"Your husband?" the girl cried hysterically. "Not your brother? . . . Mr. Newton, Mrs. Newton. . . . Your husband you say! Then he lied to me. He said he was not married. No one ever told me anywhere that he was married. Names can be the same when people are not related. I did not think of such a thing when they told me about Joy and you. You were so good, they said. How can he be your husband when you are so good?"

Shaken by the force of her emotion she sank against the mantel for support.

Mary felt her inward self retreating from the presence of this girl and from the Wilbur whom she knew. Even her voice seemed far away as she said, "What are you talking about? What do you mean?"

The girl closed her eyes as if to shut the sight of Mary from her. "Nothing. You must forgive me," she said speaking low.

"That is no answer!" cried Mary. "Tell me the truth. I demand it."

Slowly the girl looked up. Summoning her voice to a whisper, she asked, "You want to know?"

"Yes! I want to know!" Mary tried to rise and found she could not, she was trembling so violently.

"I have lived with him."

"Lived with him?" echoed Mary.

"At Sage Springs where he has a trading post," the girl went on. "I thought maybe some day he would marry me. I was all alone. My people did not want me. White people did not understand me. I was unhappy. I could not live like an Indian. He came to me with soft comforting words. He whispered love to me. He seemed so big and strong. He said Indians were better than white people. He wanted to be friends with the Indians, that was why he left all white people and came to the post. I lived with him. Even my family did not care that I lived with him. Then I found why, and why he would be friends to the Indians. He sold them cheap whisky for which they paid him gladly too much. I hated him then, and his friend Hanley of whom he talked. Together they smuggled in the whisky. White devils both of them! Just the same I asked Wilbur Newton to marry me. I found I *had* to get married. He refused, sent me away, gave me fifty dollars for a doctor. Said no decent white man married an Indian girl. I wanted to kill him then. Maybe it is better to tell you than to kill him. I do not care if he loves you. I am through with him. He is a rattlesnake—poisonous—poisoning my people. Maybe your hate will kill him."

A terrible moan escaped Mary. It had been rising to stifle her, gathering in force with each incrimination of Wilbur poured forth by the Indian girl.

Then she felt hands upon her. The Indian girl was kneeling by her side. Involuntarily she shrank from her touch.

"Mrs. Newton, forgive me," the girl pleaded. "I did not know he was married. I did not know you were waiting for him here. Why should you care for him so? He leaves you here and makes love to another woman, an Indian. There is, then, something worse than being an Indian who is an outcast among her people. It is any woman an outcast from the love of her husband. Hear me when I say that my heart breaks for you. I thought it could break no more."

Mary bent an intent gaze on the tragic upturned face, her mind for the moment clear of agony, recording what was taking place without effort.

"Me for money, you for lust! From the tricky Northerner to the hungry-hearted Indian girl!" she cried aloud. An ugly passion was born in her in that moment. Like the girl who knelt by her side, she wanted to kill Wilbur Newton. Degraded himself, he had dragged her down with him. Her passion mounted like a flame until her very body seemed to burn and sway under its feverish thrall.

An anguished cry from the Indian girl came to her dully, "Mrs. Newton, take your revenge on me if you will, only do not look like that—like someone who has seen death! I could kill myself for sorrow!"

Then Mary's faculty of reasoning returned, replacing a strange suspension of thought. She knew she was not alone in her despair, that she shared her experience and pain with this girl of an alien race. Her arm slipped protectingly around Magdaline's shoulders. The taut body relaxed into the voluminous protecting folds of native dress and, like a child, Magdaline's head sought Mary's lap. They sat in silence until they heard a car driven under full power tearing restlessly down the avenue. It startled Mary to terrifying recollection. That might be Wilbur. Any car coming into town might bring Wilbur. She had sent for him. He was coming. It was too awful to contemplate. She tried to rise from her chair.

She grasped Magdaline, compelling the girl's attention. "You must go on to Flaggerston. Stay until I come; it won't be long. You can't go through your trouble alone. I will help you. We must face our trouble together."

So she persuaded the girl to rise, and herself stood and waited for strength to return to her unsteady limbs. Then gently she urged Magdaline to the door. Neither of them said a word. Black eyes with a haunted look was all that Mary could see in the dark, oval face that for a moment was turned full toward her. The Indian girl was quickly on her way, gliding with noiseless tread down the path to the gate.

Mary went to the kitchen. Why, she did not know. She went to the cupboard, took out a pan, looked at it, thrust it

back, shut the cupboard door. Consciousness of her purposeless act drove a dry sob to her lips. She talked to
herself in an excited whisper. "What am I doing? What can
I do? How can I change it? . . . There's nothing to do. I'm
his wife. I sent for him. I wrote that I wanted him! Oh,
dear God, what made me write that I wanted him?" The
sound of the words amplified. "Five days—six days—it's
too late! He has the letter. And I sent John away. I sent
John away. And he's never coming back again!"

An exclamation of dismay cut Mary's poignant cry.
Alice, unseen, had mounted the back steps with Joy and
was standing suddenly transfixed a few feet from the
door.

Mary heard her, saw her. Alice was approaching now,
words trembling from her lips as she came.

"What's happened, Mary? What is it? I thought you had
company, that you were talking to someone. You look
ghastly."

"Everything's happened! Everything! And nothing can be
done," moaned Mary, feeling even more poignantly than
before the hopelessness of her lot.

Alice moved away toward the door. "I'll get Katharine,"
she said. "She stopped in to visit a minute with Mrs.
MacDonald. She'll come right away.

"No, you go, dear," Alice added, her eyes upon Joy who
was edging toward Mary. "Go to Mrs. MacDonald's and
tell Aunt Katharine Mother needs her at once."

"Joy won't go! Somebody hurt Mudder!" declared the
child defiantly.

But the sight of Mary shrinking from her hysterical
demand for a kiss was so terrifying that she fled without
further appeal.

An hour later Katharine was packing a valise. While she
worked she spent part of the time in strange meditation,
and the rest meeting Alice's inquiries. She was basking in
the vindication of self for her long-established dislike of
Wilbur when Alice interrupted by asking how long she
would be gone.

"I can't tell," Katharine replied. "My idea is to get Mary
away so if Wilbur does come she'll be gone. It would kill
her to see him now. She's a sick girl. She's been under a
fearful strain for months. Her idea to send Billy Horton to

find John is absurd to me, but I'm pretending to believe in it so I can get her away."

"And suppose you ran into Wilbur at Castle Mesa," Alice went on. "That could happen. You don't know where he is, or what has happened."

"Darling, give your sister credit for having a thought for emergencies. I've fixed it up with Billy. We'll have a little engine trouble at the ridge. He'll walk down, ostensibly for help, really to see if Newton's at the post. If he is, Billy will find all the beds at Shelley's occupied and we'll go around by way of the far road and camp. Billy's taking a camp outfit along. If the coast is clear we'll sleep at Shelley's. We'll be arriving late and decamping early."

"And if that awful man descends on me?" asked Alice with a shudder.

"You know nothing. Take Joy and go at once to Mrs. MacDonald. He'll not follow you there. And in such event board with Mrs. MacDonald until I return."

Katharine felt Alice's hand on her shoulder arrestingly and looked up.

"You're a very dear, Katharine, always doing for others and never for yourself," Alice said sadly.

"And what do you think we're put in the world for?" asked Katharine with a laugh.

"Some of us to fight t.b. and disappointments," Alice returned.

"Disappointments?" echoed Katharine.

"Oh, not in things concerning myself, but concerning others, things for others that would really be best for them."

"The narrow, provincial little self again, objecting to poor Mary!" thought Katharine. "Joy will take all your attention while we're gone," she said gently. "Perhaps you'll forget whatever it is that disturbs you so."

Presently Billy arrived driving an automobile borrowed from Mr. MacDonald. Joy came in to say that Billy and Mother were ready to start as soon as Aunt Katharine joined them. The child was happy again. With the nature of proceedings very vague in her mind, she was averse to Mary's leave-taking. However, to be left with Alice had for Joy almost as much virtue as being at peace with Mother.

Mary had a deathly pallor. Her eyes were frightened, betraying the condition of her mind. Having said good-by to Joy and Alice, she shrank back within the shadow of the automobile, as if to hide her shame from prying eyes. Katharine caught one of Mary's listless hands in hers. It was icy cold. She retained it, and Mary did not protest.

"Wherever man puts his foot, though it be an Eden, tragedy stalks," mused Katharine to herself. How different this journey over the illimitable stretches of the desert! She dreaded it. The trail became a place of danger, a place where almost anywhere they might encounter Wilbur. Mesas were obstacles that prolonged distance except for the crow's flight; beetling walls suggested impending catastrophe, and jagged peaks the pain of spirit, and the light breeze in the sage, so sad and melancholy, seemed like the sighing of an imprisoned spirit weary of its eternal strivings. She kept her eye on the time. With satisfaction she watched the sun lower. Billy put the car to a strenuous test as he raced over uneven roads and high centers, and on through brush wherever a stretch of mud, left by fitful showers, forced a detour. Mary sat in deep silence, which Katharine did not disturb.

By sunset they had covered considerable mileage. Night would be kind, concealing them under its dark mantle. Still, they were on the highroad. There was to be a moon. Katharine had almost forgotten about the moon. It came up like a slowly opening eye discovering their flight.

Mary sank farther into her corner. Later she peered cautiously out to see how far they had progressed. Suddenly her body stiffened, swaying against Katharine, and her hand grasped for a hold on Katharine's skirt.

"Look! A rider!" she cried. "He came around that butte. He's crossed the road. See him there in the sage?"

Katharine followed the direction of Mary's strained gaze. Then she, too, saw. Mary's hand, unmerciful in its strength, was clutching flesh. Mary spoke again before Katharine could answer.

"That's not an Indian! Did you see him cut through that clearing? He rides a big horse. You don't suppose he's—" She left the inference to Katharine .

"Wilbur? Yes. It might be," Katharine replied promptly. To Billy she said, "Drive as fast as you can through here!"

"And stop for no one," Mary added.

But the lone rider had swerved far from the trail. He moved out and away through the brush, widening the distance between them at each lope of his horse. Mary relaxed her hold on Katharine, and at last, with an accompanying sigh, her hand slipped free.

Katharine said, "That man seems as anxious to avoid us as we are to avoid him."

19

JOHN stepped out of the Flaggerston post office a disappointed man. No one knew of an Indian girl calling recently for mail; no one had seen or heard of a person of her description. He was sick and dizzy. Two days' ride at a killing pace for both horse and rider left him the worse for wear. He needed food, a doctor, sleep. But no sleep would he take till he had found Magdaline. He calculated that Flaggerston was such a small place one on the alert was bound to see every able-bodied inhabitant and identify any strangers before a day's end. There was no reason to despair.

Food was his first consideration now that he was through at the post office, so he went to a restaurant on Main Street, and choosing a seat by the window sat down to enjoy a substantial meal. Opposite him was a man with a newspaper, in which, as a page was being turned, John's eye caught a headline: COWBOY MARRIES INDIAN GIRL. "Everybody's doing it," thought John grimly.

Ravenously he ate. Meanwhile his gaze swept the street for a glimpse of a Navaho girl. He saw only white people: cowboys, young girls, women with market bags. His meal over, John left the restaurant for the Main Street Hotel where from a comfortable chair he could continue his surveillance through the plate-glass front of the lobby. It would be a while before a doctor had the pleasure of ordering him to bed. He was less dizzy now that he had eaten, but desire to sleep was more urgent. He wanted Magdaline. He kept telling himself that he wanted her, in order to counteract the lethargy that was stealing over him, and the heaviness of his eyelids. He registered in his mind everyone who passed. Pretty girl. Skinny woman. Sleepy-looking Mexican. Boys scheming mischief. . . . The train. Always someone going away. Magdaline going away. Not on the train, however. To Mexico. . . . More boys—almost ran that woman down. . . . A cowboy. . . . Damned familiar cowboy!

"Damned familiar cowboy," John repeated aloud. He leaped to his feet and strode into the street, conscious of following eyes. "High-Lo, the beggar!" he muttered.

High-Lo it was! Some girls turned to look slyly after him. No wonder they turned! Handsome beggar!

"Followed me!" said John emphatically to himself.

He caught up with him quickly and hailed him with a whack on his shoulder. High-Lo swung around abruptly. His surprise vanished in a smile.

"What are you doing here?" John asked angrily.

"Lookin' for you. An' darn well you know it."

"Had to follow me!"

"Had to stop you from marryin' Magdaline."

"You can't."

"Yes I can. Fact is, I *have*."

"You're crazy."

"Evidently you haven't seen the morning papers," returned High-Lo complacently.

"What are you driving at?" demanded John.

"I married Magdaline myself, yesterday."

John stared at High-Lo, confounded.

"Congratulate me, you duffer."

"You married Magdaline yesterday?" said John when at last he spoke. "How could you—yesterday?"

"With the help of a parson. . . . You see, you didn't leave me at Black Mesa. I left you there. Pulled out at two in the morning. Framed it with Weston who loaned me his car. I talked straight from the shoulder to Weston. He knows everything now. But I didn't tell Weston I'd marry Magdaline. Said I'd send her away. I meant it then. Then I knew you'd follow quick an' maybe find her. You'd be all the more determined. Nothin' to do but for me to marry her. It was a pretty good idee at that! It come to me on the desert."

"But, you locoed fool, you don't—" John stopped.

"Love her, I suppose you were goin' to say. No more did you. At that I guess I did care more. Didn't she help save my life? Even if she was follerin' you when she did it, that don't change things none. An' didn't I go make her a quirt that you never gave her? Never made nothin' for a girl before that. Now I'm goin' to make her a bum husband. She's got the worst of the bargain."

Something like a sob rose in John's throat. "Laying down your life for me, eh, High-Lo? My madness drove you to this extremity? Man! Why did you do it?"

"Could I let you do it? Could I take the least bit of a chance?" There was a beautiful light in High-Lo's eyes. His nostrils quivered as he spoke. "Couldn't you see folks would say the kid was yours? What if we went to Mexico? It would leak out someway, an' your goin' would look the worse. With me, they'd laugh, sort of pokin' fun. They'd expect it of me. They'd put it down to just plain deviltry. But you? You're different. An' you were forgettin' the other girl. I'd die 'fore I'd have her makin' you out a skunk. She never would smile again then."

"It's for life," John said dully. "You're not the kind to quit her because she's Indian and it'd be easy."

"No more'n you would. You weren't thinkin' these things for yourself. Why are you thinkin' them for me? Look here! I'm a pretty lucky fellow far as the wife goes. Get on to me with an educated wife! No educated white woman with brains like Magdaline would look at me twice. Think of the good to my kids with an educated mother. What if she gives them a dark complexion? I can stand that. What I come from for stock don't offer 'em much in other ways. The best'll come from her. 'Course, there's Newton's kid. . . . I don't like that much. Hope it's a boy who can some day knock his father's block off!"

John conprehended slowly. "Newton's kid!" he gasped.

"That's right. You didn't know?" said High-Lo. "Yes. Magdaline gave me the straight of it. An' say—she run across Mrs. Newton in Taho an' spilled it to her. She didn't know there was a Mrs. Newton, pore kid! Like to drove her crazy. John, there's justice operatin' somewheres, but everythin' is pilin' up on that pore little woman you jilted."

High-Lo's words splintered John's thoughts like glass. "My God!" he cried. "Where's Newton now? Where's she?"

"We're goin' to find out, buddy," said High-Lo. "We'll ride back hotfoot, after you get some rest."

John, trying to laugh, made a strange choking sound.

"Rest?" he struggled to say. "How can I rest now? For God's sake take me to her!"

He felt suddenly deathly sick. The street whirled around beneath him. He reeled against High-Lo. Then everything went black. He was plunging downward into this darkness, and High-Lo, far away, was saying, "Get me a car. This man's sick. Yes. To the hospital."

Opening his eyes upon the white walls of an all-white room and upon High-Lo talking to a woman in white, John remembered the boy's last words. He was in bed. His clothes were off and replaced by a nightshirt. On his shoulder which still throbbed was a neat new bandage. He strained to hear the lowered conversation in which he caught his own name.

"I'll ask the doctor." That was the nurse.

"I'm sure you can't keep him more than a couple of days." That was High-Lo. He continued. "Be worse for him to stay. He's got to settle up some affairs that are worryin' him, an' he'd go loco waitin'. He's strong! Long as there's no poison in the shoulder, a little rest'll fix him. He's been killin' himself with a long ride and short food an' lots of worry."

Just then High-Lo saw that John had come to. He saluted him with a comic gesture.

"Now we've got you put," he said. "Taken your clothes away. Don't worry, cowboy. I'll get you out soon. Got to have some sense about yourself. Golly, I feel like a wife-deserter! S'pose I bring Magdaline around for a minute."

"It might be awkward," said John weakly. "She's told me things. Guess you told her why you were marrying her, too. She knows you stopped me, doesn't she?"

"She knows more'n that. She knows about you and Mrs. Newton. Say! She worships Mrs. Newton more than ever since I told her. An' she wants everything to come right for you, John. Let me bring her."

John capitulated. Tumbling gray patterns in the kaleido-scope of events were shifting about to give place to a brighter design.

An hour later Magdaline came. There was a look of peace about her, in her quiet smile, in the softening lines of her face.

"High-Lo says soon we go to Taho with you," she said in a calm, quiet voice. John remembered her then as he had seen her when she was administering to High-Lo that memorable day at the pass. She would mother High-Lo. She would live for him from now on.

Magdaline seemed to divine his thoughts. She nodded her head as she observed his ruminating, as if to say, "Yes, it is so."

Presently she spoke. "By accident I have found my way out into the place where light comes through the canyon, and I see that maybe not so far down there is a way into that light. I believed in your wisdom, John Curry. Now I will do my best to make High-Lo happy, seldom sorry. He has been good and brave like you."

20

HIGH-LO won the doctor's confidence, and John was dismissed from the hospital in two days.

Accompanied by Magdaline, they journeyed to Taho, where they found Mary had fled. MacDonald informed them that Billy Horton had borrowed his car to take Mrs. Newton and her friend to Black Mesa. So far as he knew, Newton had not been seen in Taho. John was satisfied that they must go to Black Mesa at once. Late evening of that same day they reached Castle Mesa, where they spent the night, and next morning they arrived at the post.

Weston rushed out to meet them. On High-Lo's presentation of his wife, he was aghast, but soon collecting himself muttered, "Thank God!" and pumped John's hand vigorously.

"Mrs. Newton here?" asked John.

"Yes, and Miss Winfield," said Weston. "That Horton fellow brought them. He's gone back."

Mr. and Mrs. Weston were troubled. Beany, who had returned, seemed unhappily out of place. An Indian girl slipped through the living room with a tray in her hands, and a minute later John recognized Katharine's voice down the hall, "Yes, thank you, Mrs. Newton is feeling better."

John looked around helplessly, praying for someone to speak.

Weston relieved the strain. "She collapsed after I told her you'd seen Newton and chances were he had her message. And when she found that you had gone—you understand I couldn't tell her why—she just went to pieces. Miss Katharine's been nursin' her. She'll have to break it kind of slow

228

that you've come back. Things are pretty near bein' consid'able mussed up."

"No one's seen Newton?" asked John.

"Ain't showed up here. Beany rode over to Sage Springs. No sign of him there neither. Believe me, we didn't want him. Just wanted to get a line on him. Let him show up! He'll get a closed door here."

Katharine joined them at lunch. She took John's presence for granted. Magdaline and High-Lo she received happily. The gloom broke a little with Katharine there driving them to talk and think of commonplace things.

After lunch High-Lo and Magdaline went to the hogan on the hill which the boys had shared last year as a dressing room, and which Mrs. Weston turned over to them, for Magdaline needed rest, and High-Lo wanted to make sure she would be comfortable. Mrs. Weston took up some sewing, Mr. Weston and Beany went over some accounts, and John had an opportunity to talk to Katharine. It was not long before High-Lo joined them. They agreed then that Katharine should tell Mary that John had come. Meanwhile Katharine entertained them with stories about Joy and about Mary's strenuous winter experience.

Suddenly the sound of a shot split the air. Then followed an ear-piercing shriek.

John and High-Lo stared at each other.

"What was that?" they all asked simultaneously.

Instantly Weston, his wife, and Beany were on their feet. Then John tore out of the room with High-Lo close behind.

At the kitchen door stood the Indian maid waving arms frantically toward the hogan. "Up there!" she cried.

"Magdaline!" groaned High-Lo.

A riderless horse wheeled away as they approached. John remembered in a flash that very horse wheeling from him once before. Wilbur Newton had ridden him then. He heard the thud of other hoofs bearing down his way, but his eyes were on the hogan door. As he made it, he felt High-Lo at his heels.

John stared in horror. High-Lo's cry shook him as deeply as the thing he saw. On the floor, arms spread wide, face ghastly and drawn, lay Wilbur Newton dead. And near by on the bed, her feet still close to the dead man's, her hand still grasping the revolver, was Magdaline, swaying in dry-eyed agony. She seemed slow to comprehend that they had come. When they entered, she sprang to her defense with the fierceness of an animal at bay.

"I killed him!" she screamed. "He would not let me go! I killed him."

Voices sounded outside. A figure glided into the room and knelt swiftly at Newton's side, only to back away dismayed. It was Pete, the Navaho guide, come strangely from a tragic past into a tragic present.

Magdaline shrank from High-Lo, who leaped over the body to reach her.

"He would not let me go!" she reiterated wildly. "He held me tight!"

Then High-Lo was beside her drawing her head down to his shoulder. "High-Lo, I did not mean to kill him," she sobbed.

"Sure, you didn't," said High-Lo. "Everybody knows you didn't. Nobody's goin' to hurt you. Just tell us what happened."

Now the others had come. They stood stricken to silence. Magdaline's sobs seemed terrible in that stillness.

"Tell me what happened," High-Lo repeated gently.

The girl looked up, at the same time pushing her disheveled hair from her eyes, and with her hand clutching High-Lo's arm, her eyes intent on his, she spoke dully with fearful haste.

"I was on the bed. I heard somebody. Then Wilbur came crouching into the room. He was looking back, always back. I sat up. Your belt and gun you left there on the floor. I picked it up quick to put beside me so he could not see it. He heard me. He turned frightened. Then he cried my name, glad-like. He came very close. Talked very fast. Said an Indian had been following him everywhere for days. He said he was starving—said he was afraid—said I must hide him from the Indian. I did not know what to think. He has lied to me before. I hate him. I looked in his eyes. Somehow he made me look in his eyes. I saw there something terrible—as though he wanted to take possession of me again. I wanted you then, High-Lo. I was so afraid. I got up to go. He came so close. He took my hands. He said he loved me—he had come to marry me. I was so frightened. I tried to scream and I could not scream. I tried to pull away. His arms came around me tight and his face so close, and he pushed me back on the bed. Your gun was there. It came into my hand, High-Lo. I did not know it. It was there so quick without thinking. When I felt it, I knew I was safe. 'I can get to High-Lo,' I said to myself. I kept saying, 'I can get to High-Lo,' and it made me strong so I could push him up. But he stood in front of me again, when I got up, with his eyes making me look at him and his arms clutching. And I kept saying, 'I can get to High-Lo,' and I cried it out to him, and the gun was there between us, tight against me, tight against him, and my finger pressed when I said, 'I can get to High-Lo.' There was the sound then, and he fell add I saw the smoke and the blood and smelled cloth burning. That's what happened, High-Lo."

Her hands went fluttering to her neck as if something were choking her.

Pete spoke up. "I follow Hosteen Newton. One day go Sage Springs. Hosteen Newton in post. Door locked. Hosteen Newton go when Pete sleep. Pete follow Hosteen Newton to Black Mesa. Hosteen Newton dead."

He brought a stained crumpled letter from his blouse and handed it to John. John shuddered. He was receiving a bloody weapon; for verily, the letter had been both Hanley's and Newton's undoing.

Magdaline was wearing out her terror in sobs which she smothered on High-Lo's shoulder. Mr. Weston and Beany covered Newton's body with Indian rugs. Then John caught a suggestion from Weston to send out Magdaline and High-Lo. He heard Katharine and Mrs. Weston leave. He was so stunned by the recent shocking event and the extenuating circumstances that there seemed no time beyond the stupefying present. Silently he communicated Weston's hint to High-Lo. High-Lo swept Magdaline into his arms and strode from the hogan. Then Weston advised John to go.

"Leave this to us," he said. "We'll box him. Coroner will have to have a look in, an' the law go its course. But don't be worryin' none."

John wanted to go. There was terrible revulsion in the thought of laying even a finger on the carcass of the coward whose fear had driven him to his doom.

Mary's voice, plying frantic questions, came to him as he approached the house. Slim in a flowing dark wrap, her black hair enveloping her face like a cloud, she was begging that someone tell her why everyone was running around like mad. When she saw John, she stood like one transfixed. He looked at her helplessly and murmured, "Mary!"

That seemed to release her. She was a breathing demanding creature again. She rushed toward him authoritatively. "You tell me, John. They won't."

Conscious that she intuitively knew, and that uncertainty and evasions would be worse than the truth, he said, "Your husband is dead, Mary. Don't ask for particulars now. There's time enough to know them."

"Someone shot him. I know. But you didn't do it," she said with a strange calm.

"No. Not I," John returned firmly.

She smiled the most tragic smile he had ever seen.

"I want to cry," she said, "and I can't."

Then she turned from him still smiling, and walked past the others, ostensibly serene, as quietly and calmly as a nun.

Not a word passed between the group in the room until a door closed down the hall. Then Katharine said, "I had better go to her."

"It's Magdaline who needs attention," said Mrs. Weston, nodding toward the couch where she lay clinging to High-Lo's hand. "Take her to my room and stay with her. I'll be in soon."

High-Lo obeyed. John dropped heavily into the nearest chair.

"The end is not yet in sight." Mrs. Weston nodded her head in the direction High-Lo had taken with his burden.

John agreed wearily. He heard steps outside. Weston entered. He was the color of ashes.

"Bad business, John," he said. "Got to clear it up quick. Beany an' I are going straight to Flaggerston with the body in the truck, an we're takin' Pete. I'll report all the details to the sheriff. Come on yourself tomorrow an' bring High-Lo an' Magdaline. Make a clean sweep—Hanley an' everything. A couple of deaths in a liquor clean-up won't mean much nowadays."

"You're right," said John. "Pete's a good witness in the first shooting case. My wound will speak for itself. Pete has Hanley's gun. He took it to use in case Newton got gay."

"Sure he has it?"

"Did you ever know an Indian to throw away anything useful?" John asked tersely. "As for Magdaline," he added, "she'll be her own witness. Let her pour out the tragedy of her life. It will be a good thing for our executives to hear."

"You've got a clear case, but the law has to take its

course," Weston concluded. "What bail is needed, if any, Miss Katharine an' I will supply. You know her. She'll do anything to help you folks out."

"You bet I know her!" ejaculated John. "God bless her, is what I say, and all of you. I've sure found the time when I need my friends."

After the truck with its grim freight had left, the silence of unrelieved tragedy pervaded the house. Mrs. Weston, absent for a long time, at length appeared before John in the living room where he restlessly paced the floor.

"Magdaline won't be a mother now," she said in her quiet direct way. "That's over. She's in no condition to appear in court for days. You and High-Lo must go without her tomorrow. Miss Katharine will bring her to Flaggerston later."

"Nature, cruelly kind," muttered John.

Unable to restrain his anxiety about Mary longer, he asked, "And Mrs. Newton? How is she?"

Mrs. Weston gave a backward glance down the hall. "Here's Miss Katharine. She's just looked in on her. She'll tell you."

When the Eastern girl entered the room, she saw Curry's mute question in his eyes.

"I'd give everything I own if she would only cry," said Katharine. "It's you she needs. Go to her. Third door to the right."

John went. He was in the room, without memory of having knocked or entered. He was at the side of her bed kneeling, begging forgiveness.

"I wondered if you were coming!"

Her cry pierced his heart. His head sank to the pillow into the dark cloud of her hair.

She was whispering to him, her words falling in hysterical haste. "I love you. I need you. I can't go on without you!"

Her cheek was against his, soft as velvet. He heard a convulsive sob. He felt something wet slip down the relaxed smoothness of her skin. She was crying.

21

Mr. Weston was right. The trials were called early and dispatched speedily. Mary, saved by Dr. Kellogg, who voluntarily testified under oath as to her blameless character, did not have to appear in court. Newton was declared a scoundrel of whom the community was well rid, and Hanley's name was blackened for all time. The most prominent women of Flaggerston, amazed to discover that the estate of an educated Indian girl was commonly less fortunate than that of her mother, flung high the banners of reform.

Meanwhile, at Black Mesa, where Joy and Alice came to join her, Mary lived in sad-glad expectation from mail to mail. At first John avoided any mention of the trials. Mary loved him all the more for this consideration; but recognizing the major part she had unwittingly played in the tragedies, she would not be spared the details of their reparation. After her protest that she must know everything that was taking place at Flaggerston, his letters gave full details of the court proceedings. Thus she suffered with him, prayed with him, shared his hope, and, at last, the final victories. A day of rejoicing was at hand. The valiant ones were soon to return. The fifteenth of June brought word of their coming.

"Let's celebrate!" suggested Beany at breakfast the next morning, while the others nodded approvingly. "Every cowboy's back, an' the season's not begun. Let's have some Indians come over for races, and a sing and dance at night. Pop Weston's partial to it. He's so glad to have things smoothin' out, he'd give the post away."

The only word of protest came from Mary. "Suppose

they don't come until evening?" She was thinking how tired they would be.

"All the better," spoke up Beany. "They'd hit right into high doin's. That's the idee. We want to have things altogether different from what they was when they went away."

Mary read Beany's mind. It was he who had instigated the destruction of the hogan where Wilbur had met his death; and now he was scheming a whirl of excitement to change the once solemn prospect utterly.

"It's really a great idea," Mary said. "Could you gather the Indians in time? It's tomorrow, you know."

Beany ventured a scathing look of scorn. "What's Pop Weston got a bunch of riders for?"

Accounting that remark, the deeds were as good as done.

During the following day, from noon on, Mary's ear was attuned to catch the sound of an automobile. It took considerable restraint not to precede the others to the ridge to scan the trail. When Stub came in to say the folks were about to leave, she could have kissed his plump, beardless cheek. Indeed she wanted to embrace the world.

More than three hundred Indians, men, women and children, had answered the summons; a race meant exchange of jewelry and money, and a dance gave like advantages. On the level desert floor, where greasewood and brush were sparse, they had laid out their racecourse, and they moved over and around it, some mounted, some on foot, bright splashes of color against the black wall of the mesa. Tryouts were in progress, as shrill cheers indicated even before the moving forms of the riders became visible. Other Indians were encouraging betting among the groups on the sidelines. Somehow gambling did not seem a vice among these childlike people. They mobbed the cowboys, who, ever good spenders, had helped to make up the purse, and were willing to part with even more silver to add flavor to the betting.

It was thrilling to witness the races. But the growing excitement that stirred Mary had its being in that day's one great expectation for her—John's return. The desert floor stretched for weary miles between her and the man she loved. She saw only the league-long distances, not the race; she watched for a whirl of dust on the motionless plain.

Long, almost endless seemed the day. Westward mountains eclipsed the sun, the colors of the afterglow faded, the gray of evening enclosed distance in dim obscurity, and still John had not come.

The Indians made a great brushwood fire and smaller individual campfires. Mrs. Weston, Alice and Mary prepared food for the hungry cowboys and joined them at the repast. Only Mary could not eat. Everyone pretended not to notice her lack of appetite. Flame licked the great pile of brushwood, a beacon light for John. Mary's ear tried to pierce the sound of its crackling for the vibration of a low distant motor. She understood the meaning of eternity, of never-endingness. At last she heard the long anticipated sound. She imagined she had cried out to the others, the wild voice within her was so strong. It did not matter if she had.

Presently Beany shouted, "Hoo-ray! The folks are comin'! Put an eye to them lights!"

Calm as she appeared, Mary's swelling heart threatened to burst with its child-like song: "I heard them long ago! I heard them long ago!"

They were camped near the road. The car came to a stop in the circle of their firelight. There was a general exodus from the car; people were crowding around. Mary distinguished only John, whose roving eyes did not rest until they found her. Now he was coming to her, his dear, glad smile still a bit uncertain. Her fingers, fluttering like her heart, sought his protecting grasp. Neither spoke. Almost at once they were separated by the boys and High-Lo and Magdaline who could scarcely wait their turn to speak. There was no hint of sadness in this homecoming. They had relegated the past to oblivion, as if their lives now lay only in the happy future.

The voices of Indian men rose from the direction of the large central fire. The sing was in progress, and the women and girls with the younger men were circling the firelight ready for the dance. John sought Mary, and they went hand in hand to join the Indians. They stood behind the squatting figures and smiled at each other over the intrigue going on about them.

"It's not the best dancer, it's the wealthiest dancer an Indian girl wants," John explained. "The idea is that a girl nails a man who isn't quick enough to escape her and makes him dance until he buys himself free. They'll go for the cowboys, too. Cowboys pay in cash. They prefer it to jewelry. Watch the fun."

Here, there, girls voluntarily, or urged with a whack or push from their mothers, made a beeline each for a particular man, who, the minute he realized his danger, fled. Should he be captured, the man was dragged to the center of light where his dusky captor, keeping to the rear, clung to the waist of her partner's garment, turning him dizzily round and round, herself supplying a tapping step as she circled with him. Thus they slowly spun to the staccato song of the men, which rose and fell in a strange, wild cadence of boldly accentuated notes. The song had no ending. Couples quit whenever a bargain was consummated. Girls refused to be bought off cheaply. They argued as they danced. Everywhere men were dodging. Now and then a cowboy came sprawling into the ring. There was always someone dancing. Magdaline dragged in High-Lo, and a general shout went up.

Mary felt a pressure on her hand, to which John still clung. He leaned close and whispered, "A deep and abiding affection has sprung between them. I think High-Lo will be happy."

Again Mary looked their way. What she saw was a tall, handsome cowboy and a slim, stylishly dressed Indian girl pirouetting in and out among the other dancers. They stopped and the girl delivered an imperious command, only to be seized in a great bear hug, the toll she evidently had exacted, and she was borne from the lighted circle in the cowboy's arms amid the renewed shouts of the crowd.

John drew Mary from the shifting firelight to the shadow and obscurity beyond. Hand in hand they walked away, continuing to the corral and up over the ridge to a place where even the post was shut from view.

The desert lay in glistening serenity. Through moon-blanched luster solitary, solemn peaks and the sacred prayer rocks of the uplands loomed. A time of transfiguration had come. The hours of doubt and waiting were gone. The desert silence, vast yet intimate, enveloped them.

"Desert-bound!" murmured Mary, touched by the profound tranquility of the scene.

"Together!" added John.

Mary felt his arm about her, a gentle hand tilted her face. As their lips met, a flame of ecstasy enveloped her. There was tenderness in his embrace and shy, yet eloquent desire. She lay back presently in the crook of his arm, and they smiled into each other's eyes with the supreme consciousness of love.

"My little sweetheart. That's what you are," he said. "And soon you will be my wife, as soon as the missionary can get here from Taho."

His words were like a perfect gift.

"Whenever you say," Mary whispered. And she smiled again from the sweet security of his embrace.

It was the same day of another week.

Katharine and Alice from a lofty perch watched two riders and a pack mule moving westward far down Black Mesa valley into the heart of the desert. So close did they ride that at times one rider would shut the other from view. A near-by ring of hoofs against rock told them that High-Lo, with Joy and Magdaline, were starting back to the post.

"They'll be gone three weeks," said Alice, her eyes on the broad sweep of valley.

"And in the fall we'll have the fun of hunting twin ranches," returned Katharine. "John says High-Lo's just the man to take care of our place when we get it."

"A little gray home in the west, eh, Sis?"

"Yes, dear," said Katharine smiling.

Then Alice said dreamily, "It was a pretty wedding, wasn't it, with Cathedral Rock for their church?"

Memory of it stirred Katharine. "And the desert an organ on which to play age-long love songs."

Now the two riders were becoming smaller and smaller. There came a moment when they quite disappeared into the haze that softened the valley horizon.

"I'm so glad they are happy," Alice declared, with a gentle laugh that seemed to her sister to express more of sadness than joy. "But it is you that John Curry should have married, dear. I—I never had the courage to tell you, Katharine, until it was too late. But—but now—it's out. How I hoped and prayed that he would marry you—in the end. I truly hope that they will be happy. He is—" Alice paused a long, long time before she finished "—a man you could love!"

Katharine almost lost her composure. A mist came before her eyes and her lips trembled. She turned away from the girl beside her, pretending to fasten the laces of her boots, lest Alice see the confusion her words had caused.

"Just good friends, Sister dear," she managed to say. "And perhaps someday business partners, if he still wants my small legacy to invest. I've been happy to be admitted to his confidence—and his friendship. There never was anything else—with him or—with me. I'm happy about John and Mary. They were fated to love each other—from the beginning. . . . Come, Sister darling. There's a chill in the air. We must go."

ZANE GREY'S
GREAT WESTERNS

_____ 80447 TWIN SOMBREROS $1.50

_____ 80448 UNDER THE TONTO RIM $1.50

_____ 80449 STRANGER FROM THE TONTO $1.50

_____ 80456 THE U.P. TRAIL $1.50

_____ 80455 THE HERITAGE OF THE DESERT $1.50

_____ 80454 THE MYSTERIOUS RIDER $1.50

_____ 80453 THE RAINBOW TRAIL $1.50

_____ 80450 VALLEY OF WILD HORSES $1.50

_____ 80452 DESERT GOLD $1.50

_____ 80451 ARIZONA AMES $1.50

Available at bookstores everywhere, or order direct from the publisher.

POCKET BOOKS
Department RK
1230 Avenue of the Americas
New York, N.Y. 10020

Please send me the books I have checked above. I am
enclosing $_____ (please add 50¢ to cover postage and
handling). Send check or money order—no cash or C.O.D.'s
please.

NAME_____

ADDRESS_____

CITY_____STATE/ZIP_____

ZG-2